Other books in print by

Nik C. Colyer

Channeling Biker Bob 1 Heart of a Warrior
Channeling Biker Bob 2 Lover's Embrace
Channeling Biker Bob 3 Magician's Spell
Channeling Biker Bob 4 Wisdom of the King
Maranther's Deception Lost in the desert
Trillian Rising The phoenix of change
Flamenco Flood Trouble in Paradise
Kicking Ass and Taking Names
Poetry through the eyes of a tough guy

All books available through
Singing Reed Press
P.O. Box 1395
Nevada City, CA 95959
530 265-3566
www.NikColyer.com

Acclaim From Readers:

Colyer, Nik C.
        Guerrilla TV / by Nik C. Colyer. — 1st ed.
        p. cm.
        LCCN pending
        ISBN 978-0-9708163-9-9

        1. Fiction. 2. Political struggle- fction. I. Title.

1. Sheriff-vs-Homeland-security-fiction. 2.adventure-bucking-the-system-fiction. 3. Honorable-lifesaving-conflict-fiction. 4. Romance-love-fiction

Printed in the United States of America
10 9 8 7 6 5 4 3 2 1

This book is dedicated to
our misplaced Bill of Rights

and those few who realize what
peralous times we live in.

Author's note

September 11, 2001 was a traumatic time for our nation and we all morn the loss of our fellow citizens, but we also need to morn the loss of our innocence.

After that traumatic event I watched in horror as our leadership, ever watchful not for the good of their constituents, but for power and the all mighty dollar, quietly and systematically sold us out by secretly stripping away one then another of the rights of the people of our great country.

The unfortunate thing is no one with a real voice has called the alarm and brought this charade to light. Even when they did the media, who is owned by those who would perpetrate such a catastrophic set of events, said little or nothing.

The second travesty is that we all sit in our comfortable sofas night after night watching, and worse yet, believing the distractions the nightly news feeds us when in reality they serve only those in power. What would happen if the real truth was broadcast over the airways. Would we wake up even then, probably not. We are too busy trying to keep our heads above water as we tread the liquid of deceit.

Few said a word when people living in the United States were spirited away to Guantanamo as enemy combatants, stripped of their rights, tortured then left to rot for years in that hell hole without a lawyer or due process.

Problem is if one person is left without the law to protect them, even if they truly are the enemy, then we all are vulnerable to the whim of the small minded people in power.

Am I mad, you're damn rights I'm mad. What happened to the Constitution and Bill of Rights that I grew up to revere? Who will be there to protect me when someone decides that

I am their enemy combatant?

It seems that we are moving into dark times once again, but what would happen if someone said, "no". What if an officer of the law actually fulfilled his or her sworn duty to serve and protect all of the people in their community rather than only the business and power elite.

The following story is what could happen if a few people got together and said "no" to the tyranny of the ruling class and did so without guns or bullets, but simply by flooding the light of day on the darkness of a shadow consciousness very much alive in certain factions of our government.

Nik C. Colyer

Guerrilla TV

Nik C. Colyer

Singing Reed Press
Nevada City, CA

Chapter 1

Salton Sea

We're camped in the biggest renegade RV town I know of. Hell, we even have our own mayor. Like many of us in early January when the snows settle in along the northern states, our little town next to the shores of the Salton Sea bulge with RV's of all sizes and shapes. Myrtle and I always arrive early to get the best position and we settle in for a pleasant season watching the wintering birds, the flying kind and also the ever so numerous snowbirds. Living in Boseman, Montana in the summers we count ourselves as snowbirds too.

In the late December sun of the southwest, long before the main bulk of RV's arrive, we find a spot on the edge of the lake and park lengthwise so our galley looks at the sunrise over the lake. The ever-receding waters of the huge saline lake is thirty feet from our doorstep.

Myrtle quickly claims the few extra yards of beach front property by putting up lawn chairs and a clothesline. We have thirty-six feet of prime real estate and we aren't planning on moving an inch until May. How could we to know we would

1

be, all at the same time crashing an airplane and getting hunted by Homeland Security.

I disconnect our little beat-up Toyota truck and park it along one side, claiming a parking section off of the nose of our Southwind with its two pop-outs and a satellite dish.

We've been here two days. A nice couple, Aimee and Clint Potter move in next to us on the south side, but though it's prime property, no one parks north of us. The neighborhood fills, leaving sixty feet of beach front unclaimed for almost a week.

There are a few interlopers who park in the spot for fifteen minutes or a half hour trying to decide if they want to stay, but each time they drive off to find another spot.

The entire beach front is taken and the second row of camper trailers and fifth-wheels is quickly filling and yet the spot next to us remains vacant.

~

Turns out that the person who parks in that spot will fundamentally change our lives, and now, a short four weeks later our lives will be ending. How could I predict that I, Mrs, 'I'm never interested', would reach over and grab my husband's crotch. I want to do it right now as our kite floats over the outskirts of Las Vegas. I want to unbuckle my seat belt, toss my pants overboard and climb in his lap. I want him this very moment.

BillyBob takes my hand away. "Gotta concentrate."

I give him a playful pout and blow a kiss. I feel like a kid again and the feeling is good.

I look at my watch and it's five after six. When I put my arm down and look back at the skyline, out of nowhere, a huge jet roars past. It's not more than a hundred feet over our heads. My heart almost stops from the noise. It takes a few seconds for me to calm as the jet drops toward the airport. I look at BillyBob and laugh I'm so relieved.

He turns our little plane on a dime and drops out of the sky. "We'd better get out of here, Mert."

"What's wrong, BillyBob?"

Just as I say this, everything goes wrong. A huge wind catches us and flips the plane on its head. We drop out of the sky. I hear something thrum like a guitar string then twang away. BillyBob pushes and pulls the control stick. We're caught in some kind of tornado. The ground is still a long ways away, but it looks too close. The howling wind flips us over. Another guitar string twangs and snaps. I look above our heads and the pretty little red wing flaps like a sheet. There's nothing holding us in the air. The wind continues tossing us.

As suddenly as it came, it disappears. BillyBob goes from trying to right the plane to trying to control its plummet toward earth.

I'm holding onto the flimsy little cage. The wind howls. The ground gets bigger.

The only wing left is a small section above our heads. It might be six feet wide. The rest of the thirty-foot foil is flapping.

"BillyBob!"

He fights the control stick. At one point the plane rights itself. We are diving at a tremendous rate, but at least that insane spinning has stopped.

"Help us, BillyBob."

His teeth are gritting. His jaw is working. His eyes are scrunched. I see every little thing. It's all so clear. We're going to die and all I can see is my husband's facial expression. I guess it's a good enough thing to focus on. I sure don't want to look at that ground.

It's close. I know it's too close, but all I want is to look at his face. It might be the last time I see him. God, I love this man. If we're going to die, I need to say it once more. I yell over the howling wind. "I love you."

Maybe he doesn't hear me, so I yell louder. "I love you."

I reach over and put my hand on his tense arm. "I love you."

For a second, he glances in my direction. He doesn't say anything, not even a smile.

There's the ground. Cars are the size of matchboxes. There's no chance of landing this rocket plummeting out of the sky. We're dead. It's over. I lean over, stretch myself to his cheek and kiss him as the ground leaps into our faces.

But, long before all of that happens, we calmly sit under our full-length awning watching the little shore birds attempting to find an early dinner in the sand along the shore. I have a beer in hand. Myrtle sits next to me. We've been silent for quite a while watching the sun behind us reflect off of the clouds high above of the glass-calm water. A green canoe with a young couple crosses in front of us. We hear snatches of their conversation as they pass eventually paddling out of sight. Then, in the silence of the late afternoon, both Myrtle and I turn to the sound of a huge diesel pusher rolling slowly up our gravel road.

Without turning back to look at me, Myrtle says, "Our new neighbor has arrived, BillyBob."

I lift my cold can of beer in salute as the driver noses into the spot with a huge converted Greyhound vista-cruiser. He tips his dirty straw cowboy hat and grins through a cigar butt stuffed in his pudgy cheeks. He climbs out and disconnects a long, skinny trailer then pushes it aside. The bus is so big, it barely fits. Myrtle and I sit in stunned silence as he jostles into the space.

She turns to me. "Move the truck, Billy-Bob. It'll make it easier for him."

I take the last sip of my beer and set the empty can on our little folding table. I get out of my aluminum chair and walk over to the truck digging in my Levis. I dangle the keys and point at the truck. The big bus drops to an idle and rests until I get the truck started and pull it out of the way.

The extra room allows him to slide into place. He drops his automatic levelers and brings the polished silver colored bus to a level position in the time it takes me to re-park the Toyota.

His custom, twenty-foot-long pop-out slides six feet into open air and locks into position.

In a minute, he leans out the window with three long neck bottles of an imported beer. "Want one of these?"

I drop my empty can of Budweiser in the trash and nod.

The big side door opens on the far end of the bus and he descends the five or six steps to the sand. When he comes bounding around the front of the bus, half-chewed cigar in his right hand, three long necks in his left, he yells in a warm southern drawl, "Howdy, I'm Frank Deluchi."

We pull out a third folding chair and he sits with his back to the lake. With a small bottle opener he pulls from his hip pocket, he opens the bottles and hands them to Myrtle then me.

Once we introduce ourselves, I ask, "where you comin' from?"

He gives me a smile. "Last night I stayed outside of Palm Springs under the wind generators. Man, was that noisy."

I take a short pull from my bottle. "I mean originally where are you from? Where did you grow up?"

He takes a breath, releases it slowly with a soft whistle. "Been on the road for three years. Lived in Atlanta, Georgia, but that was a coupla' lifetimes ago. Mostly, I never spend more than a few days in any one place."

Myrtle says. "That's gotta be lonely."

He turns to her and smiles. "No ma'am. It makes me more willing to cut through the bull and get right down to business."

Myrtle gives him a suspicious smile. "Business?"

It probably didn't look suspicious to Frank, but having been married to her over twenty years I know that look.

He lifts his bottle. "The business of being neighborly."

She sighs. "Oh."

"Doesn't mean I don't have business to take care of, but not here and not now."

Her second, Oh, isn't quite as filled with relief.

We spend the rest of that afternoon sitting under our foldout canopy, watching the birds and boats, talking about light-hearted events and telling jokes. Frank stays for dinner and once he's back in his bus, both Myrtle and I agree it's been an entertaining evening.

Chapter 2

Ultralight

The next afternoon Frank springs his little surprise.

Myrtle and I wake from our nap. I crank up the generator to put coffee on and I'm lolling on the sofa waiting for it to brew. Frank opens the doors of that odd trailer and bangs metal pipes as he scatters them along the shoreline.

Myrtle yells from the bedroom. "What the hell is going on out there?"

I pour my cup. "Frank's building something."

By the time she walks to the front of our Southwind, Frank has assembled a thirty-foot-long, bright red sail. He opens the storage door at the back of the trailer then disappears into its cargo hold.

My curiosity is piqued. I put my shoes on, recharge my half-finished cup of coffee, open the front door and drop four steps to the hard-pack sand.

He reemerges from the trailer dragging some kind of framed cart on three wheels.

I walk over. "What's you doing?"

The cart's single front wheel rolls in an aluminum track and starts the downward glide two feet to the earth. When the rest of the contraption emerges and its other two wheels find their tracking, a three-foot propeller blade comes into view.

He rolls the cart down to the red sail and turns to me. "BillyBob, give me a hand for a second?"

I put my coffee on the folding table and walk the ten yards to the shore.

"Grab one end of the wing and help me lift it to the top of the cockpit." He points at two main bolts, then to the center of the wing.

I grab the tip and we lift fifteen pounds of gossamer wing to the top of the cart. He spins a set of large nuts into place, installs some guy wires, gives the little plane a once over, then winks. "I guess we're set. Give me a minute and I'll get the transmitter." He spins, sprints to his front door, then disappears. In the time it takes for me to retrieve my cup of coffee, he reemerges with a black leather attaché case which he mounts on the bottom of the frame in a special bracket. Once he makes sure the case is secure he points at the seat next to him. "Go for a ride?"

The guy looks absolutely insane. He's actually going to take that thing into the air. I shake my head as the little engine makes its first revolution, spits a puff of exhaust and spins to life.

"It's up to you, but it's a hell of a lot of fun." He searches for, then buckles a double cross shoulder safety harness.

I back up five paces as the engine revs, kicking up dust as the sound gets louder.

The little plane rolls along the beach. I look at Myrtle who stands at the door of our RV, then back at the plane and the wild-eyed pilot. Everything suddenly fits. I run and grab one of the crossbars. Frank looks up with his aviator goggles and gives me a toothy smile. The sound of the engine drops to an idle.

"We got to go fast. Myrtle's going to have a conniption."

His smile widens. He points at the seat next to him and hands me a pair of goggles. I climb aboard and the little whiny engine resumes its scream as we to roll along the beach. I look back at Myrtle running toward me with an angry snarl on her face.

Frank backhands my shoulder lightly. "Buckle up."

I wave at Myrtle as the little plane picks up speed bouncing along the slight dips and valleys of the flat beach. I turn again as Myrtle stops and puts hands on her hips. She's breathing hard.

I snap the last harness clip and the sandy beach falls away as the little plane leaps into the air like a jack-in-the-box. We reach an altitude of maybe fifty feet before Frank levels off and banks slowly out toward the water. A minute later he reaches full circle and faces the line of RV's along the shore. By the time we pass over our section of beach we must be three hundred feet.

He maintains a gentle angle upward as we climbed in an ever ascending circle.

He yells as his hand makes a spiral in the air. "We'll get help from the rising air."

I nod, not exactly understanding what he's saying, but totally fascinated with the feeling of floating like a bird. I've flown before, but never out in the open air with nothing to protect me from the elements. I look past my feet through a few thousand feet of nothingness at the bank of motorhome roofs. It's exhilarating.

Frank points at a gauge. "We'll level off at three thousand."

I nod, still not sure what he's saying until the engine goes quiet. The moment the engine is off, the wind whistles past my ears. The plane takes a dive toward the ground and Frank pulls on the stick until we float in a controlled glide.

Frank puts the plane into a slight right turn toward the water and points for me to take the controls. When I put both hands up in refusal, he grins. "It's no big deal, just keep the thing going straight and level. Make small moves. If you get into trouble, I'll be right here."

I tentatively put my hand on the little bar sticking out of the framework.

"Don't grab the stick, hold it with your fingertips. This plane is balanced to glide. Let go of the stick and it will find its own equilibrium."

The plane shifts and rolls slightly with my every move, but quickly I get a feel for the controls and we float along through the warm air.

Frank opens the brief case and plays with the keys of a laptop-computer-looking thing. He removes a DVD from a sleeve in the lid and inserts it into the player. He looks at his watch, waits for the right moment then touches a button and the little screen lights up. It's a newscast with Dan Rather. I'm not sure if it's the evening news that night or some recorded version from a past news hour.

"What's that for?" I ask in an innocent gesture of interest.

"The news, of course, with Dan the Man no less."

The plane bucks and I have to concentrate on keeping it level.

Frank pushes my hand away from the stick. "Let's catch this thermal." He banks the little plane to the left and passes through the bump we'd felt the moment earlier. He cuts the plane sharply and my stomach tingles as we rise. For five minutes, Frank cuts in and out of that bump in the air, then has me take over the controls again. "Bought more time without having to restart the engine." He points at the altimeter. "We rose 3000 feet."

"No kidding."

Three times during the hour, Frank takes the controls and whips the little plane into another thermal, giving us a wild mouse ride of rises. At the end of the hour, he looks at his watch, clicks another set of keys in the computer, then sets the little plane into a gentle glide toward earth. As we drop, I point at the one-gallon gas tank behind our heads. "Efficient on fuel."

He waves his hand. "Only the wind up here, but when we get close, I'll to start her to get a little more control to land. A tank of gas lasts me weeks and I go up every day."

"Every day?"

"I'll explain once we get on the ground."

The gentle glide drops into a steeper decent toward the shore next to our RV. When he turns the key and pulls the rope-start, the engine roars to life and the bicycle riding silence of wind through the wires is lost to the whine of the propeller. The plane drops quickly to within fifty feet of the beach. Frank levels out, pulls a bar in the center between us and the plane relaxes into a kite-like glide the last thirty feet to earth. As the wheels touch the hard-packed sand, we're parallel to my Southwind. By the time the machine stops and Frank kills the engine, we're a few feet past his big bus.

He unsnaps his harness, tugs at the straps of his black briefcase, grabs it and walks straight for his RV.

I'm left struggling with my strap as Myrtle steps into my line of sight. "BillyBob Harding, what the hell were you thinking?"

I look at her as the harness unsnaps. Her hands are on her hips and she has the familiar cock to her head.

"It was great. You should try it next time he goes up."

She points east. "You could have crashed in the water and drowned. Remember, you don't know how to swim."

I stand and stretch my arms. "We didn't crash, now did we and I had the time of my life."

She still has an aggravated glare as Frank steps over with three frosty bottle beers oblivious to Myrtle's mood.

"Hey, It's way past six and we better get started on happy hour before we miss it altogether. Let's relax at your table and I'll tell you about the briefcase."

She rotates to him. "You could have killed my husband."

He laughs and points at the plane. "In that? That thing is as safe as riding a bicycle. I've had that type of plane for five years and not once have I ever had a problem with it."

"But you. . ."

For the first time in a long time, Myrtle is flummoxed into silence. He grabs her hand, snaps his heels together like some military General, bends and kisses the back of her hand tenderly, like she's the most important person in the world. When he lifts his head, he looks her squarely in the eye. "Madam, I'm sorry if I caused you even the slightest concern."

He doesn't release her hand, but simply turns to stand next to her and slides her hand in under his elbow like he's taking her to a ball in a full tux. "Let's retire to your picnic table and may I offer a token of my apology?" He nods for me to follow.

I swear, for the first time in all of the years I've known her, my Myrtle placidly follows, hand clutching his elbow. Did I get a glimpse of her glassy eyes?

The two promenaded to the picnic bench, me in tow with the beers and he seats her like we're at a seven-course meal.

She's dazzled.

When he bows at the hip, then shows her the bottle of beer across his forearm like it's a hundred-year-old wine, she smiles for the first time. The spell is broken, but her mood has shifted and she's back to herself, enjoying the attention of the stranger.

With the same waiter flair, Frank pulls an opener from his back pocket and snaps the cap from the bottle all in one smooth movement.

"Would madam like a chilled glass?"

Her smile turns to a grin as she let out a slight snicker and nods.

As if by magic —I never saw him carrying a glass— he pulls a tall tapered beer glass from behind him and expertly pours the amber liquid down the side of the glass ending up with a small head by the time it's full. He sets the glass in front of her and the bottle next to it.

She picks up the glass and looks through it like it's magic. "Thank you."

Frank and I sit across from her as he flips the caps from the remaining two bottles and unceremoniously hands me one.

He lifts his bottle. "Let's have a toast to another successful broadcast."

Although I have no idea what he's talking about, we all three click glass, then take a drink of the frosty beer.

When he sets his down, he looks at us and smiles. "Great beer."

I nod.

"Bet you're wondering what I'm up to."

I look at Myrtle, then back to Frank. "The thought crossed my mind."

He takes another sip. "About five years ago, I inherited a substantial amount of money from my stock broker father. He worked himself into an early grave and never enjoyed one penny of his hard won fortune.

"Determined not to follow in his footsteps, I cashed in a

minuscule portion and bought this bus. I wanted to see what America was all about."

I point at the bus with my thumb. "You've been traveling five years?"

"Actually much longer, but the last five in the bus."

Myrtle says, "For the last year we've been doing the same. I like it."

"I knew you'd understand."

After a moment's silence, I ask, "so, what have you found in your wanderings?"

He takes another drink of beer finishing the bottle, then sets it on the table. "Most of America thinks the nightly news is the gospel truth. They think what's being shown on their television is unbiased and above board as news should be."

I shrug. "I don't think so. It might have been unbiased in the fifties and sixties, but that was before it got bought up by big business with their agendas. I hate the news."

Myrtle nods in agreement.

Frank smiles. "I hoped you'd say that."

I down the last swallow of my beer. "You have more on the subject?"

His smile turns to a sly grin and he winks. "Seeing how I had all of that money and really nothing to spend it on, I decided to give back something to my country that's been so generous to me."

I wait in silence because I have no idea where he's going with the conversation.

"Let's have another beer."

I get up, go inside to our fridge and pull three iced Texas beers while he goes to his RV carrying back the black briefcase. Once they're open and on the table, he takes a small sip and looks at us. "Seeing how the news is so one-sided, I decided to even the score a little."

14

Myrtle motions toward the lake. "How would you do that?"

He points back to the little motorized hang glider, then sets his case on the table and opens it. Inside is the laptop-computer-looking thing.

"You messed with that when we were in the air."

He smiles, pushes the "on" button and the screen lights with the standard logo of most computers. When it's running, he slides in a DVD and turns the suitcase around so we can see.

Peter Jennings comes on the screen sitting in front of the CBS news backdrop. Everything looks like a regular broadcast until Jennings says his first words. I'm mesmerized while he lays out the exact nature of the take over of our government. How it all started in the early part of the twentieth century and how the plan is coming to a close in our new century. Other than the content, the five-minute broadcast is so realistic, even I, who knows something is up, can't tell.

Frank sips his beer while the broadcast brings us up to date. It ends with a website: www.zeitgeist.com

Myrtle asks, "What is Zeitgeist?"

"It's a three-hour movie. I got most of my material for this disk from it."

When the screen goes blank, I'm sitting with my jaw open. "When did Jennings broadcast this?"

Frank smiles. "Never. He'd be run out of the business if he ever said even one word of this."

I ask, "how did you get it?"

"It's amazing what enough money, some good acting and a few techie geeks can do. I have three guys back in Madison, Wisconsin working full time producing a new one of these every week and when this little machine broadcasts, it overrides selected channels for a twenty-mile radius. Except for the content, no one knows anything is different."

Frank points toward the sky. "I broadcast from up there, of course."

Myrtle gives him a pained smile. "Why are you showing us this?"

He points at the airplane. "The Federal Communication Board would love to get a bead on us, so I have to move every few days."

"Us?"

He grins and takes another sip of beer. "Oh, I forgot to tell you, there are over three hundred of these little suitcases floating around the lower forty-eight. My techie guys produce and send out a new copy once a week to each of the brave souls who have joined me. We have all the main newscasters speaking truth."

Myrtle squints her eyes. "Newscasters?"

"Okay, not them, but actors who look like them.

Myrtle shakes her head. "Are you nuts? A person could be put in prison for something like this."

He crosses both arms. "Not exactly. I've got a lawyer on retainer. He says the FCC can fine someone pretty stiffly and confiscate their equipment, but that is about as much teeth as the agency has.

"I have a legal fund set aside to not only fight the bastards in court, but also to pay immediate bail and any fines they can levy against us."

Myrtle points at him. "You've said the word 'us' twice now. Why am I'm getting the feeling that this second us includes Billy-Bob and me?"

Before he answers, I interrupt. "You been caught yet?"

He shakes his head. "No, I'm a little more slippery than those guys would want. I do keep a whole team of Homeland Security agents fully employed though."

Myrtle asks, "has anyone been caught?"

"One couple who stayed in the Salt Lake area for two weeks broadcasting every day. They deserved to be caught. We got them out that same day."

"So, they did go to jail."

"For one afternoon."

Myrtle has a pen in her hand and is doodling on a napkin. "What happened?"

My legal fund bailed them out. The fine of twenty thousand was paid and their equipment was confiscated. I got them another suitcase a week later and they're doing things a little smarter these days. If you plan on staying someplace, just don't broadcast until the last three days of your stay. It's that simple."

I say, "I assume that you're telling us all of this because you want us to have a suitcase."

He nods, then stands. "There is no pressure here. I'll go back to my bus while you two talk it over."

He walks back to his bus. A small gust of wind on a perfectly silent day kicks up a little dust.

I turn to my wife. "What do you think?"

"I don't like it. I've never broken even one law in my entire life and I don't want to start now."

I take the last sip of my second beer. "True, but you saw the program. It sheds light on the very things we've been talking about. I mean, what other way to wrestle the airwaves back from corporate America than to steal them."

"We'll be breaking the law."

"Look honey, I won't do it if you aren't one hundred percent behind me, but I'd like you to take some time to think about it. Looks like Frank's going to be here for a few more days, so we have time."

"I don't like it, BillyBob."

"Just think about it. We'd have a real chance to make a difference for ten or twenty thousand people at a time.

17

Remember those peace rallies that seemed to go nowhere. Here we could make real changes."

She gets up and pours half of her beer in the sand. When she goes into the RV, I follow her. Through the window I notice Frank struggling to break down the airfoil in a building wind. I kiss my wife on the cheek. "I'm going to help Frank."

She says nothing as she washes the dishes.

I go outside as the wind kicks up another notch. It's not hard enough to knock things over, but desert winds can get nasty quick. I run over and help him unsnap guy wires and disassemble the foil.

By the time we have the wing put away, the wind gets unbearable. All we can do is push the little plane next to the bus, tie it to the back wheel and hope the gusts don't change direction.

We run into his bus as a big gust rolls in from the west and buffets us. Inside, Frank points at the couch. "Have a seat BillyBob, I'll get you another beer."

"Two in one day is my limit, Frank, so I'll pass."

"Have it your way," he says and pulls a frosty one out of the fridge.

Once he settles across from me, I ask, "what are you doing?"

"Like I said, it's time to take our airwaves back and I don't know any other way."

"Couldn't you have just bought a few radio stations?"

"Believe me, I tried, but the important ones are all sewn up and no one is selling. Back in the late seventies all of the stations were bought up by right wing zealots. The remainder of them were swallowed up by the turn of the century. There are no TV or radio stations to buy."

"So, this is the next best thing?"

He smiles. "It's so much better anyhow, because I get to rub their noses in the truth and there's nothing they can do about it. The more people like yourself who take this project on, the more the airwaves are free again for truth rather than the spun material the status quo has to offer and the more the regular Joe gets to open his eyes."

"If we were to take this on, how long would we have to keep it?"

"As long as you like. When you're done, there's an address to send your transmitter to and you're out of it. The other thing you can do is find someone who wants to take over or you can recruit new people. New recruitment has blossomed over the last six months. Imagine, some day there will be so many transmitters out there that the real news will be the only thing to see."

I point at the little airplane. "How hard was it to learn to fly one of those? I've always wanted to fly, but never felt I could afford it."

Frank laughs. "I'll take you up tomorrow. You already know about the controls. Landing is a little more tricky, but in a few days you'll have it down."

"I'd like that."

"We'll go up and broadcast the morning news. It's my favorite time of day."

I fight my way back to our RV in the howling desert wind. When I close the door, she looks up from the kitchen table. "The guy is a bit of a whack job."

"May or may not be true, but one thing for sure, he's hot on this broadcasting thing."

"BillyBob, you can't be serious about that suitcase?"

I sit across from her and look at a pencil sketch she's been working on the last few days. "You have to admit, the stuff we've been watching on television has lacked a certain kind of basic truth these last few decades."

She looks at me. "I say we drop it, end of story."

I see the set in her jaw and I know I'll have a long uphill climb getting her convinced, but it's worth a try. "Look Honey, let's keep the conversation on the table until we talk this whole thing out."

Two hours later we're still at it and I haven't made any headway. Somewhere in the middle of the third hour, she finally says, "do what you want, BillyBob, I'm having nothing to do with it."

"Are you serious, Myrt or are you just wanting to end this conversation?"

"Both, BillyBob Harding. I'm tired of fighting you on this and over the last twenty-five years if I've learned anything it's when you have your mind set on something, really set, then I'll never hear the end of it until you get your way. I also know that you don't often set your mind on anything, so in the bigger picture of things, who am I to stop you?"

I grin. "Thanks Honey, you're a pal."

"Don't thank me. If I had my way that suitcase would be down the road when Frank leaves."

I take a deep breath and ready myself for the next volley of no's. "I'm going to learn to fly one of those little planes."

"Jesus Christ, BillyBob, what are you thinking? You make a mistake in one of those and that's it. Flying is a very unforgiving sport."

"I know, Myrt, but I always wanted to fly and I could never afford it. This is my perfect opportunity to give it a try. Who knows, maybe I won't like it."

She rolls her eyes and gets up from the table. "I swear BillyBob, meeting that Frank Deluchi guy just might be the worst moment in our marriage.

Chapter 3

up

Early the next morning, I'm up and looking out the window onto the calmness of the lake. Frank is reassembling the gossamer wing and once I've made two cups of coffee, I take them out with me and meet him on the sand. When I hand him the cup, I ask, "What time do you get up?"

While attaching the last guy wire, he smiles. "I've always had a hard time sleeping. It's gotten worse now that I'm older. I'm usually up at four."

"Four o'clock? That's crazy."

"I know, but it's the time my eyes open and my time here on earth is limited. I figure why waste it trying to sleep when my body is not that interested." He snaps the wire like a guitar string and a low thrum rings out. "These babies have to be tight, but not too tight."

While I take a sip of my coffee, trying my best to wake up, he takes a swallow of his, then steps to the far side of the wing and tightens the opposing wire. "It's a perfect morning for flying, don't you think?" He points toward the lake.

I look over the calmness and though the sun has another hour before it climbs over the distant mountains, the thin layer of clouds to the east reflects an iridescent peach hue off of the lake.

Frank points up. "I say we watch the sun rise from there."

I take another sip. "Let me get a jacket."

I walk ten yards to the RV, open the door and climb the three steps inside. I take a last drink of my coffee and set the cup in the sink. As I step out of the RV putting my jacket on, Frank pulls the starter rope and the little engine sputters into a whine. Frank positions himself in the seat I was in yesterday. He yells over the sound of the idling engine. "You going to fly it?"

I stop short of the plane by ten feet and shake my head.

He laughs, "It's like driving a boat."

"I don't think I'd better—"

"Look BillyBob, there's nothing to it and besides the controls are in the center. I can take over if you have any trouble."

I nod, get in the driver's position and buckle up. He points at a plunger. "Pull that out and we'll get going. I pull and the engine whines as the plane rolls along the shore. I'm nervous, but Frank talks me through it. "Feel the control stick with your fingertips. As the plane comes up to speed, it's going to want to jump off the ground. Your job is to keep it on the ground until we reach take off speed. Just allow the stick to relax in neutral position by letting go, then grab it with your finger tips and push it forward a quarter inch."

I let go of my death grip on the controls and the stick jumps back to its neutral position.

"Now, BillyBob, just your fingertips."

I move the stick back slightly and the plane jumps off the ground a foot.

Frank grabs my hand, pushes slowly forward and the

wheels land back on the ground. "Hold it there for another ten seconds, then pull back ever so slightly."

The plane is fighting to get into the air, but I continue to push the control stick forward.

"Hold it a little longer, little longer, just another second. Okay, now, let go of the stick."

I let go and realize I had the stick pushed almost all the way forward. It bounces back toward me and springs into the neutral position.

The wheels leave the ground for a second then touch the sand once more.

Frank yells, "pull back a quarter inch."

I pull back and the little plane leaps into the air, ten feet, thirty feet, fifty feet like it's nothing.

"Okay, Billybob, let the controls go once again."

I let go and the plane that was flying at a steep angle levels out and pulls away from the shore.

"Give the controls a slight nudge to the right."

I follow his instructions and the plane rolls right.

"Now, try left."

I do and the plane responds while I laugh out loud. "I didn't know it was so easy."

"That's what I told you," he yells over the sound of the engine. "Let's get some altitude. Pull the stick back slightly and to the left. Feel for cross currents. When it pushes the plane one way or the other, turn toward that current."

I have no idea what he's talking about, but I'm having the time of my life. The RV's below my feet looks like toys.

"Keep it climbing," Frank yells over the screaming engine.

The controls are amazing. With the flick of one finger, I turn right or left, drop or climb.

At one point, I feel the plane veer to the right.

Frank yells, "Did you feel that?"

I nod.

"Swing the plane around and face it into the direction of that gust."

I'm still nervous about making sudden movements. I turn and when the plane is facing in the right direction, it makes a leap that leaves my stomach a hundred yards below us.

"Once you lose the current, turn and re-find it, just like the buzzards."

I drop one wing and catch the current again and feel the lift. I do this five times until our RV's looks like little pinheads in the sand. Franks shuts the engine. In the relative quiet I turn to him.

"It's okay, BillyBob, I turned the motor off. We have lots of room between us and the ground and this thing floats like a kite. You keep catching that current and we could stay up here for days."

When I feel the plane falter, I bank around and catch the current again lifting us to a new level.

"This is fun."

Frank smiles. "You're damn rights it's fun."

He opens the briefcase and fiddles with dials and switches. He looks at his watch and at an exact time pushes a button and looks out toward Palm Springs. "I love broadcasting in rich neighborhoods. It frightens them so much."

"Why?"

"Mostly because they have so much to lose. My dad was that way. He worked himself into the grave because he was afraid that he might end up on the streets. The guy had more money than I could spend in three lifetimes, but he was worried about being homeless."

"I spent my youth worried about the same things."

"Well, hell, BillyBob, you probably had a right to worry."

I look at Frank. "Dad was a machinist for a union shop in

Detroit. He made good money, but no matter how much he brought in, it was never enough. The sad part was just about the time the last of us kids left the house and my folks were getting ready to enjoy their retirement, the whole Detroit steel wars happened. After almost thirty years with the same company and six months to retirement, the company was sold, Dad was reevaluated and laid off and the bastards figured out a way to keep dad's retirement."

Frank put his hand on my shoulder. "It's a fucked up world."

We float around in silence for the half hour it takes to broadcast, then he closes the briefcase. "We can go home now."

"I'm having a gas up here. Is there any reason to go straight back?"

"We can stay for a while, but I haven't had breakfast and I'm hungry."

"How sharp of a turn can I make without hurting the plane?"

"At this speed, you could do a little maneuvering, but don't get your speed over thirty-five knots or make any radical turns."

Just for fun, I push the stick forward and the nose drops out of existence with me following. The wind goes from a gentle breeze to gale force in seconds.

Frank yells, "When you get ready to pull this thing back into a level flight, do it very slowly or you'll rip the wing off."

"Gotcha." I pull back on the stick and the nose comes up slightly. The wind subsides a bit as the plane shutters.

"Feel that vibration? You must keep the plane from vibrating. Let go of the stick a little."

I do as he says and the wing relaxes. We're still pulling out of the dive, just not as fast as I'd like. It takes another hair-raising ten seconds for the plane to slow enough to level out. I take my first breath when the wind returns to the gentle breeze of before. "I guess I won't be trying that in the near future."

Frank smiles. "You'll need a fighter jet for that kind of stuff."

"Now that we're okay, I can say it was fun."

"The operative word here is okay. This little plane wasn't built for much maneuvering.

"I get that now."

Frank wiggles around behind me. "I'll start the engine. You'll have more control when landing."

Before he yanks the cord, I say, "I'm not landing this thing. I wouldn't have the first idea how to get it on the ground."

He laughs. "Since you took it up, it's your job to put her on the ground." I'll be right here and talk you through it.

My RV is the size of a carton of cigarettes when the engine fires. The plane lurches forward.

He points over my shoulder at his silver bus. "See the red windsock on the top of my bus?"

I nod.

"It tells us which way the breeze is flowing and how strong it is."

I turn to him. "There's a breeze blowing south, right?"

"Which means you need to approach the beach from the south and head directly into the wind. Give yourself a lot of room. Maybe go down the beach a half mile."

I bank the plane over the water and fly along the beach.

Frank taps me on the shoulder. "Swing the plane around and line it up on the beach, then slow the engine a little so you can lose altitude."

I push the plunger in toward the control panel and the engine relaxes. The plane dipped toward shore and everything on the ground gets much bigger.

"Looks good, BillyBob. Now, keep her lined up and let's

get within twenty feet of the ground."

He points at the airspeed indicator. "Keep it at thirty-five knots."

I fight the stick a little as the plane slows.

"Let go of the stick for a second, BillyBob."

I let go and the plane stops fighting.

"Take the stick with your fingertips. Handle the thing like a feather not a baseball bat."

I take the stick again and the controls are feather-like.

When we get to what I think is twenty feet and we're skimming along the beach, Frank yells, "Now, drop it down to five feet. Don't let the wheels touch. You'll feel a ballooning effect that forces the plane to stay in the air."

I drop foot by foot until the plane starts fighting to stay in the air.

"Do you feel it?"

"Yes."

"Stay just above that effect and get yourself evened out, then slow the engine to idle."

I'm shaky as I push the throttle and the engine relaxes.

"Fingertip control," Frank yells.

I loosen my grip on the stick and the plane gets a little squirrelly as it drops the five remaining feet to the ground. When it hits it does so with a smooth precision I can't believe.

When we roll to a stop in front of Frank's bus, I turn the ignition key and the shoreline drops into the silence of the early morning. A few campers are milling about, cooking breakfast, going for walks, but none had such an exciting morning as me.

I unbuckle and climb to my feet while Frank unstraps the briefcase. He gives me a big grin. "Is that just about the best time you've had?"

"I never knew flying a plane could be so much fun."

He smiles and pats the little gas tank. "Better than sex, especially these days."

Not having had sex with Myrtle in three months, mostly because it just isn't in my thoughts the last five years or so, I give him a winsome smile. "I couldn't agree with you more."

We walk up the shore toward my RV. Frank turns toward his bus. "I've got some things to do."

"Sure, Frank. I'm kinda hungry. I'll see you later."

I open the door and climb into my motorhome. Myrtle sits at the table sipping a cup of coffee. "Have fun?"

"Myrtle, you can't believe. . ." and I tell her every detail. She doesn't look impressed. In fact, she's annoyed.

I pull out my favorite cast iron skillet and light the stove. In a minute the pan is hot enough and I get what is left of a dozen eggs from the fridge, all the time trying to tell her about the intricacies of flying.

Once in a while I look back at her and that sourpuss expression hasn't changed.

"You going to get one of those flying things?" she finally asks. I knew the question was coming.

"Don't think we can afford one. Don't know how much they cost, but on my pension we'd be eating rice and black beans for months trying to pay for it."

"That's good," she says. "Those things are death traps."

"But, honey, you got to go up with Frank this afternoon. It's the most exciting thing since. . ." and I can't think of anything else but sex, but I don't dare say the word, knowing Myrtle's been feeling a little unloved lately.

She gives me a look. "You'll catch me up in one of those things sometime in the next century."

"You don't know what you're missing."

She ignores me.

Once my eggs and toast are ready, I sit across from her.

"Have you given much thought to the broadcasting briefcase thing?"

She grimaces. "We'll be living like fugitives."

"Honey, we won't use it until we're ready to move to our next place. We aren't ones to stay in one place long anyhow, right?"

She takes a sip of coffee. "I thought we were going to stay here all winter."

I give her a sheepish grin. "I'm already bored with this place."

"Billy-Bob." She says with such a plaintiff resolve, I want to stay all winter just to appease her.

After a moment of silence, she says, "You're really set on this?"

"I always wanted to do something that mattered. This seems like the perfect way and we can still have our life."

She huffs. "If you let me decide when we're leaving any given area, then I'll let that contraption aboard."

"You sound like a sailor."

She smiles. "The minute that thing gets in our way, either of our way, then we send it back, agreed."

I lick my baby finger and cross my heart, then hold my finger out. She licks hers and we grab each other by the last digit and pull away hard. For thirty years, since college, it's been our binding contract.

"What about the plane?"

I shrug. "What about it. I'm sure Frank'll be gone tomorrow. He said only three days in one place once he broadcasts, so my flying days are limited. I'm going up this afternoon with him, that is if he'll have me."

"Three days you flying is about all I can stand."

I look at her wrinkled face and remembered how lovely she was all those years ago. She's still good-looking, but age

29

plays a dirty trick on women.

She says, "if we accept the briefcase we'll have to move in the next day."

"This year the neighborhood seems a little less friendly. I wouldn't mind going to Joshua Tree Park. I'm already tired of the lake."

"Okay."

I half stand, lean over the table and give her a big smooch. She really is my best friend. I know how much she likes being here. Hell, she talked about it all summer and by fall when we were headed this way she continued to bring up memories of past years. It's a big deal and she's giving it up for me. What a gal.

I put my dishes in the sink. "We could give the briefcase to Henry and Sarah on the other side of the park and stay for as long as we want."

She gives me a glare. "Why would we put them in harms way?"

"Frank said the FCC can pinpoint the location of the transmitter only while it's in operation. If we stay and Frank leaves, they'll ask a few questions then move on."

She gets a soft look. "Could we stay, BillyBob? I was really looking forward to it."

I stand and take her in my arms. "We'll stay as long as you like."

After an hour of floating in the air in that gossamer, we have another great dinner with Frank. There is lots of laughter and storytelling, one of my favorite things.

We take the case and hide it under our bed.

The next morning, before dawn, Frank's bus starts and he pulls out. I thought that might be the last we'd see of Frank Deluchi.

When I get up later that morning and look outside, in the

spot where his bus was parked sits the little red plane and its trailer. I step out of the van and walk over to it. A bow is tied around the drivers seat with a card attached to it. I open it:

BillyBob;
"I don't often find a fellow flier. It was more than a pleasure. I'm leaving this for you as a token of my appreciation for the fun we had."

Frank
P.S. Find another place to store that briefcase for the next few days. Sometime the FCC shows up two or three times just to waist more of our tax dollars.

Chapter 4

Broadcasting

I smile as I open the yellow slip of paper folded in with the card. The title is signed to me.

I go back to the RV and retrieved the briefcase, then get on my scooter and drive two miles through the maze of RV's, trailers and fifth-wheels to Henry.

When I get to his motorhome, he's sitting at the outside table with a dirty T-shirt and big belly, smoking his ever-present cigar in front of his huge Executive Vista Cruiser. Once retired from the crumbling Detroit automaker mess, he'd sold his home of thirty-years and bought the overly priced, new, forty-five foot, diesel pusher. He's been on the move for ten years.

I park the scooter next to his motorcycle and with the briefcase in hand, I walk over and sit across from him. He smiles. "What brings you over this time of the morning, BillyBob? Something to do with that suitcase I'll bet."

I lift it slightly as I sit across from him. The sun is peeking over his neighbors old beat-up Airsteam.

"Could you hold this for me for a few days?"

He takes it and sets it behind him next to the big wheels. "Cup of coffee?"

"Sure."

We sit at that table for the next two hours, greeting passers by and eating pastries with our coffee. I like hanging out with Henry.

When his not-so-friendly wife emerges, I find an excuse to get away and drive back to Myrtle who sits at the table looking over the mirror lake. She's talking with Sara, one of the permanent residents of Slab City. Her Ancient motorhome died in place and she never could afford to have it repaired, so it sits, year after year gathering not only desert dust, but old broken bicycles, defunked tape recorders, bankrupt TV's, destroyed toys her two kids discarded, worn out shoes, used up washboards, leaky tubs, empty soap boxes and a dozen stray cats. The woman is a walking junkyard, but the uniqueness of slab city is that we all live together if not in peaceful harmony, at least in a reluctant stalemate. As long as I don't have to look at her mess, I guess I'm okay with her collecting the crap. She lives on the slab 365 days a year and there is something admirable about her tenacious ability to get through a desert summer when Slab City is all but empty of us winter snow birds.

I dismount my scooter. "Hi Sara, how's the kids?"

She turns and shades her eyes from the mid morning sun. "BillyBob."

With Sara and I there is a tentative truce. Since she knows I'm not asking about her two trouble-making brats, she doesn't answer. I never expect her to answer.

I go into the RV and grab myself a cold soda, then sit on the couch as the two women return to their talking. It's a time-honored exchange of information. I've learned that women have a deep need to stay in contact and the only way is to talk. If Henry and I said more than a hundred words in the entire two hours I sat at his table, I'd be surprised.

The day is calm and the water flat as an ice rink. I continue to look out at the red airplane sitting next to our space in the empty lot.

Finally, I can hold out no longer. I have the bug and that's all there is to it. I toss my aluminum can under the sink, walk outside and over to the gossamer wing and its little gas-powered engine.

Frank hadn't given me much time to get used to the contraption, but it looks harmless. The thing lands at little more than a fast walk, what trouble can I come to?

Like Frank showed me yesterday, I check the wires, the oil and gas, checked the steering and make sure the three dinky wheels have air, then sit in the right seat and yank the starter pull rope. The engine coughs and comes to life. I taxi the plane down to the edge of the shore, wave at Myrtle and Sara, both with worried looks on their faces, crank up the motor and roll down the shoreline until I leap into the air. God, it great to feel the air currents rather than sit on that damn shore listening to those two women yack their brains out.

The little plane climbs out over the Salton Sea and its brackish waters. I bank left then right looking for currents but finding nothing, so the whine of the motor will have to do for now.

Once I reach four thousand feet, our RV and the thousand other vehicles parked around us take on a fantasy quality. I kill the engine and feel the little plane relax into a slight breeze as I sweep and search the skies for the next current.

I'm in the air for an hour, learning the intricacies of the little plane and reveling in the silence of flight. At one point, I look back at our campsite, the size of a pack of cigarettes and notice three cars sitting in our driveway with huge numbers on the roof. I've seen too many cop movies to not know who's come calling.

I bank the plane toward the shore. Myrtle will be freaking out.

Once I get close to the ground, I slide the plane back behind the spit of land a few hundred yards south of our campsite. Without much effort, I land the plane behind a series of RV's bellied up against the shore, but far enough away to allow me some room. Once I stop, I pull the key and unstrap myself. I walk quickly around the outcropping and along the shore toward my RV.

Myrtle sits behind the outside table while three cops stand talking to her.

"What's going on?" I ask as I walk up.

Myrtle doesn't falter one bit. She looks at me as if nothing special is going on. "The authorities are looking for Frank Deluchi. You know, the guy in the huge pusher parked next to us the last few days."

I sit across from her.

The detective gives me a once over and pulls his badge. "You Mister Harding?"

I nod.

"We've been looking for Frank Deluchi for some time. Have any idea where he's gone?"

I give him an innocent look. "No idea, officer. We shared a beer yesterday afternoon. He never even said he was leaving, but that's how it goes here in Slab City."

"How's that?"

"People come and go all the time."

He grimaces. "That's the problem now isn't it."

"What do you mean?"

36

"Transients don't give us much to go on."

I give him my best smile. "Guess not."

The cop asks a series of standard questions, trying to build some kind of lead. If I knew the answers, I'm sure not going to tell him doodly squat, but with most questions I really don't know much about Frank.

After an hour, the police force folds up their dog and pony show and drives off.

I turn to Myrtle who had a huge smile on her otherwise poker face. "What are you grinning at?"

She gets up and stretches. "That was the most exhilarating thing I've done in I can't tell you how many years. I almost wish they come back so we could do it again."

"Myrt, you surprise me. I rushed back thinking you'd be flipping out."

She climbs the two steps into the RV, turns and gives me that look. "Just the opposite, but if you don't get in here right this minute and strip your ass down, I'm going to attack you out there on the bench."

For the next hour, we move our way slowly from one piece of furniture to another to the bedroom. We try positions and maneuvers we hadn't tested since we were teenagers. Since we're older, we have to be a lot more careful, but the old spark is back and I mark a little note in the back of my brain to figure out a way to get her in this mood again.

Two weeks go by and I practice flying every chance I get. I still can't get Myrt to go up with me. The suitcase stays at Henry's. Late on a Friday, she walks out to meet me as I taxi the plane up the shore and onto the concrete pad next to our RV.

A nice, portly couple parked in Frank's spot with a little class "A". There's plenty of room to slip the wing in sideways without taking the plane apart.

We haven't really gotten to know them too well. They keep their own company when they're around, which isn't much.

Once the engine is off, Myrtle says, "Let's do a broadcast tomorrow night then take off for parts unknown."

I give her a big smile.

That evening, after dinner, we begin the long process of packing everything in preparation to move.

By the next morning, knowing it might be the last flight until we find a new place, I go up and stay in the air until hunger drives me back to earth. By the time I get out of the plane, Myrtle has a couple of sandwiches and some chips on our table.

I sit and start eating talking with my mouth full. "It was amazing up there today. Come up with me sometime."

Myrtle grins. "Tonight when we do the broadcast."

I look at her with surprise. "What's it with you and that broadcasting thing?"

She smiles and takes a bite of her sandwich.

By three, I've retrieved the suitcase from Henry and find the DVD that came in the mail last week. By five, I'm ready.

I clip the briefcase into its special carrying rack, buckle Myrt in and give her a kiss on the cheek. "Get ready for the thrill of your life."

"Let's just get this over with."

I pull the rope and the engine whines to life.

When we're off the ground, she grabs my jacket and holds tight. I give her a smile and yell over the screaming motor. "You're strapped in, you'll be fine."

She gives me one of her nervous grins. I could tell this first flight wasn't as thrilling for her as it was for me.

We climb to two thousand feet and I turn the engine off.

"What the hell are you doing, BillyBob? Turn that motor

back on right this second. This isn't a carnival ride."

I grin and let go of the stick. "The plane pretty much flies itself, Honey."

"We're going to crash."

"It's okay, we can float like this for hours. Isn't it better without the sound of the engine?"

She looks down. "We're so high."

I make a slight bank into a thermal and the plane rises. "All the better to reach more homes and more TV's." I look at my watch. "Speaking of which, it's five of six, time to unpack that briefcase."

She reaches down and unbuckles the lid. "What now?"

I pull the DVD from my jacket pocket. "Put this in the slot on the side then we wait till exactly six o'clock. This thing has commercials and everything."

She slides the disc in and the machine comes to life.

I point at the square red button. "When I say, press that button and that's it for a half hour. It turns itself off."

I look at the watch Frank gave me that resets its time by satellite and the digital seconds click one at a time from forty-five, forty-six, forty-seven. I wait to a few seconds before, then point at Myrt. "Hit it."

She presses the button and other than a little green light at the top of the laptop and the fact that the police will be showing up sometime in the next few days, I can't tell if it's broadcasting or not.

It's early March and night comes a little later, so we have time after the broadcast to dally around a bit, but Myrtle eventually points toward the RV. "Let's get back, I'm cold."

I want to make her first experience a good one, so I drop into a gentle glide and head for our stretch of beach.

When we reach the ground and I pull the plane into its parking place, I start to take it apart. Myrtle takes my hand.

"That can wait."

"Myrtle, Honey, we've got to pack it in and get out of here."

She gives me that look. "We're all packed. We have an hour, don't we?"

"I don't know, they could be here any minute."

"Ain't it exciting."

I unclip the briefcase then she pulls me into the RV and has her way with me for a second time in two weeks. It must be a record. It's not as rambunctious as last time after the cops left, but I'm not complaining.

After all these years, Myrtle surprises me once again with a kinky affinity for danger. She's really has a feel for it. God, I just hope she doesn't take up robbing banks.

After our romp, I take my truck and scooter over to Henry and leave it with him, who knows, maybe until next year. I know he could use it.

Once back I disassemble the plane, put it in its trailer, hook it to the back of our RV and by eight o'clock we pull away from our spot next to the Salton Sea and meander out of Slab City onto the highway. We head north toward Las Vegas, a city certainly in need of some real news.

That night we stay on a hill overlooking Blythe, California.

As we're going to sleep, Myrtle says, "We could stay here for the day and broadcast this evening before moving on."

I look at her and see that wild-eyed glimmer. "You're really like this bad girl stuff, don't you?"

She smiles. "I like the sex."

"Myrt, I'm not complaining, but do you think this much sex is good?"

Her smile turns to a grimace. "All I know is I like it and for now that's enough."

I shrug. "We should have taken this up years ago."

Her smile returns.

After the broadcast we make love until dark. Exhausted, I put the plane away, then we move north, driving far into the night, past Needles, Nevada before we pull off of the highway and into a turn in the road far enough away from traffic that I can sleep.

The next day, we make a long pull up a twenty-mile grade, crest the summit and Myrtle points. "Vegas."

Up until the last few days, Las Vegas never interested either Myrtle or myself, so we'd never seen it.

"It's spectacular," she says.

"Like a crystal formation in the middle of the sand."

I look at her as I let off the gas and allow the big RV to coast down the long hill. "I'm not sure I want to go into that mess."

"Yeah, me either. Let's find some kind of campsite up here on the hill. We could do flights over the city and come back to the sand."

"Just outside of Henderson, we find a campground and a campsite bellied up next to Lake Mead. Like the Salton Sea, the shore is reasonably flat and with a little effort in clearing rocks and debris, Myrtle and I create a landing strip right in front of the RV.

"Can we take it up," she asks.

"It's mid day, Myrt. We can't broadcast until six."

"I don't want to broadcast just yet. I like it here. Maybe we can stay for a week or two and the last three days we broadcast. I just want to feel the wind in my face."

I smile. She's got the bug.

We unpack the trailer contents and with the help from our new neighbor who just happens to saunter over to see what's happening, we reassemble the plane by five.

When the little engine cranks up, the entire neighborhood comes out of their trailers and motorhomes. We wave and roll along the beach until the red light weight wing leaps into the air and starts toward the heavens.

"Let's work out to the middle of the lake, BillyBob."

Without saying a word, I put her hand on the stick to help her get a feel for flight.

"No, BillyBob, you do it."

"I am doing it, Honeypie, you're just helping."

She smiles and relaxes into the banks and twists until we're high enough to shut off the motor.

Once we're back to the silence of the sky, she says, "I never thought I'd say this, but I could stay up here forever."

It's almost dark before we're forced, by hunger, back to our landing strip. We're greeted by the neighbor, Todd and his wife.

"That's quite a contraption," he says as he shakes with his rough machinist hands. "This here is my wife, Sally."

She's a small woman with short-cropped gray hair and the bluest eyes. I immediately wonder if she has a pair of colored contacts. "Hi," I say as Myrtle is extricating herself from our flying machine, something we've come to call it.

I shake Sally's small hand and point. "This here is Myrtle."

The two women shake.

Sally says, "We were just starting happy hour. Want to join us?"

I look at Myrt, knowing what she really has in mind but she says, "never pass up a beer. Got any chips? I'm starved."

I sigh inwardly with relief. Don't get me wrong, the sex is great. It's just that I'm kinda' worn out.

We follow our two new friends to the front of their class "A" and sit across from them under the canopy at a park picnic bench. Once our beers are open and Todd and Sally mix up two Bloody Marys, I ask, "where are you from?"

Todd points North. "Northern California in a dinky town called Burney. It's too cold for Sally's arthritis, so we spend our winters down in the desert."

"On Lake Mead?"

Todd laughs. "In the area. Our favorite place in the winter is Death Valley. The people are friendly and there are so many interesting things."

Myrt chimes in. "Really? We cruised through there a few years back and we saw nothing."

Sally sniggers. "That desert is special. You have to stop for a while before it reveals itself."

Todd finishes his sip. "There's a place in northern Death Valley where rocks travel by themselves. You can see their path, sometimes a hundred yards long, but nobody moved them. It's the weirdest thing."

Sally looks at Todd. "If you're going to tell them that tantalizing little tidbit, then you gotta tell them how hard it is to get there and how desolate that particular valley is."

He laughs. "She's right of course. It's a forty-mile drive down a horribly beat-up old wagon trail and once you're there the entire valley is a dried up old lake bed with nothing else to offer but these hundreds of rocks. You wait for them to move while you're there, but it never happens."

Sally rolls her eyes. "He waited two days."

Todd turns to her. "Come on, we had fun."

She turns to Myrt, points at me with her thumb and whispers. "The least fun I ever had. Stay back at camp when he gets that particular bug up his butt."

Myrt turns to me. "We have a secret weapon."

Todd looks at the red wing. "That little plane would make the journey a cake-walk. In fact, it would make almost any journey pretty easy."

I grin. "I'll take you up tomorrow."

His eyes glisten. "Really?"

I nod.

Sally gives him a dirty look. "Todd, you go up in that death trap and you'll never get laid again."

Three days later, while Sally is in town with Myrt, I take Todd up and he loves it.

One night after dinner Myrtle says, "Let's do our broadcast and move on, BillyBob. There's too many speed boats on this lake."

I pick up a few dishes and take them to the sink, then look back at her. "There's always too many speedboats."

She piles up more dirty dishes and hands them to me. "Let's pack it in tomorrow, get one last flight at six and move north."

"We could make three broadcasts."

"One is good enough for me. I don't like being even close to Vegas. Too glittery."

I smile. She's definitely a Midwest kind of gal. Cornfields and grain elevators are her speed. The first day we were here, we went to a grocery store on the outskirts of town and she was appalled, especially with gambling right there in the store. She couldn't get back to our motorhome quick enough.

The next morning, we start the long, slow process of packing, not that we have a lot of stuff. It's more like we don't move that fast and find a lot of distractions to sidetrack us.

I take the plane up at noon and float over the lake for a few hours until Myrt puts the red flag out. It's our signal.

I land within feet of the canopy and kill the engine. I unbuckle, walk to the motorhome and open the door. "What's up, honey?"

She gives me a worried look. "There was a news flash on the radio about two guys here in Vegas getting caught with one of our broadcasting boxes."

"Yes?"

"They've got them under arrest as a terrorist."

I climb the three steps into the RV. "Terrorist?"

She nods. "They caught them because they stayed in the area too long."

"Jesus, terrorist?"

"Something about due process being suspended because of the new anti-terrorist bill."

"What's that mean?"

"I don't know for sure. I can't remember my civics back in high school, but I know due process is a cornerstone of the Constitution."

I sit on the couch. "I guess we send this case back."

She glares at me "Not on your life. Those bastards just pissed me off. We just need to be more careful that's all. One broadcast then we move on."

"You were already planning that."

She smiles and opens the fridge. "Want a beer?"

"I'm flying tonight."

She drops a cream soda on the table and pops herself a beer. "I drink alone then. I don't mind, I need it."

Chapter 5

Jake Ballard

I've been following Frank Deluchi's almost non-existent trail for two years. Just about the time we get a bead on him, he disappears like smoke, then shows up in an entirely different state.

I have three boxes of files on him. From hundreds of interviews, all we know is he drives a bus, but damn there are thousands of buses in the Southwest.

"Jake, we got another."

Eddie Severs, my partner, hangs up the phone. As much of a slim chance I believe we have on catching this guy, Eddie is even less inclined.

"How many does that make this week?"

"Shit, Partner, I have no idea. There are maybe fifty active broadcast units at any given moment. I'd say three or four hundred. This one's broadcasting in Vegas. We going out there?"

"Let the locals see what they can dig up."

His tight-skinned, angular face drops into frown. "I've

never actually been to Las Vegas."

I shuffle some papers on my disaster of a desk in the precinct from hell. "Yeah, and so?"

He picks up his filthy ceramic coffee cup his daughter made in high school and takes a sip. "Hear it's pretty cool."

I reach out and snap my fingers for the new file. "It's glitzy that's for sure, but other than gambling it's pretty hollow."

"Heard the women were spectacular."

"Yeah, and you'll pay dearly for each and every one."

"Hookers?"

"Hookers are the cheap ones."

His forty-five year old face turns into a grin. "Spoken like a true divorcée."

I open the file and glare at him. "Hey, fuck off, asshole. Not like we aren't in the same boat.

I'm half way through the text when I spot the names.

"You find something, boss?"

"I think I know these people. They're from Florida, my home state. Maybe we're going to Vegas after all."

His face turns as gleeful as it can for a middle-aged man who can't quite get his feet under him after a particularly difficult divorce. She took the kids and everything.

I submit a work order to go to Vegas. It's work related, but that isn't why I want to be on the scene.

Late that night, Ed and I jump on the red-eye and land in glittery Las Vegas as dawn breaks.

Ed, sitting next to the window, nudges me. "Would you look at that sunrise?"

"I just got to sleep."

"Hey, you've been snoring for an hour and we're landing in ten minutes. I figured you'd want to see this. It might start your day off a little better."

I look out the window and admire the brilliant burgundy

of the distant clouds. "Starting my day off better would have left me sleeping for that extra ten minutes."

Once we disembark and walk into the terminal I see a thin man with a summer short sleeve shirt and a pencil thin mustache holding a sign that reads, "Lieutenant Jake Ballard."

I walk over to him. "I'm Ballard."

"Oh, good." He speaks with a high squeak. "I wasn't sure I had the right plane. I'm Sammy."

Up close, the dark circles under his eyes make him look like a junkie or a coke head. The bloodshot glaze confirms my impression. We shake.

He points. "Let's get your bags and I'll take you into town to the precinct."

As we walk along with the hundreds of other passengers, I ask, "how come the special treatment? Usually we find our own way to the station."

He smiles. "Captain's orders. Something about you being from Homeland and all."

Ed chimes in. "See Jake, I knew being Homeland Security would pay off someday."

We ride in the back of one of the cleanest cop cars I've ever seen.

Ed bumps my arm and points at the never-ending line of casinos. "I'm here tonight."

"I'm in bed."

I look at Sammy through his rear view. "Speaking of bed, did we get a room somewhere close?"

He looks in the mirror. "Next door to the precinct. We got you a spare car too."

Ed says, "will it be as clean as this one?"

Sammy sniggers. "This is Vegas, they're all clean."

∾

Jake never wants to go anywhere. He takes his Humphrey Bogart swagger and his Jimmy Stewart stature and goes to bed. I don't get it. The guy could have any woman any time and he wants to sleep?

I look at Sammy in the car mirror. "You into partying?"

"Got a wife and two kids."

"Well, shit. I'm in Vegas and I got a car full of nothing. I'm going out. I could give a rat's ass about you two."

Sammy pulls into the station and parks below the building in the security lot. Once the engine is off, he turns to us. "Leave your stuff in the trunk. Once you're done, we'll get you a car and transfer everything."

We get out and go up the elevator to the fifth floor. Once the door opens, we step into a precinct office out of the movies.

Ed sweeps his arm. "Fucking-A, it's spotless."

Sam leads us around a half dozen cubicles to the Captain's office.

The Captain looks up with his mid-fifties flushed face, teeth too big for his mouth and beady brown eyes.

He barks a command. "Sergeant Slackard, you're twenty minutes late. Care to explain"

Sammy stands at attention. It's not a full military attention, but rigid and attentive just the same. I look at Jake.

"Traffic out of the airport was impossible, Sir." Sammy snaps the Sir like it was his last.

The Captain looks at a file on his desk. "You two are here to interview our terrorists?"

Jake gives him a crisp, "Yes, sir."

"They're in lockup."

Jake points at the folders. "We haven't had a chance to go over your files."

"Well, boys, this ain't no Sunday revival. Get your asses to work and get up to god-damn speed."

I'm ready to rain all over this dickhead's parade, but Jake's level head saves our asses. He pulls out his badge. "Sir, with all due respect, our office sent me out here to review your suspects. In the morning, when we're rested, we'll have a look at your files and ascertain whether we'll take jurisdiction or not."

The captain starts to say something, then his face goes pale. "Fine. Do what you goddamn well please."

The rooms they have for us are reasonable for government work. After trying to coax Jake out one last time, I find myself at the Flamenco eating dinner alone.

The place is packed and it's hard to even find a blackjack table in my price range. I know a full house is not the time to sit at a table, but I want to play cards. I sit next to a fat guy with a rank-smelling cigar on my left and on my right a soccer mom with a yellow bandanna and cheap earrings. Fatso doesn't move an inch, but bandanna slides her chair over a few inches to give me room.

"Thanks." I toss a five-dollar chip on the table and slide it into the play box like I knew what I was doing.

I draw sixteen, then hit once and get a king. The second hand, I draw a twelve and hit three times for a twenty-two; out again. The third time the dealer hits twenty-one and I'm ready to get out of there when soccer mom's leg rests against mine. I drop another chip without changing expression. The cameras are on us and a pickup in the casinos is a big no-no in Atlanta, so I assume that same rule applies here.

The dealer pulls a twenty-one. I toss my cards and turn to her. "Let's get out of here."

She drops her cards on the table, grabs her small stack of chips and follows me through the throng of humanity. Once we're on the street, she takes my hand like we're old friends and says without turning her head to look at me. "Wait 'till we're out of sight of the cameras."

We saunter slowly along the sidewalk until we're between buildings. She stops and turns to me. "They can still see us, so no wrong moves. She pulls out a tourist map and we pretend to study it when she says, "are you affiliated with the police in any way?"

I've just struck it rich and I'm not about to let on that I'm a cop. "Nope."

Still studying the map, she says, "hundred bucks for a half hour or a thousand for the night."

Since Sharon left last year, getting laid is more than a problem, especially in my line of work where there are department ethics to deal with. More than getting laid, I'm lonely.

"How about I pay you the hundred for the next hour and we just hang out for now."

She turns to me and smiles. "I knew I liked you when you sat down. What's your name?"

"Eddie Severs. I'm in from Baltimore."

"Kinda cold up there this time of year?"

"That's why I'm here."

She smiles. "I'm Sara Summers and originally I'm from Bisbee, Arizona. I've lived here a year."

I take the map from her and start folding it carefully. "I'm sure you know of some bar or a restaurant we could settle into without the cameras."

She smiles her crooked little smile. With her button nose and Donna Reed blonde hair, she puts her hand in the crook of my arm, pulls in close enough for me to feel the softness of her breasts. We walk to the end of the street and cross with five hundred other gamblers.

It isn't five minutes of walking along side streets, then down a back alley when she turns us into a broken parking lot and up to a one-story building with a blue neon sign that says, Blue Mango, that is if all the letters were lit. As it is, it reads, "UE GO".

Although the outside is rough, and I've checked my pistol three times during the walk, we step in and I sigh with relief. It's a regular bar with about ten people sitting around. She leads me to a table in a dark corner and we sit facing one another.

I look at her and in the half-light she's beautiful in a mom sort of way. The bandanna and fifties-style dress gives her an innocent look, kind of like Sharon back when we were young and in love. I still don't know why Sharon decided to leave. She gave me all the reasons about finding herself and needing to be on her own and feeling cornered, but I never could figure out what any of those reasons meant. After nineteen years, she just up and left.

I try to get my head out of that depressing subject as the bartender steps up with napkins and a small bowl of pretzels. "I'll have a Corona and the lady. . ." I point at her and with a bit of an embarrassed face she says, "Coke."

Once the bartender leaves, I look at her. "You don't drink?"

"I'm allergic."

I'm positioned with my back to the wall, looking toward the bar. A middle-aged blonde sits by herself. A guy the size of a house sits six tables from us. He's not nursing his drink, but downing it. The guy's a cop I'm sure of it, but he's in street clothes. Everything is calm until some dickhead football type bursts out of the bathroom, half-stumbles across the room and sits three stools from the blonde. The guy looks like pure trouble. He turns to the blonde. "Hey Babe, you want some company?"

She doesn't look at him.

After his second attempt, the cop says, "leave her alone."

Mr. Football spins on his stool and glares at the cop. "Fuck off!"

"She doesn't want to be bothered."

The football idiot leaps off his stool and charges the cop. "You got more to say?"

The cop stays seated, but it doesn't look like he's backing down.

Sara looks at the commotion.

The cop speaks in a quiet tone, "just leave her alone."

Football Player's right fist comes from around his back in a long, sweeping arc. He means to shatter the cop's face. The cop lifts his beer bottle butt first to meet the fist. When it connects, the bottle doesn't break, but I hear a number of bones crunch. It happens so quick, I can't tell what's going on, but in a few seconds Mr. Footabll is writhing on the floor and the cop's kicking him unmercifully. He's kicked four or five times before the barkeep tries to pry him off. "Come on buddy, you got him. That's enough. Stop before you kill the guy."

The guy can't stop. It's like he's been waiting all day for something and he isn't about to give it up so quickly. I know lots of guys like this back on the force in Baltimore. Cops always seem a little more tightly wound, but who am I to judge? I've been here many times.

He lands one last bone-crunching kick to Football's chest and I'm on my feet. I turn to Sara. "Wait here a second." I step over to the scene as the bartender pulls him away for a second, but he's so hyped that he turns on the kid and almost punches him.

I move fast, ready to help the kid out, but Blondie gets off her stool and walks between the two men. "Thank you, stranger," she says in a soft voice. "You can stop now."

The guy noticeably relaxes.

I pick up a leather billfold and it flips open. Sure enough, his badge flashes off of the overhead lights. The identification reads, "Thomas Goreman".

"You dropped this," I say as he's heading for the door. He stops. I bridge the ten-foot gap to hand him the wallet. Neither of us have to say a word. We both know we're cops and that's all we need. He nods and disappears through the front door.

Football groans. I walk over and look down. "You need an ambulance?"

Out of breath, he manages to say, "no, no ambulance. I'll be all right."

I turn to the bartender who says, "as long as numb-nuts here pays for the two broken chairs, I don't need to call the cops."

"I'll pay, just give me a minute."

I walk back to my table and Sara. When I sit, she looks at me. "You sure you're not a cop?"

I get an embarrassed face. "I work for Homeland Security, here on assignment to check on some people."

She stands and gathers her stuff. I'm talking fast. "I'm, I'm from Baltimore. I'm not in this bar for any other reason than to hang out with you. Leave if you have to, but I've been lonely and I thought a little time spent with you would be nice is all."

She stops, takes a breath and sits. "My girlfriend told me to run if I ever came across a cop."

"I'm off duty right now and if worse comes to worst, I can protect you from the cops."

She gets a soft look. "Really?"

I pick up my beer and take a sip. "I don't like to lie, but I liked you right off and we both know what would have happened if I'd told you the truth in front of the casino."

"I would have left."

"Look Sara, it's the first anniversary of my divorce. I don't want to be alone tonight."

Her face gets soft, which makes her even more appealing. She reaches across the table and takes my hand.

Chapter 6

Crash

Sitting at our fold-out picnic table in front of the RV, Myrtle gives me one of those looks. "We going up this evening?"

"Sure, Honey." I'm getting used to the wild sex after.

"We're doing this for our country."

"Yes, I know. Our fellow Americans sit on couches and recliners night after night watching the nightly news. They think that America is about honesty and truth and never consider that maybe what's being fed them like baby's pabulum is so far from what's really going on that no one knows the bottom of the snake pit."

She gets a flushed look. "Keep talking like that and you know where you're going to end up."

I pause a moment, take a gulp. "Jail?"

She grins. "No, silly, in bed putting to full use that other tool you have."

I smile. "Let's save that for after the flight when things are at their optimum."

She stands, walks over to my side, turns my head and plants

a long, lingering kiss on my lips. "This is foreplay."

Who am I to complain? It's been years since she's even been interested. Her renewed libido is gravy on an otherwise perfect marriage. Knowing that nothing lasts forever, I'm riding this one for as long as she's interested.

Later that afternoon, we pack the motorhome and prepare for a quick getaway. While putting things away, I ask, "where are we off to?"

She turns to the kitchen, gets the map out of the drawer, sits at the table and opens it. "I thought maybe Death Valley, but we can't broadcast, so let's revise our little plan." She points at Lake Havasu a few hundred miles north. "A lot of people winter in that area. We park next to the lake and when we're ready to move on, we do another broadcast."

After I finish inspecting the map a minute, she carefully folds it. She's always the one to carefully fold things. She puts it back in the drawer and looks at me. "For now, BillyBob, let's finish packing, then get airborne. I like that little plane of yours. Maybe you could show me how to fly it."

I grab the box of DVD's and carry them across the RV. "I can show you what I know, which ain't much."

"It'll be a good start."

"You really like this flying thing."

She gives me her secret smile. It's apparent only during those special moments when she's truly happy. She picks up the bread on the counter, opens the cupboard and slides it in a box I built three years ago out of some paneling scrap from our remodel back home.

∾

After BillyBob and I finish packing the bus, we strap ourselves into the little kite-like airplane. He starts the engine and we leap into the air. I never thought I'd like flying so much, but being out in the elements with just a skimpy little frame below us and the silly looking wing above somehow makes the entire experience more real. Broadcasting a pirate signal in the face of the huge machine called the United States and doing so for truth and justice also gets to me. It rekindles my old hippie days of demonstrations and sit-in's. That was before Kent State. It was when we all felt so invincible. Martin Luther King was still alive and the world seemed so much more able to handle civil disobedience. It reminds me of my youth and all of those love-in's and the wild sex in the back of a Buick or on the grass next to a Harley. There were a few years when I ran as wild as the wind. Part of me misses those years and a much bigger part is glad I made it out alive. I never thought I'd make it past thirty anyhow and who trusted anyone over thirty? I never in a million years thought I'd ever get to pushing seventy.

Something about opening that suitcase and disrupting the signal for all of Las Vegas is sexy. I know BillyBob doesn't mind.

So, here we are climbing above Lake Mead, the spires and glitz of Vegas coming into view and I don't know why, but I yell, "let's go really high, BillyBob, so we can broadcast to the Mexican border."

He looks at me and grins. "Signal's not that strong. We'll be lucky to reach the north edge of Vegas itself."

I'm disappointed, but we're affecting maybe a million people with Frank Deluchi's message and I guess that'll do.

A minute later, BillyBob cuts the noise and we float in the warm breezes high above the lake.

BillyBob starts his incessant search for air currents and we rise high above the lake until the entire RV camp looks like a dot. Vegas is really an amazing scene from so high up. I want to get closer. "Can we fly over the top of Vegas?"

He turns the kite and floats toward the crystal city in the middle of so much sand. The wind in my ears and the sun setting behind the distant mountains leave me breathless.

I look at my watch, then open the case and insert the DVD. At exactly six o'clock, I push the "on" button and all of the dials and indicators come alive. It really is a marvel of engineering and so simple.

I can't help myself. I reach over and grab BillyBob's crotch. I want to do it right now as our kite floats over the outskirts of the huge city. I want to unbuckle my seat belt, toss my pants overboard and climb in his lap. I want him.

BillyBob takes my hand away. "Gotta concentrate."

I give him a playful pout and blow a kiss. I feel like a kid again and the feeling is good.

I look at my watch and it's five after six. When I put my arm down and look back at the skyline, out of nowhere, a huge jet roars past. It's not more than a hundred feet over our heads. My heart almost stops from the noise. It takes a few seconds for me to calm. The jet drops toward the airport. I look at BillyBob and laugh I'm so relieved.

He turns our little plane on a dime and drops out of the sky. "We'd better get out of here."

"What's wrong, BillyBob?"

Just as I say this, everything goes wrong. A huge wind catches us and flips the plane on its head. We drop out of the sky. I hear something thrum like a guitar string then twang away. BillyBob pushes and pulls the control stick. We're caught in some kind of tornado. The ground is still a long ways away, but it looks too close. The howling wind flips us over. Another guitar string twangs and snaps. I look above our heads and the pretty little red wing flaps like a sheet. There's nothing holding us in the air. The wind continues tossing us.

As suddenly as it came, it disappears. BillyBob goes from trying to right the plane to trying to control its plummet toward earth.

I'm holding onto the flimsy little cage. The wind howls. The ground gets bigger.

The only wing left is a small section above our heads. It might be six feet wide. The rest of the thirty-foot foil is flapping.

"BillyBob!"

He fights the control stick. At one point the plane rights itself. We are diving at a tremendous rate, but at least that insane spinning has stopped.

"Help us, BillyBob."

His teeth are gritting. His jaw is working. His eyes are scrunched. I see every little thing. It's all so clear. We're going to die and all I can see is my husband's facial expression. I guess it's a good enough thing to focus on. I sure don't want to look at that ground.

It's close. I know it's too close, but all I want is to look at his face. It might be the last time I see him. God, I love this man. If we're going to die, I need to say it once more. I yell over the howling wind. "I love you."

Maybe he doesn't hear me, so I yell louder. "I love you."

I reach over and put my hand on his tense arm. "I love you."

For a second, he glances in my direction. He doesn't say anything, not even a smile.

There's the ground. Cars are the size of matchboxes. Houses and trees the size of shoe boxes. There's no chance of landing this rocket plummeting out of the sky. We're dead. It's over. I lean over, stretch myself to his cheek and kiss him as the ground leaps into our faces.

$\sim$

We walk out of that bar arm in arm. Sara leads me down the street toward the crowds and other casinos.

"Do you have a hotel?"

I nod. "It's back up the strip a mile or so."

"Can we catch that cab?"

A yellow taxi barrels along the street toward us. I step off the sidewalk and put my hand up. It screeches to a stop and we get in.

"Queens Motel," I tell the crusty old Greek or Italian who is so overweight his car lists to the driver's side. Without a word, he pulls the shift into drive and bolts to the strip, turns left and merges into traffic seamlessly. Five minutes later he pulls into the motel.

"Room seventeen," I say. "Close to the back."

Sara was fidgety during the ride, but now that we're close, she's jumping out of her skin.

We get out and I pay the driver, then I turn to her. "You okay?"

"Fine."

I sense something's wrong, but women never say. I mean, look at my ex. She never said a word until she was walking out the door. All those years and she never said a word. Even at those last moments she didn't say much. It wasn't until we were in divorce court that the real truth came out. Even then, she never spoke, her cut-throat lawyer told the stories. I was an asshole and that was all there was to it.

Trying to second guess Sara, and I hate doing that, I ask, "We could sit by the pool for a while if you want."

She whips her head around to face me and gives me a relieved look. "Could we. . . just a few minutes?"

I take her arm and walk her to one of the five cheap aluminum lounge chairs sitting around the pool. She sits while I pull one up next to her.

When her breathing calms, I ask, "you going to be okay?"

Tears well up in her eyes. She takes a deep breath. "Truth be known, I. . ."

The suspense is killing me, but when it comes to women isn't there always a lot of suspense? I've learned not to push. I wait for her to finish the sentence.

She reaches over and takes my hand in her little fingers, then toys with the garnet ring I got last summer in New York. "I. . .Well, I. . .I'm not really. . ."

Holy shit! She isn't a woman at all, but some fag-assed cross dresser. My stomach suddenly turns into a knot. I'm ready to punch her/him out and walk away.

"I'm not really a call girl," she says. "Okay, there I said it." She points at my room. "I really can't go in there with you."

I snigger. "You're not a call girl?"

"I'm broke and I've been broke for some time. I've got two kids and we're right on the edge of getting evicted."

I take a deep breath. "You're not a call girl?"

I start to laugh with relief when I hear a buzzing above my head. It's like a mosquito, but louder and the sound is coming at us fast. I look up and a red flying garbage can with what looks like a bed sheet flapping behind it hurls toward us.

"Holy shit."

It might be five hundred yards above our heads, but by the time we're up and running for protection, it closes the gap.

I stop under the concrete stairs and turn just in time to watch it and two people dive dead center into the deep end of the pool. The subsequent cannonball splash looks like it empties half of the water. It drenches us both.

As soon as the water recedes, I drop Sara's hand and run for the pool. I kick my shoes off and shed my new sports coat. I leap into the water and taste the gas. I swim to the bottom.

Both people are floating listlessly in their seats. I grab both belt clips and release them, then pull the people free. I break the surface and gasp for a breath. Sara helps by dragging the woman to the shallow end. I pull the guy onto the pavement and he's choking. I grab the woman and pull her out next to the hacking man. She' still. Sara is next to me. "Turn her on her side."

Water dribbles from her mouth. Sara positions herself and jambs her knee into the woman's ribcage. Water gushes. Sara does it again, then again.

She flips the woman onto her back. She grabs her nose and puts her mouth on hers and breathes twice, then starts pushing hard on her heart. I check her pulse and she has none.

A few breaths, then another series of heart pushes. She repeats.

A small crowd gathers. I yell, "someone call an ambulance."

For the next fifteen minutes, Sara continues breathing. Finally, the woman coughs, sputters and starts to show some life. By the time the ambulance arrives, both people are on their knees hacking pool water.

As I sit back on the lounge chair, Jake steps up. "What the hell is going on?"

I point at the couple coughing. "They dropped out of the sky and landed in the pool."

He looks at the red cloth spread over the pool covering the pyramid shaped framework. "I can see that. How'd you get involved?"

"Sara and I were sitting out here." I tell him the shortened version of the story, leaving out the hooker part. As I finish, two black and whites roll into the motel and park.

As the couple are put into the ambulance, the two cops tie a rope around the frame of the wreckage and hoist it to the shallow end of the pool. As it sits there half submerged, Jake walks over to it. "Can we pull this thing all the way out?"

The bigger of the two cops says, "We're waiting for the tow truck."

Jake pulls his badge and shows it to them. "It looks pretty light. I'd like to try, if you don't mind."

It's lighter than I think. Since I'm already wet, I get in the water and guide the twisted frame up the steps as the other three pull on the rope. We drag it onto the patio and Jake walks over to the passenger side, kneels and unlatches the case.

I step over. "Is it?"

He has awe in his voice. "I'm almost certain."

"I've seen pictures, but never one up close."

He picks up the case and sets it on the patio table. "If those two are terrorists, then we're in big trouble."

"Why's that?"

Jake picks up the case and drains a few cups of water by tipping it on one edge. "Because those two were regular mom and pop citizens. I was expecting an extremist fanatic, not some old hippies."

He turns to the short cop. "We'd better get that couple under arrest for now until I can figure out what's going on."

The cop steps away and clicks his shoulder microphone. A moment later he comes back. "Looks like they got out of the ambulance on Fifth Street."

Jake shakes his head. "Okay then, let's get a net around this city. These two are fugitives and Homeland wants them for questioning."

The cop walks away again as Jake pushes the "on" button. The machine comes to life and the screen glows.

I point at it. "Holy shit, the thing's waterproof too."

Jake pushes the eject button and a disc slides out of the side. He takes the DVD carefully by its edges and studies it.

"We may have prints."

The short cop returns. "We've dropped most of the force on them."

Jake shows the cop the disc. "We'll need some prints lifted from this."

The bigger cop has the pool skimmer net dipped deep into the water. He fishes the pole around a moment, then pulls up something black. "I think it's a wallet."

He drags it to the surface, then hoists it around to us without looking at it.

Jake opens the wallet and pulls out the driver's license. "Cancel the net. I think we've got 'em." He hands the wallet to the short cop. "Get me as much as you can on this guy. I want to know everything, his birth, where he lives, the name of his dog, everything."

The short cop takes the wallet. "Yes sir."

"Can we have that in an hour?"

"Can do, sir."

The Vegas cops are trained well. I like the "sir" crap. I feel important. I wish Baltimore PD had half as much respect. Those bastards won't give us the time of day.

Jake turns to me. "You ready to go to work?"

I point at Sara with my thumb. "Can I have an hour?"

"Half hour."

I walk over to Sara and pull some cash out of my wet wallet. "I got to go to work."

She whispers. "Don't pay me anything, especially right here in front of Vegas Police."

I flush with embarrassment, then point across the street. "I got a half hour. Can I buy you a cup of coffee?"

Her worried look softens. "I'd like that."

After I change out of my wet clothes, we walk across the street into a dingy twenty-four-hour joint and sit in a booth.

The place smells like sour milk.

"Two coffees," I say when the waitress arrives.

I turn to Sara. "Things got a little out of whack over there."

She reaches over and touches my hand. "That's sweet."

She pauses for a moment and takes a deep breath. "I'm sorry, I can't go through with our agreement."

"It's okay. It looks like I'll be in town for another few days. Mind if I call on you?"

She gives me a suspicious look. "I can't—"

"No, not for that. I liked this last hour. Well, save for the bar fight and plane crash."

She sniggers.

"Maybe I could take you out to dinner or lunch, or we go for a walk in a park. I really don't care."

Her face softens. "That would be nice, but I'm still looking for a job, so anything during the day is probably going to be out."

"Dinner then. No expectations."

"Tomorrow night, Eddie?"

"Looking forward to it."

I pause, then asked my stupid question of the hour. "How did you decide to take up this particular profession in the first place?"

"My best friend is a call girl. She kept saying how easy it is. She told me what to do and how to dress. I thank my lucky stars that I met an understanding person like yourself. I could have gotten myself in a real pickle."

I look out the window then at my watch. "My half hour is up. I gotta get to work."

She takes a napkin and writes her phone number across the center. "Call me around six. I'll meet you somewhere."

I take the napkin and fold it, then stand and put out my hand to shake. "I look forward to tomorrow."

She shakes and gives me a radiant smile. "Me too."

I turn, walk out of the restaurant and wait for traffic to clear before I cross the street. Just before I step off the curb, I turn and give her a wave. She smiles again and waves back.

Jake's got a Cheshire grin. "Glad you could make it back."

"Hey, fuck off. What do we have?"

"They got in a cab and went south out of town. The cab dropped them just outside of Henderson and that's where we lost them."

"We're combing that area, I assume."

He doesn't give my question a response, but turns to the briefcase. "You got to see this, Eddie. This little broadcasting unit is amazing. I don't think I've ever seen something so well made and so simple to use. If this is what we're up against, then we got some real problems."

"The real problem, Jake, is there are thousands of reports out there from all corners of the country and they all couldn't come from this one unit."

"Exactly," he says. "Someone is churning these things out by the hundreds, the big question is, why?"

I point at the disc in his hand. "I'd say we look at the disc and see what they have in mind."

Jake closes the lid. "On the laptop in my room."

We walk to his room, slip the disc into his computer, and immediately the disc starts smoking. Jake pulls it out as quickly as possible, but not quick enough. By the time he gets it out the information part of the disc has self-destructed.

"Well shit," Jake says. "It probably messed up my disc drive."

A big cop steps through the door. "We got a lead on their RV. The last place they bought gas was outside of Henderson."

"Drop a net around Henderson."

"We figured they're in one of the hundreds of RV parks in the area so we already did that."

Jake asks, "You got a name?"

The cop looks at his notebook. "BillyBob and Myrtle Harding from Boseman, Montana. Other than some stupid demonstration stuff in the sixties, neither of them have any kind of record."

I look at Jake, "Just some regular mom and pop team. Man, we're in trouble."

Jake asks, "How do you mean?"

"A couple of regular citizens doing shit like this, and there are thousands of these boxes out there. We've got a lot of work."

"We catch these two and it won't take much to get their story and figure out who is heading this organization."

"We already know who, just not why."

The cop's radio squawks and he steps away to answer it.

I turn to Jake. "What would make these two want to do such a thing?"

He grimaces. "Something we've got to find out for sure."

I point at the disc. "I wish we could have seen what was on that."

"Yeah, me too." Jake drops the disc back into the evidence bag and puts it inside the silver case.

Soaking wet, I drag Myrtle out of the ambulance and find our way away through the busy part of town. She is still a little groggy, but as soon as they find the case we're in trouble. We've got to get out of here.

I hail a passing taxi and slip into the back with Myrtle.

"Where to, Pal?"

"Henderson. I can't remember the campground. I'll tell you where to turn. There's an extra twenty if you get us there as soon as humanly possible."

He pulls the shift into gear and spins a "U" in the middle of the quiet street. "You're talking to the right guy, Mack. I know all the back alleys to get around that mess out on the strip."

I'm not exactly listening. Myrtle has passed out again and I'm having a hard time keeping her upright. I slide her to the far door behind the driver, so he can't see and slip in next to her to hold her up.

I don't know what to do, get us safe or take her to the hospital. I feel her scalp and find a bump the size of an egg. No blood, but she certainly whacked her head and I've heard from her all these years that you don't fuck around with head trauma.

The driver makes a right onto a back alley and rushes past garbage cans and alley cats as I say, "Where's the hospital?"

He looks in the mirror. "I've been listening to the police scanner. Looks to me like you've got some trouble. If that's the case, a hospital is the last place you want to go. Make that a hundred and I've got a private doctor who works out of his home and wouldn't be able to file a report until tomorrow morning. Might give you some time."

I go for my wallet and can't find it. Myrtle's fanny pack nets me a few hundred in her secret hiding place. I slide a hundred to him.

His eyes sparkle. "Had you two pegged when I first saw you."

"What gave us away?"

"Might be that desperate look. Might be the leaking bandage covering the nasty cut on your neck. My wife says I'm psychic, but shit I don't believe in that hocus-pocus crapola."

In five minutes he pulls up to an old renovated Victorian. "You want me to wait? I could turn the radio off so I don't have to check in with dispatch."

"Yes, please wait."

He turns in his seat. "As soon as someone asks, I got to tell them everything. You know that, right?"

"As long as you tell me too."

He smiles. "Deal."

I open the door as Myrt awakes. "Where are we?"

"We're going in to see the doctor, Honey."

"Doctor, why?"

I climb out with the cabbie. He's a small man with a wiry frame, but he has a gentle face. Once I get Myrtle out, he takes her other arm and helps walk her to the front door.

I ring the bell and an older gentleman with a shock of silver white hair smoking a pipe opens the door. "Don, what do we have here?"

"Hi Doc, couple's got a little trouble. Brought them to you if that's okay."

The doctor opens the door all the way and takes Myrtle's arm. "Let's take her to the back and get her settled." It's just then that she collapses. Both the doctor and I struggle to carry her into the back room and get her on the examination table.

He immediately checks her head and finds the bump. "She's hit her head pretty hard."

"Yeah, Doc, I'm worried it's too hard."

"Me too. She really needs to be in the hospital. This could be serious."

The cabbie speaks up. "Like I said, Doc, they got trouble."

The doctor looks at me. "What kind of trouble?"

"We crashed our ultralight."

"Doesn't sound like the whole story to me."

"We've been doing a bit of civil disobedience lately."

Myrtle's eyes open. "What am I doing here, BillyBob?"

The doctor gets down to her level. "I'm Doctor Bloomfield.

Looks like you banged your head. Can you tell me what day it is?"

She thinks a few seconds. "It's Saturday, I think."

He holds up two fingers. "How many fingers do I have?"

"Two. What's this about?"

The cabbie starts to walk out. "I'll be in the car."

I walk him to the front door and slip him a fifty. "This should hold you for a while."

"About a half hour. I'll keep the radio off for now."

I put out my hand to shake. "You're a good man, Don."

He smiles and descends the three concrete steps, then walks to the car.

Myrtle is passed out again when I walk in the room.

The doctor turns to me. "She really should be in a hospital."

"We can't right now."

"Maybe you could fill me in on your civil disobedience while I check that cut on your neck."

While he pulls the bandage off and rinses the wound, I tell him about the plane and the broadcasting unit. When I get to the part about overriding the signal, he laughs. "I thought the news was a little weird this evening. It seemed so very unlike the regular news. What is this Zeitgeist thing?"

"Look it up on the Internet. It's hard to explain, but once you see the documentary, you'll understand."

Myrtle awakes and reaches out for me. "Where are we, BillyBob?"

I turn to her and take her hand. "At the doctor's, Honey. You banged your head pretty bad."

She smiles at the doctor. "At least I didn't drown in the swimming pool."

The doc looks surprised. "Swimming pool?"

She point at me. "This guy flew our broken ultralight right smack into a swimming pool. Otherwise, we'd be splattered all over some sidewalk. How he found that pool, I have no idea."

He turns to me and I shrug. "I don't know where it came from, but suddenly it was there and I crashed us into it. Turns out some cop pulled us out and that's how we're in trouble."

"Crashing into a swimming pool?"

"No, Doc, crashing into the swimming pool was no big deal. It's that broadcasting suitcase."

A knock comes at the front door and a moment later the cabbie steps in. "The cops are checking all the cabs. I can hold them off for ten minutes or so, but I'll be in big trouble if I lie."

I shake the cabbies hand. "Thanks for all the help. Hold them off for as long as possible and you'd better get out of here."

"How are you going to get to Henderson?"

"We'll figure it out, but your cab will lead them right to us, so I'll thank you again. Go ahead and keep the change."

The cabbie nods and leaves the house. I turn to the doctor. "Can you give us directions of some back routes to Henderson where our RV is parked?"

"I'll go you one better. I'll take you there. I can keep an eye on your wife at the same time."

"Doc, you don't have to put yourself in jeopardy."

"Hey, I'm an old man and what can they do to me, especially if you don't tell them you told me anything. I was just giving you a ride. I'll stay at my girlfriend's house after I drop you so they can't ask me any questions until tomorrow when I come to work."

"By then we'll be long gone."

He smiles. "Exactly."

He turns to Myrt. "You really need to go to the hospital and have your vitals checked, but under the circumstances, all I can suggest is when you get to your next place, a hospital should be your first stop."

Myrtle climbs off of the table. "I'm fine, Doctor."

He gets a worried look. "Promise me you'll have it checked, because these things have a history of causing trouble."

He turns to me. "Her brain has been bruised. Any intense headaches or more passing out, you get her to a hospital pronto. For now, follow me."

He walks us through the back of the old house where he lives and hangs his smock on the hook at the back door. We step out to a small parking lot and over to a late fifties Cadillac parked under a carport.

Myrtle gets in the front and me in the back.

When he starts the engine, the purring sound takes me back to the days of my misspent youth working in a gas station in Inglewood, Colorado.

The ding-ding of the bell told the team of attendants that another car has pulled up to the pumps. We ran out to the car and more often than not filled the tank, checked under the hood, even checked the tire pressure. There was a certain pleasure to really serving the customer and continuing to maintain their car, then to make the commission selling them all of the extra products they needed. It was 1963 and Kennedy had yet to be assassinated. Martin Luther King was still a thorn in the side to everyone in power. The Beatles were moving up to take over Elvis in popularity. All seemed right in the world. Maybe it was because I was just reaching puberty. Maybe I had yet to open my eyes to the endless wars, the constant struggles humans were destined to go through living in a capitalist society. Credit cards had yet to take a full grip on our culture. Companies made good on their promises of a full pension when a worker reached his golden age. Bread was fifty cents a loaf, gas was twenty cents a gallon. Most everyone had some kind of savings account.

Ding-ding, the sound of a culture ready to serve just for

the delight of serving the next customer.

Had we been lulled to sleep or are we asleep now? Maybe we've always been asleep and those predatory creatures count on our blank stares, walking through our pathetic lives without looking at anything but the next paycheck. I certainly did it for thirty years with the engineering firm, Platt and Wilford, the bastards. They found a way to fire me six months before my retirement. Luckily I'd invested some of my paychecks during my career. I just felt bad for the poor schmuck who counted on that pension that had been gambled away.

Myrtle says, "BillyBob, do we turn here?"

"Yes, turn left."

It was a time of innocence and the feel of this leather seated Cadillac with its cushy ride, silent engine and a transmission that shifts so smooth you don't feel it certainly has taken me back.

I pull myself out of my revelry to concentrate on the twists and turns of the RV park. "Up ahead, turn right, then a quick left."

The car floats around corners I can't feel and glides along rough, sun-baked asphalt like we're on a cloud.

"Three thirty one, on the left."

Doc Bloomfield pulls over. "You'd better pack up tonight. It won't take them long to figure out where you got off to."

"Already packed."

I get out and reach through his window to shake hands. "Thanks doc, for all your help."

He grabs my hand with a strong grip. "Keep an eye on your wife. She needs attention."

"When we get to the next city, Doc, I assure you."

Myrtle steps up to the driver window. "Doctor Bloomfield, you've been an angel." She kisses him on the cheek and I detect him blush even in the semi darkness.

We wave as the silent wonder of an age gone by floats off into the darkness.

I take Myrtle's hand. "What happened to people like that?"

She smiles as she continues to wave. "Oh, they're around."

I look at her. "I remember so many more."

We get into our RV and since we prepared to go before we took that fateful flight, I disconnect the trailer as Myrtle climbs into the passenger seat. I start the engine.

In ten minutes we're moving south along the highway, getting as much distance between us and Las Vegas as possible before dawn.

Myrtle's passing out symptoms has ceased, but though she insisted that she'll take over driving during the night, I'm having nothing to do with it. "What if you pass out while you're driving?"

"I'm fine, BillyBob. You're beat and I should take over."

"Just keep me awake till we make it to Needles. We can stop there and sleep."

As the morning sun breaks over the ridge of a distant set of mountains, we pull in for gas and some breakfast at a truck stop on the Southern outskirts of Needles.

We walk into the restaurant and sit in a booth. The blinds are closed as the sun blasts in through every crack.

The waitress, a heavy set woman in her thirties brings us some water and menus, then turns without greeting us and goes back to her place in front of the cash register. She's watching the morning news on a TV above our heads. I can't see the set, but I hear the commentator. "Two people crashed their ultra-light in this Las Vegas swimming pool last night and walked away unharmed. Authorities are looking for them in connection with terrorist activities in the Las Vegas area."

I look at Myrtle and whisper. "Terrorist?"

She shrugs. "I told you."

The couple drive a golden class C motorhome with license plate numbers. . ." He reads off the numbers and I give Myrtle a grimace. "Jesus, they got our number, didn't they."

"What do we do, BillyBob?"

The waitress walks up at that second and with pencil and pad in hand says with a surly snarl, "what can I get you?"

Once we order, and the waitress walks away, Myrtle says, "We just can't keep running, BillyBob. I'm no Bonnie and you're no Clyde. I can't spend my life looking over my shoulder. I mean, what can they do, give us some kind of fine and send us on our way."

"Terrorist means more, Myrt."

"Oh, BillyBob, that's just to jazz the news up."

"I don't know, honey, they sounded pretty serious."

She huffs and gives me a glare. "You want to run?"

"Maybe we call Joseph back home. He's not a criminal lawyer, but he might know what to do."

She takes out her cell phone.

I grab the phone and disconnect the battery. "We can't make any calls from our phones. They have a way of pinpointing us through our cell."

I hand it back and she returns it to her purse. "Okay, Mr. I-know-it-all, what do you suggest?"

I dig in my pocket and pull out some change. "Give me what change you've got and I'll call on the pay phone."

She dredges up a handful of quarters as the waitress returns with two plates of greasy eggs and overly buttered toast. She sets them on the table in a haphazard manner and puts one hand on her hip. "Anything else?"

I look up at her sad face. "Does you're pay phone work?"

"Nope."

"You know where one might be?"

She points with her other hand still standing with her weight on the one hip. "Cross the street in the Texico." She turns and walks away.

I start to get up, but Myrt stops me. "May as well eat while it's still warm."

I settle in and pick up my fork as two police officers saunter into the restaurant and start bantering with our waitress.

They sit behind us drinking their coffee and joking with one another.

I finish the crappy breakfast, get up and walk past them as nonchalant as possible. As I pass, one of the cops speaks up, "Hey, buddy."

I stop and feel all of the color drain from my face. I turn.

~

I have my back to the door as my husband of thirty years and father of my children gets up to make the phone call to our lawyer. Yes, we're in trouble. I know we have some extra bills to pay for wrecking that little plane into the swimming pool, and we certainly have some questions to answer to the Las Vegas police about the briefcase. Okay, probably we violated some F.C.C. laws and we have some kind of price to pay for that, but terrorist? That has me worried. We were about as far from being terrorists as I can fathom.

While my brain is assimilating this whole mess, a voice from behind me says, "hey, buddy."

I turn and find myself sitting a few feet away from two a huge police officers. My face drains as I look directly into the eyes of the second, smaller one facing me. I turn back and cringe. I'm sure he saw my expression. Police are suspicious by nature.

Behind me, BillyBob takes an intake of air as the deep voiced officer says, "You dropped something."

Did he say my husband dropped something? He's not going to arrest us and even more embarrassing, handcuff us?

I turn slightly toward BillyBob and watch him take a slip of paper from the officer. "Thanks," he says and walks away.

In the reflection of the big plate glass window, I see the smaller cop make a silent motion to his partner and I know the jig's up. In seconds we'll be wrestled to the floor and manacles clamped to our wrists. All of our freedoms will be tossed out the window.

My husband goes out the front door. Will he get away leaving me to deal with these two? God, I feel like Bonnie and Clyde and it isn't any fun at all.

I eat my two greasy poached eggs and wait for one of the cops to recognize me.

Ten minutes goes by before BillyBob returns. He sits across from me, leans forward and whispers. "Joseph said we should turn ourselves in. It'll look better in court."

I grimace. "What would we do with our RV and I need to call the kids."

BillyBob finishes his eggs and drops a twenty on the table. "Let's go then."

I get up with him and without looking at the two police, we go through the door to freedom. We walk to the RV and get out of there as soon as possible. Once on the freeway toward Los Angeles, I point. "Pull off at the next off ramp."

When he parks on the side of a frontage road, I take him to the back of the RV and jump him even more intensely than any of the times after the plane rides. Something about the close call with authorities that continues to spark my libido. BillyBob isn't complaining.

Later, we drive away from civilization and out into the

desert headed toward Bakersfield.

"What did Joseph say?" I ask as we move across flat endless landscape ruined by dune buggies and dirt bikes.

"He said to find a small town and turn ourselves in. He was checking to see how much trouble we were in and I'm supposed to call him back later this evening."

"Does he have any idea?"

"He thinks some kind of fine from the F.C.C. and maybe probation, but we may have to spend a few hours in jail waiting to get bailed."

I smile. "That's not too bad."

"He thinks the fine will be substantial."

"Even if Frank doesn't come through with his promise, we can handle that, can't we BillyBob?"

He gets a distracted look as the RV pushes through the hot desert air and we sit in comfort in an air-conditioned environment.

"Can we handle it?"

He turns to me. "Yes, honey, we can handle it, but I'd rather not give this fucked up government a penny, if you get my meaning."

"You don't need to cuss."

We drive along for another few miles in silence before I ask, "why a small town?"

"Joseph seems to think we will get treated better. Something about the police being less stressed."

"Makes sense. So, what town?"

"Thought we'd go into the hills above Bakersfield, a place called Lake Isabella. There's four or five little towns around that lake. We could park our RV in a campground and choose which town to turn ourselves into."

"Is it pretty there?"

"We went through there four or five years ago, remember? Just after Nancy and Paul's baby was born."

"Oh sure, we stopped there for a few days at an old hot springs. It was pretty."

The rest of the day we drive in relative silence, watching the landscape go from flat desert to grassy foothills, then over a rocky mountain pass that reminds me of a smaller version of the Utah badlands. Once we drop over the pass, though the landscape is dry, large cactus and vegetation dot the land. We stop for gas at a small station along side the two-lane road. When I get out I can smell the water.

"How far away is the lake?" I ask the lanky attendant with his greasy coveralls and mechanic's hands puffy from working in petroleum products too many years. He plugs in the gas nozzle and gets it started. "You got another ten miles before you see the lake, but it's another ten miles after that to get to the first town."

"I smell the water."

He smiles. "Yeah, we get a bit of weather from that lake, especially in the winter. Pretty calm right now though."

"Which is the nicest town?"

"Isabella's the biggest town on the South end of the lake. It's got all of the stores and even a theater, but I'd say Whiskey Flat's the nicest. It's on the north end of the lake. It ain't got nothing 'cept a restaurant and a coupla' bars. Kind of a tourist town, if you know what I mean."

"Does it have an RV park?"

He grins. "They all got RV parks up the ol' ying-yang."

BillyBob steps around from the back with an oil stick in his hand. "You got synthetic oil?"

The guy turns to him. "No, but there's David Rylie's part store just down the road maybe six, eight miles. It's up on the hill to the left. Got a big sign. You can't miss it."

BillyBob ask the attendant one last question. "Which of these towns has friendly police?"

He looks at me with a curious gaze. "Well. . . I guess Whiskey Flat, since they cater to tourist, the police are the most tolerant. The chief picks only friendly cops." The gas nozzle clicks off and he turns to grab it. "I should know. Guess I've been in most of the jails. Not so much any more, but when I was younger, I raised a little hell round these parts."

He hangs up the nozzle and wipes his hands on a red rag. "Got myself a wife and kids these days. Ain't no time to give the local cops any trouble."

BillyBob hands the guy our credit card. He walks back to the dingy office.

As we climb into the RV, I say, "We'll turn ourselves in at Whiskey Flat."

"Whiskey Flat?"

I point toward the office. "He said the police are friendly there."

"Whiskey Flat it is."

The attendant takes forever. When he finally comes out, he gives us an embarrassed look and talks to BillyBob through the small side window. "The credit card company wants me to keep your card."

BillyBob asks, "really? Why?"

The guy shrugs. I don't know, they just said to cut it in half."

BillyBob digs in his wallet, pulls out his last hundred and hands it through the window.

The guy says, "Sorry, it wasn't up to me."

"No problem. I'll call my company, cause we got tons of credit. I really don't get it."

When the guy goes for change, I say, "Maybe it's the bit of

trouble we are in. Maybe they stopped our credit cards."

BillyBob gets a worried look. "Shit, I forgot. They probably seized our bank account too."

"Stop your cussing, BillyBob."

I take his hand. "I guess we'll have to turn ourselves in, because if that's the case, we're down to lunch money."

He gives me a sad smile as the attendant steps over and hands him the change. The attendant looks a bit nervous. "You folks seem like nice people and I hate the local cops."

He stops and looks around again. "The cops called and said to hold you as long as possible. I guess you're in some kind of trouble. If anyone asks, I never said this, okay?"

BillyBob nods. "Sure, okay."

"When you drive out of here go about a half mile to the next left turn, then go up the hill to the top and you'll be able to see what's coming for miles. There's a place to turn around up there. Sit and wait for the cops to go by on their way here. Once they go by, make a bee-line for the southern end of the lake. Just as you pass the first freeway onramp get off, make a left and follow the old highway to the bottom of the canyon. It might get a bit tight, but your rig will make it. Wait there until night, then you can slip out of the county."

BillyBob reaches out the window and shakes his hand. "Thanks."

The guy smiles and waves us on.

Without saying a word and my heart is racing the whole way, BillyBob turns left on the road and drives to the top of the hill. There is a huge dirt turnaround and we park looking out over the blue lake with strings of houses and businesses lined up along the ragged shoreline.

My heart is pounding as I look over at BillyBob. "Joseph said it's better if we turn ourselves in rather than get caught."

"Can we make it to Whiskey Flat?"

Far in the distance three sets of red and blue lights come round a bend and race along the highway.

"We can try. Maybe I should call in and tell them we're coming?"

"I don't know, BillyBob. Maybe we just walk in the front doors and surprise 'em."

He looks at the phone. "It probably doesn't work here."

The cars get closer, then another set of lights come from the southern end of the lake. "Jesus, BillyBob, they must really want us. Four cars and this whole area couldn't have more then ten cars total."

He smiles. "Guess we're real desperadoes."

The cop cars drift past our turn. BillyBob starts the engine and drives back to the highway, then makes a left. We drive the ten miles to the split and turn north toward Whiskey Flat.

The road meanders along the shore of the lake. When we pull into town, I point at an RV park to the right. "Pull in there BillyBob."

"They locked up our credit cards. Don't think I have the cash to pay for even one day.

There is a sign for a city park and he turns right down a road that follows the shoreline with grass all the way to a slow moving river. There are a few parallel bus parking places and we pull into the last one. He turns the engine off and looks at me. "Maybe we should have lunch first. I don't think jail food will sit with us very well."

We walk over to a corner restaurant and sit at a table next to the window. The restaurant is almost empty.

A nicely dressed young man with a day-old beard carrying two glasses of water and menus steps over to our table. "How are you today?"

If he only knew. I tell him we're fine and let it drop.

"I'll give you a minute." He turns and walks back to the kitchen.

I look at BillyBob. "I'm having a hard time concentrating. I've never been behind bars before."

He opens the menu. "Don't worry, Myrtle, Joseph is on it."

The kid comes back after a minute and stands with his pencil poised.

BillyBob looks up. "I want the club without bacon."

The kid looks at me.

"A small salad."

Once the kid is gone, I turn to BillyBob. "How can you think about eating?"

He leans in close. "It's better than jail food."

He pulls out the phone and dials a number.

"Who are you calling?"

"Joseph told me to call as soon as we decided which town."

"Thought we aren't suppose to use the phone."

"In a few minutes we're turning ourselves in. Shouldn't be a problem."

His attention goes to the phone, "Joseph?"

"Yes, we're doing fine."

"She's okay. Maybe a little nervous."

"Yeah. . .Yeah. . .Sure"

"We decided on Whiskey Flat, California."

He closes the door of the phone.

BillyBob looks at me. "We have to wait a half hour for him to get everything in place, then he'll call back."

We sit in an uncommon silence eating our lunch and waiting for Joseph to return our call.

An hour goes by before the phone rings. BillyBob put it to his ear. "Joseph?"

I slide my chair over and put my left ear close so I can hear. "BillyBob, the news isn't good. They want to keep you overnight until Homeland Security can get there."

"Overnight?" BillyBob says.

"It's not too bad. They have a pretty comfortable jail and they serve food from the local restaurant."

"There's no other way?"

Joseph takes a deep breath. "You can keep running, but isn't it better to get this over with? You fucked up, BillyBob, now it's going to cost you. All I can do from here is to get your bail lined up and get you out as soon as possible."

"How's the bail thing going?"

"I've got it ready, but the sheriff wants you overnight. It's just how it is."

BillyBob takes a breath. "Okay. Do we turn ourselves in after I hang up?"

"Make sure you don't have anything on you or in your RV that will be a problem for the police."

"Like what?"

"Illicit drugs, anti-war pamphlets, anything that might give them reason to want to keep you longer."

"Joseph, I haven't smoked a joint since high school and even then I didn't like it."

"I know, buddy, but just check yourselves thoroughly."

"I really don't have to. I don't have anything to hide."

"Any old discs from that broadcasting machine?"

BillyBob has surprise in his voice. "How did you know about the broadcasting machine?"

"It's what you're being charged with."

BillyBob looks at me, then says, "I'll give the RV a once over."

"Remember, BillyBob, I'm right here working every angle to get you out as soon as possible."

"Thanks Joseph, I do appreciate this."

The line goes silent, then Joseph says, "the minute you get out, call me."

"Yes, of course. You're our lifeline."

BillyBob hangs up and looks at me. "You heard it."

I nod. "Looks like we don't have much choice, do we?"

The walk to the RV is a death march. The overwhelming feeling of dread lay over us like a thick fog. The RV has nothing as we already knew, but it's good to check.

Chapter 7

Jack Perkins

I happen to be close to the receiving window when the couple walks in. I'd seen photos of them from Homeland and they looked pretty sinister. I've worked the force in Bakersfield, Fresno, and finally here for thirty years and from my experience, these two are not terrorists. They look more like hippy throwbacks from the sixties. He has his little goatee with his skinny Arabic frame and she an emaciated woman in her sixties.

That dickhead, Lennie is at the window and I stop what I know will be his blatant disrespect of these two by standing behind him.

"Help you?" He says with as little guile as he can muster.

The man takes her hand. "We want to turn ourselves in."

No clue Lennie gives them a curious stare. "Names?"

"Mister and Misses BillyBob Harding."

Lennie turns to me like he doesn't know what to do.

"Get them inside," I whisper.

He pushes the door button. "Step through the door."

The couple walks through and I greet them. "I'm Captain Perkins."

The guy reaches out his hand to shake. I take his and give him a smile. "You don't look like terrorists."

He gives me a nervous half grin. "My lawyer said we broke some FCC laws, but the terrorists part I don't get."

I point down the hall. "Let's go to my office?"

I follow them to my little cubical of an office and get them seated. "Want some coffee or water?"

"No thanks," the little guy says. She shakes her head.

I sit across from them and pull out the beginning of an endless stream of forms to fill out for these two.

"Can you give me your full names?"

An hour later, without much more than a question answer session and fingerprinting, I walk them to a holding cell and lock them in.

From their story, I don't get how Homeland can see these two as terrorists, but they have their own way of approaching things and who am I to question a government agency.

~

"Jake, we got em," Eddie says as he hangs up the phone. "That was some sheriff in Whisky Flat, California."

I sit hunched over two eggs, sour dough toast, no butter, and two slices of bacon. One thing about ordering the same thing every morning, I don't have to think about what I want.

I take a sip of coffee and look at Eddie.. "I was there nine years ago when I was an MP for the Navy. Some guy went AWOL and we cornered him in his parent's house back in one of those canyons. It's a nice little town in the hills above Bakersfield."

Eddie takes a bite of his waffle. "Maybe you could go there alone. I kinda got some unfinished business here."

"The hooker?"

He gets an angry face. "I told you she isn't a hooker."

I grin. "Oh yeah, right. She picked you up and you gave her a hundred bucks, but she's a school teacher. You get laid yet?"

"Jake, will you stop that. I like her."

I take another bite of my uninspired eggs. "I can't leave you behind. We got work to do, pard and it's going to take both of us. Druckmyer wants those two on the plane by noon tomorrow."

"But Jake—"

"Call Druckmyer and tell her you need some time off for romance."

He grimaces and sips his coffee. "She'd be the last person on earth to understand."

"I rest my case, buddy, but what I can do is not get on the plane until early in the morning, if that'll help. We've got to finish off the real reason why we're out here."

"How early?"

"Oh, I don't know, maybe seven."

He gets a hopeful face. "Seven is good." He opens his phone and punches in a number.

"Know her number by heart already?"

He smiles, stands and walks to the far end of the restaurant.

I reach for a ticket and waive the keno girl over. Guess I'm kind of jealous that Eddie's got a girl and I'm still pining over whatever I lost. Hell, if there was anything I ever had in the first place. As things unraveled, I realized that she hadn't been there for years.

I fill in the same numbers I've used since I came of age. I never won much, but more often than not I'd win something.

She takes my five and my ticket and rushes off without saying a word. I pretty much had my fill of women after Sandra left three months ago. I was left alone and cranky and I've been that way ever since.

Eddie sits back in his seat and takes another bite of waffle with a big grin.

"Getting laid tonight, are we?"

With his mouth full, he says, "I don't know about your sorry ass, but the odds are looking pretty good for me."

When we get back to the station, I find myself buried in paperwork for most of the day. Transferring suspects from local jails to locations unknown, usually in Egypt or Bolivia, takes tons of paperwork.

By evening, I sit in an empty bar in the Flamenco along the strip looking out at the sea of gamblers with an occasional ringing and ding-dinging of jackpots. It's downright comical how serious the faces. They're supposed to be having fun. But then, I guess I'm one of them. Eddie might be the only one in all of Vegas who's enjoying himself, the bastard.

"Get you another?" asks the hulking bartender with a

voice so disinterested someone probably has to kick start him every time he needs to move.

I shake my head, take the last sip and get off of the stool. I want someone to call, but back home it's midnight and who would I talk to anyhow? I spent the last ten years on the road and things like relationships with people consisted of half-hour meetings, overnight stays with bored hookers and an occasional AA meeting in some odd town just for a reality check.

After three or four drinks, I've lost count, I'm not drunk, but I'm certainly not sober. I walk outside and the heat of Vegas hits my face. I climb into a taxi. "Tiki Motel next to the police station."

The driver shifts into drive and punches the gas. "I know where it is." The car lurches forward throwing me against the seat, then against the far door as he pulls into traffic.

I want to say something, but knowing taxi drivers, he'll drive more wild out of spite. They certainly are universally a special breed.

When he drops me at the motel, I pay him and work my way up the concrete and steel stairs to the second floor. My key is a little difficult to negotiate, which gives me an indication that maybe I had drank five or six rather than three or four. Glad I'm not driving.

I flop on the bed fully dressed and don't remember a thing until Eddie shakes me awake in the full light of day. "Hey compadre, aren't we suppose to be meeting the plane about now?"

I bolt upright, feel my head and almost toss my cookies. I

drop back onto the bed and cover my eyes.

Eddie laughs. "Thought I was the one who was supposed to be nursing a hangover this morning."

He pulls out his cell, "Maybe I'll call the plane and tell them we're going to be a bit late."

I grunt some form of approval.

"What's the number?"

"Wallet," I say, pulling out my billfold and handing it to him.

He rifles the wallet, then dials the number. "Why don't I go get us a coupla' coffees?"

I wave him out of the room, then once again slowly sit up. I find my way to the bathroom and into the shower. I can't imagine that I stand under the hot water for the entire time Eddie is gone, but I look at my fingers and they're pruned beyond belief. I do feel slightly better.

The coffee sits on the flat of the sink as I step out of the shower and towel off. The first sip is a god-send.

Eddie has my suit laid out on the bed and packed my suitcase. He looks up as I step into the room. "You look like shit. What the hell did you do last night?"

"Nothing really, just sat in some empty bar and lost count of my drinks."

Eddie steps toward the front door. "Well, you better get it in gear. The guys in that plane are none too happy that we've thrown their schedule off. I'll meet you by the pool."

Once he closes the door, I drop the towel rapped around me and dress.

We get in a cab and I hold my head while the cabbie slides

around corners, yells at other drivers, makes rabbit starts and tire squealing stops, all the way to the airport north of town.

He pulls up to the waiting Lear and slides to a stop. We get into the plane. The second the door closes, the plane taxis to the runway and gets in line between two commuter jets.

Once we're in the air, I relax in my seat and sip the second coffee Eddie hands me. It's not quite an hour flight, so I have to get my act together if I'm going to handle my charges in Whisky Flat without puking my guts.

By the time the plane sets down and we get out, I feel slightly better. I grab my suitcase and get into the waiting black Suburban.

"I need some breakfast," then motion for Eddie to do all of the talking.

There's only one restaurant in town and we sit at a window table while the driver waits outside.

While we eat, I point at the case file in front of me. "I don't like this one. Druckmyer wants us to disappear the guy to Egypt, but he's a regular citizen."

"Remember Jake, we don't make the decisions around here. In this case we're simply the muscle."

I put some blackberry jam on my toast. "Yeah, and I still don't like it one bit."

He shrugs as I take a bite of the toast.

Twenty minutes later we're in the Kern County Sheriff Station. I pull my badge. "We're here to pick up the Harding couple."

He gets a nervous look and steps away from the window. In a moment a tall man with a cowboy hat and boots to match steps out into the waiting room. He puts out his hand and shakes both of ours as he talks, "Boys, sorry you came a long way for nothing. The Harding's turned themselves into my custody and other than extraditing them back to Vegas, they aren't going anywhere."

I glare. Eddie hands him the paperwork. "Maybe your desk sergeant didn't tell you. We're with Homeland Security and we've been authorized to pick them up and transport them away from here."

"Transport them to where?"

The sheriff is a feisty one. I smile. "Look Sheriff. . ." I glance at my paperwork and read his name, "Sheriff Perkins, we've been ordered by the Federal Government to pick these two up and trans—"

"You said that. I'm just asking where are you transporting them, because if you are extraditing them back to Vegas, I'm on board with them. If you can't tell me, or you don't want me along, then I guess we've got a problem."

My head is still fragile and I'm not looking to get into a screaming match with this backwater cop. "I really can't tell you."

He puts his hands in the pockets of his levies. "These two have rights, you know. They broke the law and as far as I can tell, they have a court date and some fines to pay. Unless you can clearly show me they had other intentions, it's my job as sheriff in this county to serve and protect, that includes protecting my constituents from over zealous government agencies."

Inside I cheer him, but on the surface I have to represent

the government and Druckmyer.

I hold up one finger. "Can I have a minute?"

He nods.

I pull my phone and speed dial Druckmyer. She answers with her matter of fact voice. "Lieutenant Ballard?"

"Looks like the locals are dead set on not releasing the Harding's."

Her voice raises an octave. "Who the fuck do they think they are?"

I'm not prepared to answer that question so I stay silent.

She barks, "What's this assholes name?"

"Perkins."

"Well, put him on."

I hand the phone to the sheriff and move back a step. I know what's about to happen. The Druckmyer volcano is about to erupt and I don't want to stand anywhere close to the fallout zone.

After a moment Perkins holds the phone away from his ear. I hear screaming, but can't hear the content. When the noise stops, Perkins says, "Madam, if you are extraditing the Hardings back to Las Vegas, then I have no problems, but—"

The screaming starts again. Perkins holds his palm over the mic and looks at me. "This is what you have to deal with?"

I can't help myself. Although I want to remain passive, one eyebrow goes renegade and raises slightly.

When the screaming stops, Perkins says, "Send paperwork that you're moving my prisoners to Las Vegas and I will ride with them. Otherwise, I'm mandated to keep them here.

More screaming, then he hands the phone over to me. "She

wants to talk to you and she isn't happy."

I take the phone and cautiously put it to my ear. "Mame?"

She screams, "Ballard, you fucking stay in that jerkwater town overnight until I get some backup there in the morning."

"Yes mame."

The line goes dead. I close the phone, put it back in my pocket and look at the Captain, who's face is passive. "Knowing her, she'll drop a platoon on your head."

He frowns. "Military?"

I scrunch my face into a questioning expression. "Don't ever know what she'll do, but I do know she does what she says."

He gets a worried look, then shifts to his friendly face. "Guess you two will be needing a place to stay for the night. Whisky Flat Motel has the best prices, but Lakeside has the prettiest view and it's only a few more dollars."

"Fatima and Harriam Hissiam own that hotel. I'm sure she has a couple of rooms."

I don't know what to say. The guy's being friendly even after I dropped Druckmyer on him.

"Can I interview your prisoners?"

He gives us a relieved laugh. "Why sure, no harm in getting the real story from these two. Maybe it'll change your mind and you won't be carting them off to who knows where you take terrorist suspects nowadays."

"We don't cart—"

His interruption surprises me. It's the first time his anger rises. "Don't give me any bullshit. You're team dropped in on us two years ago and yanked one of our solid Arabian citizens for no apparent reason and we have yet to know where he is. These are folks who grew up in Whisky Flat. They are tax-paying citizens and your goons just snatched the husband like he was a stray dog. No papers, no records and we have no idea where he is. You can imagine his wife went crazy."

I look at Eddie, then back at Perkins. "There must have been something going on."

"Something going on or not, this is not how our country is supposed to run. Our citizens have basic constitutional rights and I'm here to see that no one else is going to miss out on their due process."

"I don't think you have much choice in the matter. By this time tomorrow this place will be crawling with our people and you will be forced to give them over to us."

He glares. "Wrong answer. You just lost your interview privileges."

I raise my hands in a stop gesture. "Let's back up a second, can we Captain?"

He takes a breath.

I look at Eddie. "Can you wait outside for a moment?"

"Yeah, sure Jake."

Once Eddie is gone, I turn to the Captain. "Can we go back into your office and talk private?"

He nods at the window clerk and who buzzes me through. Perkins leads me along a beat up hall and into a small office with papers strewn across the desk. He points at an old steel folding chair, then sits across from me in his badly worn office chair.

"Captain, I'm sorry we got off on the wrong foot. In a

sense, I agree these two are not terrorists."

His eyebrows raise.

"I've read over the transcripts and your right, this couple doesn't belong in some Egyptian prison. They need to pay their fine and get on with their lives. Unfortunately, my boss, and you met her over the phone, doesn't agree. I'm hoping to sway her bullheaded opinion, but I can't do a thing unless I get an interview with the Harding's."

He glares at me. "Is that where you took Fatima's husband, to an Egyptian prison?"

"I have no idea, Captain. I'm just a small cog in this very big machine."

"You could check?"

"It's beyond my pay grade."

"You're pay grade? We're talking about a man's life here and his wife has had two nervous breakdowns."

"Captain, I just can't saunter into the data banks and pull up information."

He gives me a suspicious look. "There's something that tells me that you do that sort of thing all the time."

I shake my head.

Perkins leans forward and whispers. "Tell you what, I let you interview the Hardings and you do what you can. Just tell me if Harium Hissiam is still alive. That'll be enough."

"Is he a citizen?"

"I'll get you his social security number."

"I can't promise a thing."

He stands. "Yes, of course. I say that all the time. You wait here and I'll get the Harding's into the interview room. You want them separate or together?"

"Together will be fine."

"So. . . you'll not have any information on Harium by the morning, right?"

"By morning."

"I'll be counting on you before the whole mess with the troops begins."

"Before."

He walks out of the dingy little office and I get a chance to look over the photos of two children on his desk, but no photo of a wife. He's single with a messy divorce behind him. There is a big photo on his wall of him holding up what looks like a huge bass. The lake behind him looks like Isabella, but it's hard to tell.

An array of open case photos and notes are pinned to a cork board. In the far corner from his desk under a thin stack of police business papers, with only one corner showing, I lift the papers and a large photo of Hissiam.

I remember Hissiam. I was on that case, though not at point. I'd just been hired and they were breaking me in. I was doing followup from the office.

I remember looking at the paperwork after we bagged him, got him on the plane and flew him to a prison in the Congo. Was that really two years ago? Is he still in that prison? Is he even alive? I hope so, because if I can give this sheriff some good news, it's going to make tomorrow much easier.

As Captain Perkins opens the door, I drop the sheaf of papers back over the photo.

He walks to his desk, opens the drawer and pulls out a

copy of the photo. "This is Hissiam two years ago. I'm afraid to know what he looks like now, that is if he's still alive."

I look at the photo as if I've never seen it. "No promises."

"Yeah, right, no promises," he says as he leads me out of the office and down three doors.

He reaches for the door. "I'm in there with you."

"I'd rather be alone."

"Do they get a lawyer?"

"Nine-eleven commission expressly forbids lawyers for terrorists."

"Figured that was the case. If I'm to serve and protect, and they can't have a lawyer, then I need to know what you're asking my prisoners." He smiles. "Part of the package."

Although Druckmyer is going to shit bricks, I like this guy more every minute.

"Okay, part of the package, but you can't say a word."

We walk in together and he stands in the corner.

I sit in front of the couple. "Mr. and Mrs. Harding, I'm agent Jake Ballard. We have a few questions."

The Egyptian looking guy says, "Do I get my lawyer present during this interview?"

"Sir, this is a preliminary interview."

"Agent Ballard, I am an American citizen. I was born in America. I love America. Now, as far as I can remember, I'm supposed to have a lawyer present during any interview, isn't that right, Captain?"

He stands stone-faced and says nothing.

After a moment of silence, I say, "Where were you born, Mr. Harding?"

He glares at me. "Sir, didn't I just ask a question?"

"Can you give me your social Security number?"

He laughs. "You get nothing from me until my lawyer arrives."

I give him one of my dangerous stares. "Sir, you are in a lot of trouble here. I suggest that you cooperate. It'll look much better when you go in front of a judge."

He laughs again. "You know and I know this interview will have no bearing whatsoever on my trial, unless of course, you can weasel some new information out of me before my lawyer shows up."

I've got one last card to play, but it's a big one. This card usually breaks them down. I reach in my briefcase and hand him the nine-eleven commission report and point at page sixty-one at the highlighted passage.

He reads it and pales. "I can't have a lawyer?"

"You are a terrorist, sir."

"But. . . what happened to the Constitution and the Bill of Rights?"

I give him my practiced glare. "We no longer live in that world, Mr. Harding. You both are terrorist, sir, and you must live by new rules."

He looks at the Sheriff who still stands stone-faced. "All we did was run some footage."

I don't say another word. The wife reaches over and takes Harding's hand, then looks at me. "I was born in Muncie, Indiana."

Harding slams his open palm on the table. No Myrtle, don't tell them a thing. Joseph will be here soon and he'll get us through this whole freaking mess."

The wife says, "My Social Security number is. . ."

~

I try not to crack a smile when the Homeland Security guy tries to weasel information out of my prisoners. They know their rights and I'm here to see that they're rights are observed.

To my surprise, this guy's pretty respectful. He doesn't try to muscle or cajole them. He simply goes through his list of questions, not getting an answer to one in ten. He then puts his papers back in his briefcase and walks out of the room. So far, so good, but my guess is the big guns will come in tomorrow when they toss black bags over their heads and spirit them off to some unknown shores.

I can't help myself. As I turn to leave, just for a second, when I know I'm out of the camera's range, I look at them and give them a big grin. "Good Job."

I go through the door before either of them can respond. The agent waits in my office. "You weren't much help."

"I wasn't there to help."

He sighs. "I wanted to do this the easy way, before my superior's take over. I don't think these two are terrorist either, but my boss."

"She'll give me some trouble, huh?"

"You got a hint of what she's like on the phone. Hell on wheels."

I sit behind my desk. "Two years ago I lost a valued

member of my community to you guys and I'll be damned if I'm going to loose another."

He sits. "I don't get it, these people don't even live around here. They're from Detroit."

"This entire community was pretty upset when Harium was disappeared and a lot of fingers pointed at me. My reelection promise was that sort of thing would never happen again in Whisky Flat or all of Kern County if I could help it."

The agent gets up. "I really don't think there is much you're going to be able to do about it. Tomorrow morning the entire United States Government will be breathing fire down you're neck."

I twiddle a pencil and smile. "We're ready. The only real question is. . . are you?"

He turns and opens the door. I say quick, before he leaves, "You're still going to get me some information on Harium?"

He stops and turns to me. "I promised to try, but unlike the rest of this fucked up world, I'm a man of my word."

The minute he leaves, I dial the mayor, then one of our county supervisors and finally our congressman. The ball is in motion. We've planned this for two years.

≈

I don't have much experience with police, but this sheriff guy looks to me like the angel of police. He treats us more than fairly and with the greatest of respect. Although he has to put us in separate cells, he did put me and BillyBob in adjoining cells so we could still talk to one another. That is itself is a god-send, because I'm pretty scared. Our Sheriff —and his name will forever stick in the fond part of my memories— Jack Perkins, has personally checked in on us three times today. It's more like we're VIP's at a hotel than prisoners in his jail. Maybe this is why Joseph suggested we turn ourselves into a small town police department.

I hear the clicking of keys on that steel door. I'm in here only a few hours and already I listen for the keys, hoping that someone is out there to get us out of here.

Sheriff Perkins walks in for the forth time today. "You two okay in here?"

I give him a trapped animal smile. "We're going to be all right. Can you tell me who that guy in the black suit was?"

The sheriff draws a nervous breath. "Homeland Security. They want a piece of you and they're very persuasive."

BillyBob chimes in. "You want to hold them off."

"Mr. Harding, you are certainly in serious trouble with your broadcasting shenanigans, but until they can prove to me that you actually were planning on blowing up some building or assassinating someone, I'm keeping you right here."

"We're not—"

"I know, but we're talking about the federal Government here and they have all the big guns and I don't mean that metaphorically. If they really want you, this little backwater precinct isn't going to be able to physically stop them."

"Sounds like your going to give it a try though?"

He smiles. "This county has been preparing for this exact scenario for two years. We won't be able to stop them by force, but we have a few tricks up our sleeve."

I ask, "What's that?"

"First off, politically."

I look at BillyBob and give the sheriff a quizzical look. "Politically?"

"We shine the light of day on these spooky bastards. . ."

He gets an apologetic grimace. "Sorry."

I smile. "I've heard worse."

"Anyhow, we shine the light of day on them and they won't be able to move."

BillyBob asks, "How?"

"You are about to become a political football," He crouches slightly and drops into a boxer stance then throws a few punches into thin air. "and I'm spoilin' for a fight."

He straightens. "You two sit tight and I'll keep you posted. Can I get you some reading material?"

BillyBob, always the wise-ass, says, "We're not going anywhere."

I say, "I could use a novel or two to pass the time."

"I'll see what I can do." The sheriff turns and walks down the hall.

An hour later the steel door opens and two sets of shoes walk toward us. Except for us, the jail is empty so any sound is welcome.

More welcome is Joseph who stands in front of our two cells. "You two look no worse for wear."

BillyBob leaps to his feet. "Joseph, how the hell are you? You're a sight for sore eyes."

The two men shake and I grip both of their hands as they do so.

The deputy slides a chair behind Joseph and disappears. "Thanks," Joseph says to the disappearing officer.

The steel door latches and I look at him. "You got here quick."

He grimaces. "I had to. They are about to cart you off to who knows what foreign airfield."

"Airfield?" I say.

"For some reason, you two fit a terrorist profile and the government wants a piece of you."

BillyBob says, "Yeah, we heard. What can you do about it?"

Joseph opens his briefcase. Nothing right this second, but I'm filing these papers in the morning to keep you here."

"Can't you get us out?"

He frowns. "Not a chance in hell. I'll be lucky to keep you from being put on a plane to Iran or Turkey."

I'm doing my nervous pacing thing again, but I don't care. "The sheriff wants us to stay here too. Have you had a chance to talk to him?"

"He's at dinner. The deputy says he'll be back in an hour."

I stop pacing. "It looks like he's got some kind of plan."

Joseph's bushy eyebrows raise. "Really. A cop with a plan to foil the feds, now there's a twist."

The rest of the hour we spent going over forms and paperwork that Joseph plans on filing in the morning. It's a good distraction from the boredom of waiting.

≈

Once I finish with BillyBob and Myrtle, I step into the Sheriff's office and sit across from him. "I'm Joseph Thomas, attorney for The Harding's. They say you have a plan."

He gives me an innocent smile. "I really can't say."

"It seems that we both don't want them in the hands of Homeland. Is there anything I can do?"

His face scrunches into a worried grimace. "I really can't say anything right now. I assume you'll be around tomorrow though."

I nod.

"Good, because I might need your help starting around eight in the morning."

"Is there a fax in town?"

"You're motel has one."

I stand and shake his rancher rough hand, then leave the office and the station, nodding at the deputy as I pass the front desk.

The sun has long ago dropped behind the hills, but there is plenty of light left in the day. I look at my watch and it's ten to six, so I stroll through the little grassy park across the street to the only restaurant in town.

The food is adequate for a small town and after I walk along the Kern River just before dark ending at my motel along the banks.

The Arabic woman lets me use her fax to send the paperwork to my assistant so he can file first thing tomorrow.

The night is a little too quiet for a guy who is used to the sound of distant sirens and normal noise of a city. I have to turn on TV just to be able to sleep.

The morning sun blasts in my window around six and I'm dressed by five to seven. I retrace my steps along the river bank toward town. Once I round the last bend and see town, it has been transformed into a battle zone. A few dozen military personnel mill around in the park. Three or four imposing looking hum-vees park half on the grass, though there is a high curb to keep cars on the pavement. An armored personnel carrier with a dozen soldiers sitting in the back pulls in and parks across the street.

I walk towards the restaurant and get stopped by a sentry who holds his rifle out as a restraint. "State your business."

I point at the restaurant. "Breakfast."

He shakes his head. "Off limits."

"Is there another place to eat in town?"

"All I know is this restaurant is off limits."

I turn and walk to the convenience store. A crappy cup of coffee and a Danish might just be my breakfast.

The sheriff is pouring his coffee as I walk into the store. He looks at me. "Councilor."

I nod, not yet in the mood to speak to anyone.

He walks to the register and speaks to some pimply faced kid. "Give me a half dozen mixed, will you Joey."

"Sure thing, Sheriff."

I've finished pouring my coffee and walk to the counter and set it down. "Bit of a circus out there this morning."

He grins. "You ain't seen the half of it."

The kid gives him change for his twenty. "What's it all about?"

The sheriff sniggers. "Looks like you got a ring side seat,

Joey. Keep your coffee brewing, you're going to need it."

He turns to me. "Once you're done here, we'll want you at the office."

I pull out a ten and give it to the kid while I give the sheriff a sleepy gaze. "About a half hour. Will that do?"

The sheriff struts out of the store and for the first time I realize he's wearing cowboy boots.

The kid hands me the change. "You know what's going on?"

"Not as much as I should, apparently." I turn and walk out of the store with my day old Danish and a weak cup of coffee that taste like it was brewed last May.

When I walk into the sheriff's office, the deputy buzzes me in without hesitation. "The Captain wants you in his office. He'll be back in five minutes."

I sit in that uncomfortable metal chair and gaze over the hundreds of photos and notes pinned to all four walls. It's like a collage of crime mostly in eight by ten color prints of mug shots.

When he finally walks in, I stand to shake his hand and he asks, "you like the zoo out there?"

"Look pretty chaotic."

He motions for me to sit. "It's all because I was the lucky sheriff to draw your clients. They are going to become the biggest hot potato in history and you and I are going to make that happen."

"Sheriff Perkins, I don't think it is appropriate for me to work together with you on my clients case."

"It's either that or they disappear to some Egyptian prison

and spend the next three or four years being tortured."

"Sir, I really don't think—"

"It's what happened to Harium two years ago and I vowed to never let another one of my charges slip away like that again. Harium grew up in Whisky Flat. There was no reason whatsoever for him to be a terrorist. Some pencil pushing, paranoid Washington D.C. bastard designated Harium a threat and he hasn't been heard from since. We don't even know if he's alive or not. His wife, who owns the motel you stayed in last night, has been in permanent depression ever since. You want that for your clients and their family?"

I take a breath. "Okay, you made your point. What do you have for me?"

That very second a spooky guy in a black suit and Rayban sunglasses steps into the office. Perkin's eyes shift from me to him. "What did you come up with?"

"Your citizen is alive, but I can't tell you where he is."

The sheriff gets a relieved look. "His wife is going to be pleased."

The guy steps to the cluttered desk. He looks at the sheriff. "We've got some urgent business to discuss."

Perkins raises one eyebrow and motions for him to sit in the only other chair in the room.

The spooky guy leans on the desk and in a threatening manner says, "alone!"

The sheriff doesn't flinch an eyelid. "You two haven't met, have you. "Agent Jake Ballard this is Joseph Thomas, attorney for the couple in question."

The agent gives me a dirty scowl and turns his attention

back to Perkins. "I said alone."

Perkins doesn't move. "Anything you got to say here should be said in front of their attorney, isn't that right?"

The agent straightens and gives me another dirty look. "We're bringing an entire Marine division down on the head of this little town. Is that what you really want?"

Perkins grabs a pen and twirls it. In a calm voice with a slight smile, he says, "That, Agent Ballard, is exactly what we want. In fact our entire town has been preparing for this ever since you bastards came in here two years ago. You may have the Marine Corp behind you, but we have a few tricks too."

The agent huffs, turns and exits the room.

Perkins gives me a nervous smile. "I just blew whatever pension I've built up over the last twenty years. These guys are out for blood and I really need your help."

"Whatever I can do, Captain. That was about the bravest thing I've ever seen."

"Bravest or stupidest, I'm not sure, but I'll be damned if I'm going to lose one more person to these thugs."

"What can I do?" I ask.

I point out the widow. "They're rallying the troops.

He turns. "Shit, looks like they brought in a tank."

"Looks like the whole damn Army is out there."

The sheriff looks at his watch. "We have our own troops, if they ever get here."

"Once they get in place, I'm going to have to face off with Agent Ballard. As starters, I'm going to need your help on the front steps."

"Front steps?"

"You're their lawyer. You're plans with your clients are going to be helpful."

"Legally, Captain, you don't have anything to stand on. That's Homeland out there and since nine-eleven they pretty much have free reign."

"I know, but there is one last show here and I'm playing this one hand before they haul off your clients."

"What do you have?"

"Embarrassment, mostly."

The deputy steps into the room. "They're in the office, sir."

The sheriff stands. "You going to come with me?"

I follow him down the dingy hall into the office. Ballard stands with three lawyers and two highly decorated military in dress blues.

Ballard opens a folder and reads aloud some writ that declares the government's legal jurisdiction over the Hardings. When he's done, he hands the document over to Perkins, but the sheriff doesn't take it.

The deputy hands Perkins a small book and he reads his own version of why he must protect and serve, including protecting from unjust treatment of his constituents. His speech is eloquent and firm without any wiggle room.

Ballard looks at sheriff Perkins with disdain. "You aren't going to win this one, you know."

Perkins gives him a sad smile. "Yes, I know, but I'll be damned if this time I'm not going to try."

~

I huff, turn and lead my show of power out of the office and onto the street amongst the three armored vehicles and that single tank Druckmyer ordered.

Before I can say another word, my phone rings and it's Druckmyer.

"Ballard, how have things gone so far?"

"You're not going to like the results."

"It's that fucking bastard sheriff."

"Afraid so."

"We will be landing in twenty minutes. Put everything on hold and get your ass out to the airport to pick me up."

"I already have a car there for you."

"No, you fucking idiot, not a car, you, in person, standing at attention when I open my door."

I'm about to tell her to shove it, but my better side restrains me as the phone goes dead.

I turn to General Burkheart and look at his bulldog face. "Let's put everything on hold until I get Druckmyer on site."

He looks at me. "Don't you think these people have a plan? We could go in there right now and pluck those two without much fuss. We wait and who know what barriers might be thrown up."

I shrug. "My boss says wait. . . we wait."

He shakes his head slightly and salutes. "I'm here under her command, but I'm filing a complaint."

"You met Druckmyer?"

"No sir."

"I'd save filing that complaint till after you've met her."

115

He gives me a quizzical look.

"Everything is on hold, right General?"

"Per your orders."

I walk over to Jason's rental car, and I can never remember his last name. I get in and close the door. "You know where the local airport is?"

"Yes sir."

"Let's get there, pronto."

He pulls away from the curb and winds his way through the hum-vees and armored vehicles. This thing has gotten way out of hand.

Chapter 8

Druckmyer

"Madam." The voice of the pilot comes over the intercom.

"Yetman?"

"The airport we are landing at."

The bastard is so fucking tentative, I want to run up to the cockpit and backhand him. "Yes, Yetman?"

"It's a little short."

"Short?"

"For a Lear jet."

I roll my eyes. I really don't have time for this. "How short, Yetman?"

"Fifty yards."

"We've got a fucking war to fight and you're worried about fifty yards?"

"Yes, ma'am."

"Is it impossible?"

"No ma'am."

"Stop with the ma'am crap."

"Yes, ma. . ."

If it's not impossible, I want you to put this god-damn plane on the ground."

"It'll be a bit of a rough ride."

"What the fuck, Yetman, did I just give you an order."

His non-response allows me to go back to my computer as the engines drop in speed again and the plane slows.

I don't look up again until his whiny voice breaks my concentration. "You'll need to buckle up ma'am."

I find both ends of the buckle while still concentrating on the screen and snap them into place.

~

We pull up as the Lear comes in for the final approach. I send Jason back to town and walk to the limo.

The pilot puts the wheels on the pavement less than ten feet from the far end of the runway. He hits the reverse thrusts and slams on the brakes the second the tires are on the ground. The plane pushes hard on the front landing gear, shoving the nose down toward the pavement. The tires squeal. The plane zips past us going way too fast for such a small landing strip, especially since the end of the strip drops into the lake.

I lean against the front fender of the car. "They going into the lake?"

The limo driver crosses his arms in front of his chest and smiles. "We could only hope."

"You know Druckmyer, do you?"

He turns to me and rolls his eyes.

The reverse thrusts kick in and the plane slows to a crawl. It can't be five feet from the end when it turns around. Once off of the active runway it taxis back toward us.

The driver turns to me. "It's my job if you tell her what just accidentally let slip out of my mouth."

I step away from the car to meet the plane then turn back to him. "Not like we don't all feel the same way."

He puts his hand out to shake. "I'm Bosue."

I take his hand and smile. "Jake Ballard."

As the plane slips up to the limo, I stand at attention until the door opens and that extremely overweight, poor excuse for a human being squeezes out of the door. She descends to the pavement. "Okay, Ballard, you can stop the kiss-ass and get my bags, then get the fuck in the car."

Without saying a word, I take the overnight case from the steward. He gives me a relieved look and casually salutes.

In the car Druckmyer leans forward to open the privacy window to the front seat. "No fucking point in sticking around here, BobbieSue, we got a small town sheriff to crush. Get your ass in gear."

I want to say his name is Bosue, but what is the point.

The car pulls away from the plane and rushes toward the highway. Not a word is said until we're pointed in the direction of Whiskey Flat. Druckmyer turns to me. "What have you got for me, Ballard?"

"Sheriff's pretty hunkered down, Ma'am."

"Cut the ma'am crap, asshole."

I look out the window rather than punch her. Would I love to see her nose bleeding? Better yet, wouldn't I love to see anything happen to her? A hang nail would be some consolation. Nothing ever happens to Druckmyer. With her over-sprayed bouffant hair and a quarter inch of makeup, couldn't she break one of those sausage legs or come up with a debilitating illness? Hell a common cold wouldn't be bad. She's a rock. Nothing ever gets to her and she's always there in the middle of everything, mostly messing up any chance of a peaceful resolution. God, I hate her.

"So, what's you got, Ballard?"

She says my name with a nasal insult like I'm some kind of lichen on a rock.

"Nothing other than he's got the couple and he isn't going to let them go without a fight."

"Marines in place?"

I snigger. "Enough to take out Vegas."

"Don't you laugh at me, boy."

I think fast. "Not at you, ma'am, at the General running that show. He's a piece of work."

"We'll give that fucking sheriff something to think about."

We roll into the outskirts of town and pass the first Humvee. I turn to her. "Sheriff acts like he's got something up his sleeve."

She huffs. "He might have something, but he's going to have me up his ass in about twenty minutes. Want to put some odds on who's going to come out on top?"

The driver stops at the checkpoint and rolls down his window. A grunt with a rifle leans down and looks through the window. Our driver shows him a pass and he waves us through.

When we pull up to the sheriff's office nothing seems to have changed. Perkins stands outside the door with his deputy and that lawyer.

The driver leaps out of the car and opens Druckmyer's door. Once she stands on the sidewalk without looking at the driver, she says, "wait here, BobbieSue. This shouldn't take a minute."

Behind her back, I look at the driver and mouth the word "BobbieSue?"

He shakes his head and rolls his eyes.

Druckmyer almost catches him as she spins and looks at me. "That the fucking sheriff?"

"In the middle with the cowboy hat."

She starts up the walk like a freight train.

I follow not far behind.

When she gets within a foot of Perkins, she stops and puts one finger out to point at his nose. "You want to give me trouble, asshole?"

Perkins doesn't say a word.

The lawyer steps forward and hands Druckmyer some paper. "My clients are under the jurisdiction of the local police. Until you can show cause, they will stay where they are."

She ignores him and lets the four papers scatter to the grass beside the walk. Her intent does not waver from the sheriff. "You really want a piece of me?"

The sheriff reaches into his shirt pocket and pulls out a small, very thin, white booklet then holds it out to her. I look over her shoulder and he's handing her a copy of the Constitution and Bill of Rights.

She takes it, looks at the cover and slams it into his chest hard enough to push him back a few steps. "That piece of shit means nothing to me. I am the United States Government and you have three minutes to hand over those two."

She turns, walks to the limo, leans on the front fender and looks at her watch.

The second her fat butt touches the black paint of the car, thirty people come from behind the sheriff's building. Another thirty pour out of the bar next door. A fleet of news helicopters come over the ridge and circle the downtown area at a respectful five hundred feet. From inside every building in the downtown area hundreds of people pour onto the streets. The military stands dumbfounded. Within the three-minute time limit, I estimate five thousand people mill around the square in front of the tank and the armored vehicles handing out spring flowers to the military who are swallowed up in the mass of celebrating humanity.

A juggler rolls in with his unicycle tossing six balls in the air at once.

Druckmyer turns to see the crowd as the juggler rolls up. Her face turns red with rage. She pushes herself away from the car. She slams the juggler with the palms of both hands and sends him sprawling across the sparse lawn on his back. Over the din of humanity, I hear a crack as he lands on one of the steps. He screams and grabs his arm.

I start over to him, but Druckmyer grabs the collar of my suit and yanks me. "Pay attention, Dickhead."

She looks at her watch, raises her arm and motions the military into action.

Nothing happens.

She looks behind her and waves again, this time with angry force.

Nothing.

The General steps up. "Sorry, Ma'am, we can't do anything with this many citizens in the way."

"Open fire, asshole. Open fire right this second."

The General shrugs. "Can't ma'am. These are U.S. citizens."

A middle-aged woman with bleached blonde hair rushes up to the sheriff and locks arms with him.

The General points at the woman. "And that's my wife."

Druckmyer turns to him and slugs him in the nose. "Wake up, General. I don't care if your fucking kids are in this crowd. You have your orders."

The surprise on his face is priceless as his nose starts to bleed. He fingers the dripping blood and looks at it. All of the lines in his aging face scrunch. He grimaces. He takes her left hand and spins her around. There is a second where she knows what's about to happen. She looks at me. With a wide right arc, the General slams his fist into her face. She drops like a sack of potatoes. Bouse and I help her onto her butt.

He stands stiff and motions for his next in command. "Carson."

The man steps over and salutes. "Yes sir?"

"Stand our troops down and let's go home."

"Yes sir."

"I'm placing myself under arrest and handing command to you."

"Yes sir."

The second in command barks a set of orders and the hundreds of Marines move with lightning speed. In three minutes they're gone. The crowd cheers as the last truck disappears.

Two paramedics step out of the crowd. One goes to the juggler with a splint in his hands and the second kneels to tend Druckmyer who is still out cold sitting splayed leaning against the front tire of the limo.

The driver turns to me with a big grin. "See what that General did?"

"Yeah, someone in this mess has some sense."

"No, I mean with Druckmyer."

The paramedic looks up. "Looks like she's got a broken jaw."

The driver's grin widens. He leans in close and whispers, "she's not going to be able to open that filthy mouth of hers for a long time."

I walk to Perkins and nod in appreciation, then point back at the crowd who is not dispersing. It looks like they're making a day of it. "You did this?"

"Everything but punch out your boss."

"Where did you get the people?"

"All from this county if that's what you're thinking."

"I wasn't thinking anything other than it's pretty amazing."

"Lucky for us Druckmyer is such an asshole or the General

may have followed her orders."

"You know it ain't over, right?"

He smiles. "Of course not. You're the all powerful United States Government. It ain't over until you say it's over."

"If I had my way, it would be over, but it isn't up to me."

"At least there is one sane person in this whole mess."

An ambulance weaves through the crowd and parks behind the limo. The juggler is walked to the back and Druckmyer, who is still out, is rolled onto a gurney. Once inside, the ambulance turns on its siren and pushes through the crowd.

Booths are set up in the park selling coffee and food. The mood is jubilant. What the hell, Druckmyer is out of the picture. Other than visiting her sorry ass later, I've got the rest of the day off. I salute Perkins and turn toward the crowd, walking to the coffee booth.

～

I'm about as surprised as one cop can be when the obese boss woman punches out the General, but I'm not surprised at all when he lays her out cold.

I turn to Harding's lawyer. His face is pale. "You going to be okay?"

He gives me a nervous nod. "They almost fired on us."

"Luckily more stable heads prevail, huh?"

"I've never been this close to violence."

"It can happen."

Just then Ballard steps over to us and points back at the crowd. "You did all of this."

"Everything but punch out your boss."

"Where did you get the people?"

"All from this county if that's what you're thinking."

After Ballard walks away, I turn to the lawyer and my

dipshit deputy. "Let's go inside."

The three of us walk into the relative quiet of the station. I walk them back to my office and I sit. "We got a temporary reprieve, so we have a lot to do in the next twenty-four hours."

"What can they possibly do next?"

"Covert."

"You mean like double-oh-seven stuff?"

"You need to file a restraining order against them."

"The government as a whole?"

"I think it's our only recourse." I write a number on a slip of paper. "Judge Martin has already been advised. He'll have it on record by noon. I'll serve Ballard sometime this afternoon."

He takes the paper. "You guys have a regular conspiracy going here."

I give him a worried look. "Please don't even say that word. Just file the writ and let's get this ball rolling."

He smiles and leaves the room. I turn to Alex. "You have the safe house set up?"

"Yes sir, Auntie is ready."

"Okay, in an hour, once we're sure Ballard is safely out of the way, we move them, right?"

"Yes, sir, but. . ."

I look up from trying to find the Harding's file. "But?"

"Well. . . Sir. . . you're ready to retire, but I've got another fifteen years. If I get caught in the middle of transporting prisoners, I'm pretty much dead meat."

"Yes, of course you're right. Get me a transport form and I'll fill it out, then the whole thing's on me."

He grins and salutes. "You're a good man, Captain."

By noon the crowd and Ballard are still here. By five o'clock the crowd has dissipated. Ballard sits in a rented car parked behind the limo.

The lawyer steps into the office and opens his briefcase.

I look at him. "You get the restraining order?"

He pulls out the single sheet of paper and hands it to me. "You know this thing won't stand up in court."

I give him a worried grin. "It may slow them down a little.

The lawyer says, "looks like the driving force of this whole operation went to the hospital with a broken jaw. Everyone, including that spook with sunglasses, seems to be waiting for new orders."

"Ballard's okay."

The old man raises one bushy eyebrow. "Once they get those orders, my guess is they'll move quickly."

"I'm afraid you're right, Mr. Thomas."

"Joseph. If we're going to be conspiring against the United States Government and I'm sure both of our asses are in a sling over this one, then you may as well call me by my first name."

I point at the deputy across the hall and whisper, "everyone except him calls me Perkins."

Joseph smiles. "Okay, Perkins, what's next?"

I stand and look out the window. "I'm waiting for Ballard to leave."

"What for?"

"We need to transport the prisoners to a safe house, but I just can't traipse them down the sidewalk and put them in a car."

Joseph steps over to the window and leans on the sill. "Don't look like he's moving anytime soon."

"Sure don't."

"We wait for dark and figure a distraction for the agent?"

I look at my watch. "It's the middle of the night when they will be pulling something and I want your clients out of here long before that."

"No back doors?"

"Yes, but no place to go. We're at the bottom of a thirty-foot cliff right outside the back door. The bar is the only cover for a hundred yards either way."

The lawyer brightens. "I've got a plan. It's not much of one, but we've been flying by the seat of our pants all day and what the hell."

~

"Joseph, where have you been?" I say as he and the sheriff walk into view with armfuls of clothes.

"Trying to keep you in jail."

Myrtle says, "I thought you were supposed to get us out?"

He looks in the next cell. "Right now, Myrtle, you really don't want to be on the loose. Put these clothes on."

He hands some to Myrtle and some to me.

She smells them. "These things smell like moth balls. I'm not putting these on if my life depended on it."

The sheriff says, "in a way, ma'am, your life does depend on it. We're trying to figure a way to keep you safe, so please put the clothes on. We'll be back in ten minutes to help you with makeup."

I strip and put on the smelly clown suit. They're a bit small, but I manage to slip the big shoes on.

I can't see my wife, so I ask, "what do they have you dressing as?"

"I don't know, BillyBob, something like Mary Poppins with attitude."

When Joseph and the sheriff walk in, I stand and they both snigger. Joseph walks to the next cell. "Myrtle, you're transformed."

"This better be for some good reason, Joseph Thomas or you've got some explaining to do when this is over."

A young woman steps in with a bag and walks to Myrtle's cell. "Sheriff Perkins asked me to give you a makeover."

She slides a chair to the bars and though I can't see much, I do see her pulling different colored makeups from her bag and sliding her arms through the bars. After ten minutes, she slides her chair over to me. "You're going to be a bit harder, Mr. Harding. I've never done a clown before, but I brought some photos."

Twenty minutes later she holds up a mirror. "How's that?"

"Well," I say, "I certainly look like a clown, but where's my red nose?"

Perkins walks in. "You won't need a nose if what we're planning comes off. You ready?"

"Ready for what?"

Perkins unlocks the doors and we walk into the hall and look at one another. "You do look like Mary Poppins."

Myrtle turns to the sheriff. "What do you have in mind?"

He looks at both of us. "First, since you came in under your own steam, can I get a commitment that you won't try to escape? I'll be ruined if you do."

I look at him. "Escape?"

"You're going to walk out front alone and get into a van. You won't have handcuffs or any kind of restraints. If you act weird in any way other than how we want you to, the agents will know something's up."

"How do you want us to act?"

"Half-drunk."

I look at Myrtle, then back at the sheriff. "Then I'd suggest you at least get me something to drink. Five o'clock happy hour is long gone and I'm Jonesin' for a beer."

He smiles. "We'll get you a beer after this part is over and you're safe. For now, follow me."

The sheriff walks us out a back door to face a thirty-foot

concrete wall. He turns right and we follow through a narrow dark alley, past some garbage cans and in through the back door of a bar. The owner meets us and walks us to the front door. The place is packed, so even with my clown suit and Myrtle's getup, no one pays much attention.

The sheriff points out the door. "See that brown van?"

I nod. "Yes."

"In ten minutes, stumble out there like you're half-drunk and get in the van. The keys are under the mat, but don't start it for a minute or two. Once you drive away go straight through town the way the van is pointed and Deputy Chesterman will be waiting to escort you to a safe place."

I look at him. "Why a safe place, Sheriff?"

"Sometime I'll tell you what happened today and you'll understand, but for now we have to get you out of here."

The sheriff does something odd for his position. He reaches out and shakes both of our hands. "Remember, wait two minutes." He turns, walks through the crowd and out the back door.

I look at the clock on the wall, then at Myrtle. "The cops are strange in California."

She takes my hand. "Don't look a gift horse."

The bartender steps out of the crowd with two frosty mugs. "Sheriff Perkins said you'd want these."

"We don't have any money."

"You're the reason I'm having such a busy night. They're on the house." He disappears into the crowd.

Myrtle turns to me and smiles, then takes a sip.

I take a long drink, finishing half of the mug. "Now, here is a real gift horse."

At exactly ten minutes we finish our beers, half-stumble out of the bar and over to the brown van. When we're safely inside, I look at the Sheriff's office and every light is out.

The agent and six of his people are scrambling about paying attention to the dark building.

I start the engine and slowly drive past the office then down the road. When I pull onto the highway, a sheriff's cruiser pulls in front of us.

We drive three miles, then turn up a steep road into the hills. The road is so steep more than a few times, I'm forced to put the transmission into first gear and the cruiser has to slow to allow me to catch up.

When he turns left onto a small dirt road, we follow for a mile along the side of the hill, across a makeshift bridge, through a broken-down gate and finally into a football-field-size flat area long ago carved out of the side of the mountain. A few scraggly trees try to shade the dilapidated vintage double-wide trailer. Lights turn on and an old woman opens the door.

We park next to the cruiser and get out.

The deputy leads us to the house as an old dog lifts its head from a sleeping position on the porch. It gives us a single muffled chuff then drops back to sleep.

The deputy points at us. "Auntie, these are the people I was telling you about."

She might be in her nineties. Although she moves slow, she looks at us with sharp eyes that miss little. "Well, come in children. No point in standing on the porch jawin'."

We follow her into a magical kingdom filled with canning jars and strange concoctions. Hanging from the ceiling are bundles of dry sweet-smelling plants and paper bags filled with dried herbs of dozens of different varieties.

The old woman leads us into the kitchen and moves some bundles of herbs from her table to make room for us.

"Maybe you want to go into the bathroom and take off that clown makeup before you smear it all over everything."

"Yes ma'am. Which way?"

She points to the back of the living room. "First door to your right." She turns to Myrtle. "Probably you better go help. I put out some face cream to get it off."

Myrtle follows me down the canning-jar-congested hall and we walk into another room filled with hanging herbs. I finger one of the two-inch thick stems, smell my fingers, then turn to Myrtle. "She's drying pot."

She smiles. "Along with almost every other herb known to mankind."

I look at her in the mirror. "The smell takes me back to our summer of love. You remember Golden Gate Park, that concert and you couldn't help but get high there was so much smoking going on?"

Myrtle rubs one of the flowers gently then smells her fingers. "Back then it was mostly that crappy Mexican weed. This stuff is light years beyond that."

"Yeah, but the memories are vivid."

She opens the facial cream and shows me how to scrub it into the makeup, then rinse. It takes two tries but finally that greasy white goo is off and I can wash with water.

Both Myrtle and I strip our costumes back to our street clothes and I feel like myself again.

We walk out of the bathroom and back to the kitchen, then hand the costumes to the deputy.

The old woman greets us with a cup of tea. "My nephew says you'll need to stay a few days."

"Yes ma'am. We seem to be fugitives."

She laughs and turns to the deputy. "They don't look like fugitives, Alex."

"They are Auntie, just not the kind you see on TV."

"You know I haven't had a television since I took mine to the dump in the mid eighties."

He rolls his eyes. "Yes, I know. You tell me all the time."

131

"Television is for all those dimwits out there."

His voice is patient. "Yes, Auntie."

"You ask me, we should all throw our televisions away. The world would be a better place if we did."

I look at Myrtle. "My wife feels the same way, ma'am."

She turns to me with her wrinkled face all scrunched up. "If you're going to call me by my title, then it's Auntie."

"Auntie, I'm BillyBob and this is my wife Myrtle."

She smiles and a whole other set of wrinkles comes into play. It's obvious that both sets are used often.

I take a sip of tea and the taste is familiar, yet I can't place it. I look at her. "Thanks for putting us up, Auntie."

"Alex here says you've got some trouble with the federal guys, is that right?"

"Yes ma'am, but we really don't know why things are such a fuss."

"There's such a fuss because there are a bunch of crazy people out there and not all of them are on the wrong side of the law."

Myrtle shakes her head. "You certainly got that right."

Alex stands. "I gotta go to the bathroom."

She gets a worried look as he leaves the room. In a whisper she says, "Alex doesn't understand."

I immediately get that she's talking about the marijuana hanging from her shower curtain rod.

All three of us sip our tea waiting for him to come out.

"Auntie, you know I said you can't have that stuff. We got some laws that forbid—"

She glares at him. "Alex, will you just sit down here like some regular human being and give your Auntie a break. You really don't have to be a cop all the time."

He sits and takes a sip of his tea.

Auntie smiles. "I made a special blend to help you relax."

He gives the tea a worried look.

She laughs. "No there is no pot in it if that's what you're thinking."

His face turns into a funny, childlike expression. "I wasn't thinking that, Auntie."

"Just drink your tea, youngun' then leave the three of us to our own devices. I'm sure you've got some important deputy business to attend to."

"No Auntie, I get to go home."

"Well then, I'd say you better be skedadlin' off to home."

"Yes ma'am." He stands and turns to me. "You two going to be okay?"

Myrtle grins. "Auntie can take care of us."

He pulls out a business card and hands it to me. "Call my cell if you need anything."

I take it. "I'm sure we'll be fine. Go home and get some sleep."

"Okay then, I'll be taking off. Oh yes, you're still in custody. If you decide to disappear, our whole office is in big trouble."

"We turned ourselves in. We're not going anywhere."

Chapter 9

Break In

I'm sitting on a chair, in a dark corner, almost nodding off to sleep, when I hear a soft click. I push the little button of my watch and see that it's four-fifteen. I expected these guys, but not so late. I stand in my stocking feet and walk over to the breaker panel that runs the whole building. The next sound is the creak of the main cell door opening very slowly. I wait for a moment until I hear the pat of feet on the concrete moving closer. I flip the switch and everything floods with light.

Two guys dressed in black tights with black hoods are crouched with automatic pistols strapped to their shoulders. They look up at the silver barrel of my three-fifty-seven.

"Guess it's time for you two to drop your weapons."

Without saying a word, they un-shoulder the guns and set them carefully on the floor.

"Now, go ahead and strip then step into that cell and lay flat on the floor."

Again, without speaking, they do as I say. Once they're on the floor, I close the door and lock it.

I sit on the plastic visitor chair just outside the cell and start going through their clothes. "Okay, though I already know, maybe you can tell me who sent you?"

Neither of them speaks.

I find two twenty-five automatics each of them had in a hidden pocket close to the crotch, but no paperwork.

I keep the weapons and toss the clothes back into the cells. "You may need these. It's a bit chilly in here and I wouldn't want you catching cold."

I turn, walk out of the holding cell area, close the big steel door behind me, walk to the front door and into the darkness of a predawn desert. I love it just before dawn.

I walk down the street to the Save-Mart and Sandy sits behind the register resting her chubby head on both hands watching a six-inch television. She turns the sound down.

"Hay Sheriff, getting to work a bit early today?"

I walk over to the coffee machine and pour three medium coffees. "Haven't gone home yet."

"That was some wing-ding you put on yesterday, Sheriff."

"You came down for it, did you?"

I dole out a dozen donuts and put them in a small box, then walk to the register.

She scans each item. "Wouldn't have missed it. We still got the prisoners?"

"Sheriff business, Sandy. I can't really say."

"I heard the feds were going to try and bust them out sometime last night."

I smile and sign the receipt. "Can't say."

"Oh, come on Sheriff, can't you see I'm about as bored as one human can be? I need something to get me through the rest of the night."

I smile and look around. I shouldn't say a word, but I can't help myself. I'm kinda proud of how I got those two. "A few minutes ago I locked two of their agents in a cell."

"No shit? Did they get to the Harding's?"

"Everyone knows their name, do they?"

"Well damn, Sheriff, this is a small town. Not much news comes out of this town, so when something does happen there's a whole network of telephones and texting."

She bags the coffees and I pick them up to leave.

"What're you going to do with the agents?"

"Feed them donuts and coffee."

I walk to the door.

She says, "Good luck, Sheriff."

I turn. "I'm going to need it."

I sit in front of the cell with the two cat burglar's perched on the single cot. I lift two coffees out of the bags and set them on the flat crosspiece of the bars. "Cream or sugar?"

The shorter of the two reaches for a cup. "Cream please."

I pull out my coffee and pour a packet of sugar, open the donut box and pull out the chocolate one with nuts on top. I slide the rest of the box over to the bars with my foot.

The tall, skinny guy sidles over to the bars and eyes the box. As I take my first bite, he picks out an old fashion then sits back on the cot.

"I know Druckmyer sent you."

Neither of them says a word.

"Maybe you know, but I'm not giving this couple up as terrorists. They have a court date and probably some fines, but they will not be spirited off to Guantanamo or some cell in Egypt."

Neither of them speaks.

"I'm telling you this because later this morning when I let you go, I want you to take this back to Druckmyer+++."

They both take sips from their coffee.

"They're US citizens, for God sakes. What happened to

the Bill of Rights." They have a right to a fair trial in a timely manner with their lawyer present. You never gave Harium any of those rights, now did you?"

I know I'm not going to get anything out of these two, but it feels good to spout off. I lean forward and take a second donut, then stand and leave the cell area, locking the big steel door behind me.

Three hours later, long after a spectacular desert dawn, Agent Ballard rings the bell.

I walk to the outer office and look at him.

"You have two of my agents?"

"I'd call them burglars."

"Sir, if you don't want the wrath of Druckmyer raining all over your head for the next ten years then I'd suggest you get them."

I click the outer door and it opens.

Ballard walks through. "Threats will get you nowhere, Agent Ballard."

He takes a deep breath. "Look Sheriff, we're on the same side here. Why does this have to be so hard?"

"Tell you what, Agent Ballard, you go down to the Save Mart, get me a cup of coffee and a couple of those sprinkled donuts and you can have your agents back."

He gives me a curious stare. "Coffee?"

"I didn't book them yet to save both of us a shit load of paperwork. You just get me the coffee and donuts and they're yours."

"I'm not your errand boy."

"No sir, I do know that. Just consider it one favor for another. I can book them if you want, but we don't have to do this the hard way, do we?"

He turns and walks out. In fifteen minutes he's back with a tray of cups and a donut box. He sets them on the counter.

"Didn't know what you wanted in the coffee."

"Sugar, but I got some here."

"I got a cup for my men."

"I'll get 'em."

Without a word, I let the two men out of the cell and walk them back to the front desk. When they see Ballard, he shakes his head. "You two managed to get yourselves caught?"

The taller one speaks. "He was waiting for us."

Ballard points at the cups. "Get your coffee and wait out in the car."

The skinny one speaks. "The Harding's aren't back there." They each grab a cup and donut then walk out of the office.

I give Ballard a grin. "You don't think I'd be so stupid as to leave them in harms way."

He takes a sip. "Look sheriff, we both got a job to do here. You saw what Druckmyer is capable of. I just want to get my prisoners and go home before both of us end up on the wrong side of her."

"Interesting you would say this. I just happen to have an affidavit stating that you plan to extradite them back to Las Vegas where they belong. You get Druckmyer to sign it in front of the Harding's lawyer, oh yes, and maybe twenty or thirty members of the press and I'll be more than happy to give this mess over to you."

"You know she's not going to do that. Even if she was inclined, the demand alone would send her over the top."

I hand him the document. "Knowing what little I do of the woman, I figured as much. Hell, what does a guy have to lose?"

He takes it and shakes his head. "Everything."

"Tell you what, you get me face to face with her and I'll present the deal. I've already lost my job and probably my pension, so in a sense I have nothing else to lose." I'm lying about the pension part, but what the hell.

He looks at me and shakes his head. "You don't know Druckmyer. She'll snatch your balls and eat them for breakfast, then work up some diabolical way to get you. She doesn't stop. Five years from now she'll still be raining terror on your head."

I give him a long stare. "It's already a done deal for me, right?"

"Pretty much. You and that General."

"I guess then she's the real terrorist now isn't she?"

He doesn't answer, but then I don't expect him to.

Ballard says, "Just tell me where they are and I can make this whole thing go away."

"Somehow, I don't think you have that kind of pull with Druckmyer. She seems like an independent thinker."

He looks at the document, then back at me. "Man, I'm trying to save you a lot of heartache."

"Tell you what, you bring Harium back in one piece and I'll release my prisoners to you." Another lie, but I'm getting good at them.

"Can't do that."

"It's my only other deal. Besides, you've had him for two years. I'm sure if there was information to be had, you must have gotten it by now."

"He's got to go through channels. I can't just go get him."

"Not you, but I'll bet Druckmyer could in a hot second."

"Sheriff, you're trying to muscle the wrong person."

Chesterman opens the front door and with a chipper voice says, "morning."

I turn and walk toward the back office. Once the door is open I look at the agent. "Just give the message to her and let's see where the chips fall."

～

This sheriff has some kind of death wish. I keep trying to talk him down, but he isn't budging. I wouldn't be surprised if he ended in a back alley some night. Druckmyer is going to be livid.

I walk out of the station and to my car with those two dickheads leaning against the front fender. I look at the tall one. "Nice job, Freddie."

"Look Ballard, he was laying for us. There was nothing we could do."

"Going in one at a time so you had backup, Freddie?"

They look at one another.

He glares at me. "Name's Fred Hawkins to you Ballard."

I walk around the far side of the car. They start to get in. "You two find your own way back. I got something to do now that you've failed."

I start the engine and leave them on the sidewalk, speed dialing Druckmyer as I leave town.

She answers with her normal snapping-turtle gruffness. Her voice is different though. "About time you called, Ballard.

"Heard you had a broken jaw."

She guffaws. "Just out of joint. They popped it back in and I'm right as rain. You got those two?"

"No ma'am, Hawkins and his sidekick landed in jail."

"Jail!" she yells.

"I just got them released. The sheriff has a proposal."

She barks, "unless it's a fucking marriage proposal you can tell him to shove it up his ass."

"You better look at this."

"I don't make deals, especially with piss-ant sheriffs."

"Can I come over and show you?"

After a moment's silence, she says, "Okay, get your ass sorry over here and let me hear about this proposal."

141

"Where are you?"

"Thought you were a fucking detective, Ballard."

"Yes ma'am."

I wait in silence for what seems like a minute as she pulls her typical make-me-wait act. It's okay, I'm getting paid by the hour.

In a softer voice I'm not familiar with, she finally speaks. "Guess that chicken shit General slugged me pretty hard. They got me in the hospital at the south end of the lake." The line goes dead.

I pull into an ancient gas station turned into a mechanic's nightmare. Used tires are lined up on a rack out front. Two cars are in the air, both disassembled. Two gas pumps stand on a decomposing island of concrete. I know the pumps are not operational because the advertised price of gas on the pump is thirty-three cents.

I get out and walk into the dingy little office with its smoke-stained glass. A guy in coveralls and greasy hands has his feet up on the congested desk drinking coffee.

"How many hospitals do you have around here?"

"Just one."

"Can you tell me where it is?"

"Down the road three miles or so and you see a hospital sign pointing to the right. It's up on the hill on Kennedy Drive."

I nod and get back in my car feeling like just grabbing the door knob got grease all over my new suit.

The hospital is a bit hard to find, but finally I park and walk in through the front doors to the familiar acrid smell of all hospitals.

I step over to a cute little candy striper sitting at the large information desk. She can't be more than sixteen. She smiles and her braces gleam. "Can I help you?"

"Looking for Anne Druckmyer."

She clicks a few keys on her computer and reads the screen. "Room three-ten." She points to the right. "Elevator is there."

"Thanks," I say and go toward the elevator.

On the third floor, I walk slowly down the highly polished linoleum realizing that I'm not looking forward to what's about to happen.

Druckmyer sits upright on her bed, laptop open, bluetooth plugged into her right ear. A big bandage is plastered over her left ear and a metal splint is taped across her nose.

She speaks with a nasal whine. "Where the fuck have you been, Ballard?"

I know from the twenty-eight months of being under her that no answer is the best response.

"You get those two assholes on the plane yet?"

"No ma'am, the sheriff still has 'em."

"I give you one small fucking project and you haven't got the balls to complete it."

Here's where feeding the lion works. "Once you were out of commission, things just fell apart. Guess we needed stronger leadership."

"You're all a bunch of candy-asses. Guess when I want something done, I do it myself." She puts her computer aside and swings her sausage legs out from under the covers. "Get me something to wear."

I turn to open the closet as she lifts her heft onto the floor. When the food tray crashes, I spin and she's laying on the floor.

An Asian nurse runs into the room and over to Druckmyer. "What happened?"

"She tried to get out of bed."

She checks vital signs, then rushes out of the room. In a moment she's back moving all of the broken and scattered equipment out of the way.

"You should have stopped her."

"She's my boss."

Two line backers in blue scrubs step in and take one look at her. The bigger one turns to me. "We're going to need some help."

I step over as the two grab a limp Druckmyer under the armpits and hoist her up. I grab her legs and swing them onto the bed. The smaller of the two says, "Jesus, she's heavy."

Once she's back in place and the attendants are gone, the nurse turns to me as she re-hooks cables and monitors. "Next time, you come get me before she tries to get out of bed. This woman has a concussion and she should be horizontal for at least another few days."

"I'm not going to be here much longer."

The nurse pulls up the side railings on the bed and locks them. "This should keep her in place for the moment. I'll get the doctor in here in a few minutes to have a look at her."

Knowing Druckmyer is out of commission for the rest of the day, I bow out of the room and rush for the front door.

Back at my motel, Eddie is laying on his bed talking to the hooker again. The guy's just waiting to get his heart broken.

I'm leaning on the rail outside of the room impatiently overlooking the choppy waters of the lake.

When he hangs up he steps onto the deck and joins me.

"Shit Eddie, you pay prostitutes, not fall in love with them."

"This one's different, Jake. She likes me."

I'm not going to change his mind, so I change the subject. "I think we should start the process of getting Harium Hissiam back into the states."

"Did Druckmyer tell you this?"

"No, but she's will and I want to be prepared."

"Jake, you know what it's going to take?"

I look away from the water and stare at him. "I know, that's why I'm getting this thing started now. I don't think we

144

have much time before Sheriff Perkins spirits our couple off somewhere we'll never find them."

"Jesus, Jake, why don't we just drop this whole mess? The Harding's are about as far from terrorists as I can imagine. They're just a couple of old hippies."

"Yeah, I know, but I also know Druckmyer. She isn't going to let this one go. For no other reason she'll drive that sheriff right into the ground, then kick dirt over him just because he crossed her."

"You might be right."

"I thought we'd get the wheels greased and make the deal before she gets out of the hospital."

Eddie turns, faces our open door and leans on the rail. "What do you want me to do?"

"You're the trailblazer, Eddie. Figure a way to get Hissiam back to Whiskey Flat."

"I'll probably need to go to Washington to grease those particular wheels."

"Druckmyer's Lear is at the airport. I don't think she'll be out of the hospital for a couple of days. Take the Lear, but stay in touch, because if all goes well, once she's out of the hospital she's going to want to get out of here and that plane better be sitting on the tarmac."

∼

The pilot gives me a hardy handshake as I step into the Lear. "Agent Ballard wants me to take you back to D.C.."

"We'll need to make a quick stop in Vegas."

"No problem. It's on the way and we need fuel anyway."

"Fuel?"

The pilot points out the window. "Druckmyer forced a landing on this strip that is about fifty yards too short. Landing was dicey, but doable. We've had to dump most of our fuel and extra luggage to get back in the air."

I give him a worried look. "Back in the air?"

"It'll be nip and tuck, but since we had time while waiting, we calculated this thing to the last pound. There won't be much runway left, but we'll make it."

"You sure? Maybe I should take a commercial flight?"

The pilot turns and closes the door. "Everything'll be fine, Agent Severs. We'll get you to D.C. without a hitch."

He walks to the cockpit and closes the door behind him.

I find a seat in front of the wing and buckle myself in tight. I've heard in a crash the people in front of the wing are most likely to survive, or is that behind the wing? Also, does that apply to small jets?

I look out the window at the choppy waters of the lake and realize we're flying into a cross wind. I don't know much about flying, but I do know that cross winds are not good.

Over the intercom, the pilot says, "Buckle in tight, Agent Severs, we might have a rough take off."

The engines speed up and the little plane moves forward and taxis to the far end of the runway. It turns and rests pointing down the strip of asphalt. They takes a minute to check both engines and whatever other tests they make before a flight. My heart is racing a bit as an acid taste forms in my mouth.

The engines speed to an incredible rate and rattles the plane until I think the thing is going to shake itself to pieces. When he lets go of the brakes, the screaming engines push the plane forward and me back in my seat harder then I've ever wanted to experience.

The plane bolts for the far side of the runway. Just when I think we've run out of pavement, the plane hits a rough patch and shakes again. Any second I expect to feel the splash of water. Just when all is lost, we leap into the air.

My entire digestive tract loosens up and the moment we're in the air, I unbuckle and rush for the bathroom in the back. When I get back, I give Sara a call.

"Eddie?"

"Turns out that I'm coming into Vegas in an hour. Want to flying to Washington D.C. for a day or two?"

The phone is silent. "I'm broke, Eddie. I couldn't afford a cab fare much less a plane ticket."

"How about we take my Lear?"

"Your Lear?"

"Okay, the company Lear."

"Where do we meet?"

I stand, step to the front and knock on the cockpit door. The co-pilot answers.

"Where are we landing?"

He looks at his clipboard. "Gate forty-five in the business airport."

I nod and turn back to my seat. "Did you hear that, gate forty-five."

"Yes, in the business part. I'll be there in two hours."

I wince. "We're landing to refuel in about an hour. Can you make it a little faster?"

The rest of the hour flight is eventless and by the time we're on the ground, I'm back to myself.

Sara stands on the pavement with a single bag as we pull close to a hanger.

When the pilot opens the door, she meets me with a nervous hug and a kiss on the cheek. "I thought you were a cop?"

"I am."

"Cops don't fly around in private jets."

"I work for one of the top dogs in Homeland Security. I'll spend all of tomorrow working in D.C., then we'll come back the next day, is that okay with you?"

She shrugs. "I lost my job almost six months ago and nothing short of being a cocktail waitress at the casinos has presented itself. I hate the casinos. My mom's keeping an eye on the kids. I got three days. Besides, I've never been to Washington."

I take her hand. "You've got kids?"

"A boy ten and a girl seven. Is that going to be a problem?"

"Not a bit. I like kids. You never spoke about them."

She frowns. "Learned not to. Most men hear about kids then flip out and disappear."

"I'm not going anywhere."

She smiles. "We'll see."

I change the subject. "I may not be able to spend much time with you during the day, because of work and all, but I'll be free in the evenings. Will that be okay?"

She gives me a reassuring look. "It'll give me time to walk the mall and go to the Smithsonian. We'll be close enough, won't we?"

"Smithsonian is a few blocks."

The fuel tanker pulls up and a young man in coveralls get out. Without any exchanges, he pulls out the fuel hose and fills the tanks. The smell of kerosene is in the air.

I take her bag. "How about we get on the plane and away from these fumes."

"Good idea."

I lead her on board and get her seated in one of the five leather lounge seats." I pull the door closed behind me so the fumes can't get in and sit across the round table from her. I get an excited smile. "So, how have you been?"

She gives me an exasperated look. "You should know, we've talked twice a day since you left."

"Yeah, I guess you're right."

"Did you pick up the people you went to get?"

"Not exactly. There are some complications. It's one of the reasons why I'm going back to D.C."

"Why's that?"

"Tie up some lose ends."

She gets a disappointed look. "It's all right if you can't tell me."

"No, no, I can tell you. It's just so boring I thought you wouldn't be interested."

"That might be true, but how am I going to know."

I start into the story about the Harding's and the crash landing she and I witnessed, then their escape and the subsequent debacle at Whiskey Flat. When I get to the part about the Egyptian and his time in prison, she stops me.

"He hasn't been tried?"

"Well, no. After Nine-Eleven some new laws were passed that got around the Constitution."

She gets a confused look. "You mean like due process?"

"Actually, it's in the Bill of Rights, but who's counting?"

"How can we just toss out the Bill of Rights?"

"I really don't know how, it just happened."

"It's what this country is based on."

I shrug. "I do as I'm told. I really don't know much about legal stuff."

Fifteen minutes later and a hundred questions about legal things I really don't understand, the plane starts its engines and we pull out to take off. By then Sara is overly aggravated about the state of affairs in our country. I try to change the subject a dozen times, but she won't drop it. Finally, I outright ask her to stop obsessing on it and she drops into a pout as we rocket off the ground and climb high into the clear, late morning sky.

Once we're up to cruising altitude, our steward, a good

looking young man with a baby face and short haircut, steps over. "I'm David, can I get you something?"

I turn to Sara. "You want some lunch?"

She looks at David. "Water with ice and lemon would be fine for now. I need to wash this taste out of my mouth."

"Same for me."

He steps to the front of the plane as I ask. "Did you get a dose of that kerosene?"

She flashes a glare at me. "More like a dose of disgust."

I take a breath. "Look Sara, it's just my job. I have little to say about the policy of Homeland Security or our country for God's sake. Save for Druckmyer, I don't think any of us likes what's going on."

She huffs. "If you don't like what's going on, what's keeping you from saying something?"

"It's my job. I would lose any chance for not only keeping it, but probably any other high-security job for the rest of my life. These people have so much power, I'd probably have a hard time finding counter work in a gas station."

David steps over to us and puts two waters on the small round table between us. When he leaves, Sara looks at me with a sad expression. "I wish I'd never gotten on this plane."

"What did I do?"

"It's not you Eddie. I like you plenty. I was under the illusion that I was safe in my own country."

"You are safe. You're an American citizen."

"Apparently not. If these two people you're looking at are not safe to face a trial for their digressions, then none of us are safe."

"I guess our country has run amuck, but give it some time, I'm sure things will straighten out."

She takes a deep breath. "I'm not so sure."

Chapter 10

Auntie

I awake to a bright morning not knowing where I am until I look out the filthy window of the trailer and smell the acrid scent of some desert herb hanging on a string above my head.

I shake my husband. "BillyBob, wake up."

He grumbles and tries to turn away from me, but I stop his retreat while continuing to shake him. "BillyBob!"

"What, what?"

I whisper, "we have to get out of here."

He opens his eyes and in a sleepy voice says, "We promised the sheriff we'd stay put."

"It's not the Sheriff I'm worried about. You saw the look on the faces of those government people. They were determined to get us."

He sits up in bed. "We broke the law, Myrtle. We have to pay the price. I'm sure it's going to be substantial, but we can handle it even if Frank doesn't come through."

"Those government guys weren't at the sheriff's office yesterday to levy some FCC fine on us. While you were napping yesterday I overheard the deputy talking about them flying us to Egypt as terrorists."

"Why would they take us to Egypt?"

"I don't know, but I heard him. We've got to get out of here, BillyBob."

A soft knock comes at the cheap hollow door. "You two awake in there?"

I answer. "Yes, ma'am."

"Breakfast is ready."

"We'll be out in a few minutes."

BillyBob says, "sounds good."

We're forced to remove the marijuana hanging on the shower curtain rod to take our shower, but the water is hot and towels are clean. Although I don't have my makeup kit, I feel refreshed and ready to face the world.

Once we've replaced the pot, I walk along the hall and meet the old woman in the cluttered kitchen as she pours a cup of coffee for me. "You two sleep well enough with the mugwort?"

"Mugwort?"

"It hung above your bed. Should have given you some dreams."

"Now that you mention it, I did have strange dreams."

"Good ones, I hope."

"Good and not so much. We do have this problem."

She smiles and takes a sip from her cup. "Never got a chance to get the story. My nephew called me at the last moment and without explanation dropped you. You two don't look like murderers or terrorists, so I'm guessing I'm pretty safe."

I take another sip of my coffee and notice a hint of some spice while I finger the spilled salt on the table. "Truth be known the government is charging us with terrorism."

Her eyebrows raise. "I'm sure there's a good story."

"You wouldn't believe it."

She reaches over and puts her hand over mine for a moment. "Give an old woman a thrill and don't hold back on the details."

It takes fifteen minutes to tell the whole story, including Frank Deluchi and the incredible sex with my husband after all these years. When I'm almost finished, BillyBob walks in sleepy-eyed.

Without breaking eye contact with me, Auntie gets up, finds a cup and pours a coffee, then sets it in front of him.

". . . and we ended here, not know why or how and also not knowing if we should escape or not."

"Where would you go?"

"That's what BillyBob says."

He looks at us with clouded eyes. It usually takes him two cups before he's coherent.

"I think your husband's right. You'll spend your life running from some government ghost."

I take another sip of my coffee. "Yes, but an Egyptian prison isn't quite what I have in mind either."

With one arthritic finger she motions for me to follow. I stand and we walk to the window overlooking the canyon. She points at a knoll a few hundred yards away. "There is a large oak tree standing on the edge of the precipice. Once you two have finish breakfast, go to that knoll and wait under the tree."

"Why?"

"I'm not sure, but I saw you there in a dream last night and I don't take my dreams lightly. I used to go there a lot when I was young, but though it's reasonably close, it's a difficult hike and I can no longer make it."

I look back at BillyBob and he's still in his early morning pre-coffee haze. "If you say so."

She smiles and walks back to the table. "I've got some fresh eggs from my chickens and a little toast. You hungry?"

Both BillyBob and I say the same single word together. "Starved."

After we eat, we start across the rocky steep terrain to the knoll. She's right, the journey is difficult in the best of circumstances and my pumps don't really help matters much. The whole way, especially after I slip and skin one knee, I wonder why we're doing this. We sit on a park bench positioned at the base of the massive tree and hear the thumping of a huge helicopter. It takes a moment to spot the thing in the open sky as it climbs up the canyon toward us.

BillyBob gets nervous as the mechanical mosquito gets within a mile. He takes my hand and stands. "We'd better get behind the tree."

"You think it might be coming for us?"

"I'm not willing to find out."

We slip behind the tree and watch the chopper thump its way directly at us, like its radar has honed in on two people in a sea of rock and dry field grass.

It even slows as it goes overhead then, incredibly, it lands in the middle of the minuscule flatness of Auntie's garden. I point. "They ruined her garden."

Seven dark-clad men with deadly-looking rifles leap from the helicopter as two black Suburbans race into her gravel driveway and come to a sliding halt in front of her trailer. Six men leap from the cars and rush the building.

～

After my dream, just before dawn, I get up and find my way to the kitchen, brew a cup of tea and read yesterday's paper. Not like there is much to read that isn't sensational garbage, but I like the comics and Ann Landers.

Three hours later —and I know there is plenty of time— my charges get up. The shower runs for an overly long time, but I shouldn't be worried. This young couple needs whatever conveniences they can get, considering where they might be going if my dreams are wrong and the government goons come early.

When the woman steps into the kitchen, I have their coffee brewed. It's lucky I keep a small bag in the freezer for when my nephew visits, because I haven't drank coffee in twenty years.

The woman sits and brings herself awake after a second cup. He's still a little groggy when I spring the news on them. Well, I don't exactly spring it, but I do coax them to find their way to the cliff edge out behind the house.

Once they've left and I watch them carefully pick their way across the steep mountainside, I get to work. It won't be long and I have a lot to do.

It takes almost the whole hour. I'm an old woman who doesn't move as fast as I used to. When I hear the blades of the helicopter coming up the canyon, the table is set for fourteen and I leave the front door ajar. I slowly get to my knees then lay flat on the floor with my arms spread wide.

The cars rush in my driveway and slide to a stop in front of my house. I already know the first car has crushed the new forget-me-nots I planted last week. It's okay, I planted them expressly for this purpose. Better them than my prized bougainvillea. If they must crush something, and last week's dream told me they must, better it be the Forget-me-nots.

Without knocking, three burly men dressed in black with full riot gear try to crush the front door as they burst in yelling so loud and fast I have no idea what they're saying.

One puts his knee in my neck, pulls my arms behind me and handcuffs me while the others search the house.

When things finally calm, two men pick me up by my shoulders and sit me on the sofa.

The helicopter has landed in my vegetable garden, but I don't mind as much as they do, because who they're after isn't here.

The captain sits down in front of me. "Where are they, Mrs. Flanders?"

"They left earlier this morning." It's the truth, just not the full version of the truth.

The captain points at my table with the four leaves added and the fourteen place settings. Pancakes, eggs and bacon are piled up in the center. "If they are gone, Mrs. Flanders, who were you planning on feeding?"

"You can call me Auntie, Captain Hood. Everyone does."

He ignores my invitation. "Who were you going to feed, Mrs. Flanders?"

I look at him and smile. "Why you and your men, of course. You haven't had breakfast yet have you?"

His face shifts from the stern Captain of a fourteen-man S.W.A.T. team to a regular confused man. "For us?"

"Yes sir. I've been expecting you for a half-hour. Sorry the food isn't as warm as it could be, but I'm sure you don't mind."

"One of our cars wouldn't start."

"I know. It was unexpected."

"How do you know?"

"I really couldn't tell you, Captain. Not because I don't want to, but because I don't know how I know. I just do."

He gives me a confused stare.

One of the young men steps up and gives the Captain a snappy salute. "Harding's are not here, sir."

The Captain rubs his face as a young soldier charges in from the back yard. He salutes, clicks his heals and yells. "We found no one out back, Captain!"

His second in command steps over. "We got 'er buttoned up, Captain and the Harding's aren't here." He looks at the table. "Could sure use a little breakfast."

The Captain turns to him. "We have a job to do here soldier. Breakfast is not on the agenda."

"Beg pardon, sir, but far as I can tell, our job's done. We fly back to base and eat that crappy mess food or take this nice woman up on her offer. Food looks pretty good here and it'll just go to waste."

Nine men standing around the table grunt in agreement.

The Captain looks at the table, then swings his arm.

"Okay men, un-cuff this woman and let's eat."

The young man rushes out back and brings in the three helicopter guys. When they sit, I pour coffee and notice one chair is open. I turn to the Captain. "I thought there were fourteen?"

He smiles as he takes a sip. "Jennings came down with the flu this morning."

I sit in the fourteenth chair next to the biggest of the group, a football player type that looks like he has shoulder pads. I put my hand out to shake, "I'm Auntie."

"William Tuttle, ma'am." His hand shoots out and I expect his huge paws to grip me like a vise, but he's gentle and takes my hand with his finger tips. "I'm sorry we busted your door, ma'am."

"I guess you have to break down doors at times."

"Didn't look like this was one of them times. I got a day off in two days. I'll fix your door if that's okay with you."

"You don't have to call me Ma'am. I'm Auntie."

He tries the name on like a new word in his vocabulary. "Auntie."

"I look forward to you coming up anytime and fixing my door. I turn to the rest of the men who are silently eating. "If any of you young men see your way clear to come back, I'd be delighted to have the company."

"Yes Ma'am." They all say the two words as a unit.

The Captain, sitting across the table from me, speaks. "We're not always this quiet, ma'am. It's just that William here is our meanest hombre. We're all in awe at the transformation."

William gets an angry glare. "I'll rip the balls off of anyone who mentions this back at base. . ." he turns to me. "Sorry, ma'am."

Two men sitting at the end of the table snigger.

William turns to them and in a demanding gruffness I have not yet experienced, he barks, "What?"

One of the two, obviously not concerned with his mean streak says in a high-pitched voice, "nothing, sweet William."

"The Captain says, "that's enough boys. Let's enjoy Auntie's generous meal and get back to base. I'm sure the General isn't finished with us today."

"Yes, sir," they say again in unison.

When the stack of pancakes is finished, I retrieve the backup stack from warming in the oven and re-pour coffees.

Twenty minutes later, the Captain wipes his mouth with the paper napkin and stands. Twelve men stand with him. He turns to me. "Ma'am, it has been a pleasure. You certainly made our day."

The other men, standing at attention, give me a military stiff nod and the Captain files out with his men in tow.

I follow them to my shattered door as the helicopter engine starts in the back. The cars back up and one of the men gets out and kneels to carefully fluff the dirt of the track in my garden and attempts to right the crushed Forget-me-nots. When he can't, he looks at me with a childlike face and shrugs.

The helicopter lifts off the grounds and starts back to the lowlands as the cars wind their way out of my driveway.

I walk to my back door and look at my row of crushed lettuce and slammed snow peas from the wind of the blades.

The helicopter is far in the distance dropping down the steep canyon when I wave at the couple.

They emerge from behind the oak and begin the perilous journey back.

By the time they walk onto the flat of my property, I reestablish the row of lettuce and start water into the trough.

The young woman asks, "how did you know they were coming?"

I drop the hose into the next row. "My dream last night."

"Your timing was incredible."

I smile. "I've always had good timing. Why don't you come in and have a glass of lemonade? I squeezed it fresh and the lemons are from my tree."

They follow me into the house with the fourteen dirty plates and the smashed door and dirty boot prints all over my rug. The young man turns to me. "What happened here?"

I start piling the dishes. "I fed 'em."

The young woman laughs as she piles the dishes. "You fed them?"

"They hadn't had breakfast, so it was the only hospitable thing to do."

The young man shakes his head. Even after they busted down your door and raided your house?"

I shrug. "They were hungry."

The young man walks over to the door. "The least I can do is fix this door."

I put the stack of dishes on the sink. "I don't think you'd better."

He runs his fingers along the shattered jamb. "Why, Auntie? I certainly know how to fix doors."

His wife points proudly at him. "BillyBob was a

journeyman carpenter in his younger years."

BillyBob, I'll need to remember his name.

"Because, BillyBob, one of the young men is coming up in a few days to do the repairs. It might look a little suspicious if suddenly it was fixed."

He looks at me. "One of the S.W.A.T. team men?"

"Supposedly the meanest of the lot. His name is William."

BillyBob shakes his head.

I smile. "They're men. If I've learned anything in my ninety-three years, I've learned that you feed a man and he'll follow you like a puppy."

"Not me," he says.

"Okay, maybe not you."

~

We sit in the office all the next day waiting for something, but nothing happens.

The next morning, my radio squawks as I'm driving around the East side of the lake. I pick up the mic and answer.

"Captain, we might have a problem."

I wait out the silence, knowing that my deputy is a little slow on the uptake.

"I got word that S.W.A.T. out of Fresno is on its way to our safe house."

"I still think everything will be okay, but I'm worried about Auntie. She's pretty old and that kind of drama might kill her."

"Not much we can do about it now."

"No, there isn't, but I thought you'd swing around and check up on her after you take care of the Freeman issue."

"It's the Freeman's again? I might be there all morning."

"Well, I'm the only one here and I can't get away."

"What I know of Auntie, she'll be fine. She has the sight."

"Yeah, but she's old, and those S.W.A.T. guys aren't a gentle lot."

"I'll look in on her when I'm done."

I check out with him and put the mic away. Either the Freeman's call us or one of their neighbors calls us at least once a month with some kind of domestic dispute. No one ever gets hurt, but they do seem to scream a lot and over the years more than a few guns have been fired.

I turn off the highway and drive up a pothole-riddled gravel road for a quarter mile. I park under a huge oak tree next to a hundred dead cars of varying degrees of disassembly. The rusted single-wide trailer stands in a clearing. Rex, the pit bull is chained to Ford Pinto with no tires and all of its glass missing.

Rex, as usual, goes absolutely crazy jumping at me and almost ripping his own head off when the chain snaps him back. Does he stop? He keeps right on leaping headlong at me, though I'm still twenty yards away from the furthest reach of his chain.

Bud, the husband, opens the squeaky front door and yells, "Rex, shut the fuck up!"

The dog relaxes, goes back into the Pinto through the windshield and curls up on the ragged front seat.

Bud Freeman looks at me, then climbs down the three steps to the bare earth path strewn with dead washing machines, rusted transmissions, bald tires and twisted steel objects of unrecognizable origin. The place is a disaster.

Bud takes a drag from his cigar. "Did my neighbor call you?"

"Someone called, Bud. You two at it again?"

"It's no big deal, just Betty and me getting into it a bit."

I walk a little closer, knowing that old Rex will stay put as

161

long as Bud is within eyesight. "That same someone said they heard gunshots along with the screaming."

"It's them fucking raccoons." He points behind the trailer. "They keep gettin' my chickens."

His coop is an old step van that stinks to high heaven. He took me back there a few years ago when the neighbors accused him of burying someone under it. God, that was a mess. We were mandated to dig out the plot next to the van only to find a huge hog half-decomposed. It wasn't the smell of the hog, which was bad enough, but the chicken coop itself.

"You got yourself a raccoon, did you?"

"No, sheriff, the little bastard got away and with my prize Bantee, too."

"You know I got to ask, Bud."

He sighs. "Yeah, I know." He turns and screams, "Betty, get your fat ass out here right this second if you know what's good for you."

I wince at his vulgar verbal abuse of his wife. Unfortunately there is no law about verbal abuse or this guy would be serving a life sentence.

The front door opens tentatively and Betty pokes her jowled face out. "I'm okay, sheriff."

"Betty, you know I need you to come all the way out, right?"

"Will you get the fuck out here, bitch."

She opens the door and squeezes through it, then steps down to the earth in a faded house dress with a ragged robe hanging limp over her obese body. As usual, she looks fine, but my job mandates that I make sure. Bud and Betty are screamers. The neighbors hate them. What else is new?

I tip my hat. "Mr. and Mrs. Freeman, have a nice day."

I turn and walk away from the scene, happy that I don't have to play marriage counselor for those two this time.

Bud screams loud enough for the Franklin's who live

within eyesight and earshot of the car graveyard. "Sheriff, you tell those nosy neighbors of mine to shove it up their asses."

I ignore his obvious attempt to engage me and I get into my car, carefully wiping my feet first on a raw edge of tin from an old, broken ironing board. One of Bud's chickens saunters up and pecks my sock.

I shake my head, close the door, start the engine and drive away from the Freeman compound of desolation.

Once on the highway I open my window trying to air out the car, or is it my head? I'm just lucky he's not my neighbor.

Since I'm over half-way around the ten miles of lake, I continue the loop and stop at the Piggly Wiggly for one of those famous pastrami sandwiches on a Kaiser roll.

After I order from Matilda in the deli she asks, "so, Jack-o, what's up with all the military yesterday?"

"You really don't want to know."

"Things are slow right now."

I give her the shortened version, knowing that if I hold back some of the juicy details, my sandwich will end up dry and lifeless.

She slathers the mayonnaise. "Where are the Harding's?"

"Undisclosed area."

"Come on Sheriff, you can tell me."

"If I did you could be charged as an accessory."

"Yeah, like that's ever going to happen."

I smile. "Already so many people are in on this little caper, the whole county could be charged with conspiracy. You want to be added to the list when the doo-doo finally hits the fan?"

"Okay, you got my attention on that one. Just tell me if they're going to give Harium back. His wife's been a mess ever since he was snatched."

She drops the meat in the slicer.

"Thin sliced, okay Matilda?"

She turns back from the machine and jokingly turns the knob to thicker. "How's Harium doing?"

"They say he's alive. It's all I could get out of them."

"You'll keep us all informed?" She turns the knob back and starts pulling paper-thin slices.

"Once this whole mess is over, I'll do an interview with Jason in the paper."

She brings the fifteen or so slices over and lays them expertly over the bread, puts Dijon mustard on the opposite piece and closes the sandwich. When she folds the paper around it and cuts it in half, she says, "You come over to my place sometime and I'll cook you a decent meal."

I knew it was coming. She always asks.

"I don't think that would be a good idea."

She hands me the sandwich and shrugs. "Can't blame a girl for trying."

I give her a smile. "Thanks for the offer, Matilda. You'll be the first woman I'll contact when I am, but I'm not ready just yet."

"Jesus, Jack, that was five years ago."

"Yeah, but she died so suddenly."

"Hmmm."

"Thanks again, Matilda." I turn and walk to the checkout just a little sad that I still haven't let go.

Joe and Janet's tall, skinny kid stands idle behind the checkout. I can never remember his name.

When I walk up, he talks as he rings my Coke, a bag of chips and the sandwich. "Big deal yesterday."

"Yeah, we had a run in with the Marines."

He rubs his faint, blonde goatee. "Who actually won?"

Just like a twenty-year old to make everything black and white with that kind of question. "Don't know yet."

I hand him a twenty and he counts my change. "It was my

day off yesterday and I was there. Looked to me like we pretty much kicked some Marine butt."

I put the change in my pocket and slide the remaining bills in my wallet. "Maybe we won that little skirmish, but it was only a single chess move in a much larger game. "Unfortunately, they got lots more manpower. I'm not so sure we'll be able to hold out too much longer."

He pops a small bag and puts my things in it. "I hear you might get Fatima's husband back?"

"I doubt it, but it won't be for not trying."

He grins and starts to ring up Old Lady Trescot's groceries. "I'm rootin' for you, Sheriff."

I walk out to the car and put the bag on the passenger seat.

When I pull onto the highway and drive to a deserted stretch, three military trucks come from behind and box me in, slowly forcing me to pull to the side of the road.

I pick up the mic. "Come in Alex." But all I hear is static. They must have some kind of jamming equipment.

Once stopped, I lock the doors, unbutton my shirt, take the sandwich out of the bag and slide it down next to my belly button. If I'm going to be abducted, I'm not leaving lunch behind. I re-button my shirt.

Six storm troopers leap out from behind the front truck with rifles pointing at my face. They surround my car. I put my hands in the air.

A small man dressed in some kind of black cape with overly dark wrap-around sunglasses and a short horse-riding crop casually steps back to my car from the front of the truck. He gives me a sardonic smile and motions for me to roll the window down with a rotation of his kid-gloved right hand. I roll my window down a half-inch.

With a syrupy voice, he says, "Sheriff Perkins, I presume." I nod.

"We would ask you to step back into our van?"

"Do I have a choice?"

His smile does not change. He nods and one of the troopers turns his rifle and smashes my side window, grabs the lock and opens the door.

The spooky guy in black gives me a little bow. "'Fraid not."

I get out before the troopers drag me out. They take my gun and force me back to a huge RV-type bus with no windows. The door automatically opens and I step up into a command center only seen in the movies. There must be thirty guys operating various pieces of equipment.

Mr. Spook points for me to sit in a leather lounge chair facing the windshield. He sits across from me.

Another box truck drives in front of my car and in a few seconds, it drops a ramp, hooks to my cruiser and pulls it out of sight.

I realize I have not seen one car on an otherwise busy part of the road. No witnesses to my abduction.

My voice is a bit shaky. Now I know how it feels when I arrest someone. "What do you want?"

The driver of the bus closes the door blocking any outside view and the entire procession pulls away from the side of the road. No one talks.

After twenty minutes the bus comes to a halt.

Spooky finally speaks. "We wanted to show you how easy it is to make you disappear. Next time we come for you, it won't be so friendly. We have unfinished business with the Harding's and you're going to give them over today."

One of the men opens the door and Spooky points out. "You can go."

I cautiously step down to the pavement and realize I'm standing in front of my own office. I walk to the front of the bus as my cruiser is being unloaded from the truck. With rubber knees, I step up the walkway to the front door and open it. Alex stands behind the desk. "Captain, I've been calling you for twenty minutes."

Without answering, I walk back to my safe little office, sit in my familiar rickety chair and take a few breaths.

Alex steps in behind me. "Captain, you don't look too good."

"I was just abducted."

His face gets a worried look. "By aliens?"

The stupid question brings me fully back into my office. "No, you dope, not by aliens, by Druckmyer and that crowd."

He sits. "Druckmyer? I thought she was in the hospital."

God, this guy is dense.

"She ordered my abduction, probably from the hospital."

"Where did they take you?"

I pause for a moment before I answer. "Here. They brought me back to the station as a lesson. They want the Harding's and they'll go to extreme measures to get them."

He gives me one of his famous blank looks. "Back here?"

I'm tired of answering his stupid questions. "Don't you have something better to do?"

He stands. "Just checking on you, Captain."

"I'm fine. Now why don't you get to whatever it is that you do."

He turns and steps out of the office.

I yell, "close the door!"

Once the door is closed, I remove the uneaten sandwich, put my head on the desk and fall asleep.

It can't be a half-hour later and the phone rings. I pick it up and try for a professional voice but fail. "Sheriff Perkins." I sound like I've been sleeping.

"Did you get my message?"

It's Druckmyer. I only heard her talk once, but that gravel

based froggy voice is unmistakable.

"Loud and clear."

"What are your plans, Sheriff?"

"I'm still recouping from the shock. I need another hour or two."

Her voice is syrupy friendly like the spook she is. "I'll give you a two hour reprieve, Captain. It'll take that much time to get my troops in position. Call me here." The phone goes dead.

I stand and go to the dinky bathroom across the hall and splash water in my face. It's like they not only kidnapped me, but drugged me too. The only problem is, I ate or drank nothing. Maybe it was in the air.

"Alex!" I yell.

He clumps down the hall and the door opens. "Sir?"

"Get the mayor."

He turns and goes back to the front office.

In a moment he buzzes my desk. I dry my face, go into my office and pick up the phone. I click the line and Johnson's gravely voice come through. "Jack, what's up?"

"Carson, we need to talk."

"What's going on?"

"I'm sure this line is tapped. Meet me at our usual place."

"See you there."

I stand, check for my gun and realize at some point they gave it back to me, but I don't remember when.

I step into the front office and Alex looks at me with a worried face. "You going to be all right, Captain?"

"Just hold down the fort, Alex. I'll be back."

He tosses me a radio and I almost don't catch it.

Outside the afternoon sun hits my face and I pause to feel its freshness, then walk across the street, around the corner and into the park next to the Kern River.

The bench closest to the shore is slightly under water from an early spring melt, but three other park benches are okay and I sit on a dry one. The flowing river clears my head.

The mayor, in his lanky frame and those ridiculous spit-shined cowboy boots sits and pulls a pack of cigarettes from his thin plaid cowboy shirt. He tilts his white Stetson hat and removes the Ray-Ban sunglasses. "Jack, you look like shit."

"Try getting abducted and see how you might look."

His mouth drops open to reveal his Hollywood capped teeth. "Aliens?"

"No, damnit. You and my deputy have been watching too many science fiction movies. I was kidnapped by Homeland Security."

His face goes from surprise to a furrowed brow worry far beyond his forty-seven years. "Homeland?"

"These guys are serious, Carson. They gave me two hours to produce the Harding's."

"Holy shit."

"That's what I said. I know we have some contingency plans, but we never counted on them going this far."

"I'll talk to legal, then the other board members."

"Well, you'd better get on the stick, because I don't think I have much time." I hand him the radio. "I'll stay in touch with this, but until you guys get this figured out, I'm disappearing. You'll be able to get a good signal at Jackobe's Auto Parts."

"Why Jackobe's and why don't I just call your cell?"

"Because once my two hours are up, I won't want to be found. They can't trace a radio signal; they can a cell call."

I stand. "You guys need to figure out something quick."

He stands and shakes my hand like any good politician will do. "We're on it, Jack."

I walk back to the office. Alex is still leaning on the

counter with a blank stare in almost the same position I left him. He looks up as I walk in the front door. "Alex, you still got that dirt bike?"

"Yeah, sure, but why?"

"I want to borrow it."

"It's at home."

"Take your car and when you get home change into Levies and that red long-sleeve shirt you wear on Saturday nights."

He gives me a curious look, like I've just gone round the bend.

"Just do it and get back here with the bike as soon as you can."

"Okay, Captain. Be back in ten."

"Park the bike out back and bring your full faced helmet."

He saunters toward the front door.

"Quickly." I yell.

He scampers out the door and races down the walk.

I go to my office, open the little closet behind the door and strip to my skivvies. I guess I've gained a little weight since I've used my spare change of clothes, because I have to leave the top button of the Levies undone in order to get the red shirt to tuck in. I better start chilling on those early-morning donuts.

The front doorbell rings and I force the button closed and walk into the office expecting to berate Alex for not leaving yet.

A woman in her mid forties stands with a worried look.

I step fully into the room. "Can I help you?"

"You're the sheriff?"

"Yes, ma'am, Captain Perkins."

"My son went missing yesterday afternoon."

I'm thinking the timing on this problem is about the worst it could be. "How old is your son?"

"Sixteen."

"I pull out form 1799 and pick up a pen. "What's his name, ma'am?"

"BillyBob Harding."

I look up. "Is this a joke?"

Her piercing brown eyes glare at me. "No sir, this is not a joke. My son has been missing for eighteen hours and he's never been gone like this before."

"Is it possible he's out with some friends?"

"He's diabetic and his insulin kit is still in the bathroom. In the next few hours, if he doesn't get his daily dose, he's going into shock."

"Does he have some way you can contact him?"

She taps her thin fingers on the countertop just once. It's a nervous unconscious movement and she checks it immediately.

"He has a cell phone, but it's been out of service since yesterday morning and I'm worried."

I write in the name, BillyBob Harding, but I already know what happened.

Alex steps in from the back. I turn to him, "Mrs. Harding here has lost her son. Can you take the rest of her statement?"

I turn to her. "I need to leave ma'am. Sergeant Chesterman will take care of you."

She huffs. "What, my son isn't important enough?"

"No ma'am, that's not it. What I have to do may have a bit to do with your missing son."

I point at the name I wrote as Alex looks over my shoulder. He lets out a short gasp. "Holy shit."

I take his helmet and it's a tight fit on my head as I grab a radio and walk out the back door.

The small Yamaha starts without a glitch and I go west along a back trail out across the desert hillside, hill climbing up steep, open terrain until I get a mile away.

I stop and look back over the little town I've come to love. I turn the radio on. "Come in Alex."

"Yes, Captain?"

"Checking the radio. I'll keep in touch."

"Yes, Captain."

The second I click the radio off, a helicopter rises from a spot beyond the Kern River and heads directly toward me.

I keep one foot on the ground and pop the clutch, spin the back wheel in the gravel to make an about face. I race another hundred yards to an ancient Valley oak. I pull the bike under its branches and behind the massive trunk before the helicopter is close enough to spot me.

With its blades chopping the air, it passes over me in a straight line for the top of the hill. After another minute the sound of the blades are far in the distance.

I drive off toward the south, stopping three times under trees and bushes when I hear the chopper approaching. Finally, it drops back to its original landing pad and I can finish my cross-country journey unhampered.

When I pull down the driveway, Auntie is waiting on her rotting wooden porch. She looks up as I park the bike. "They're looking for the bike. Maybe it's better to put it in the shed." She points at a beat-up tin building barely big enough to contain the dinky motorcycle.

I push it over and in among shovels and rakes.

When I walk back, she smiles so big her wrinkles disappear for a moment showing for a second how beautiful she was in her youth. "Auntie, I need—"

"They're after you too."

"Yes, ma'am. I—"

"You need a place to hide for the next few hours."

"Yes ma'am."

"Well, come on inside, Jacky and we'll get you fixed up."

She's called me Jacky ever since I was a toe-headed kid. For years I hated it, but now it's a name of endearment.

I follow her in, noticing the shattered front door.

The Harding's are sitting at the kitchen table.

Auntie sits me at the head of the table and sets a glass of ice tea in front of me. "We have another half hour, Sheriff, then the boys from the military base will be visiting again."

"Again?" I ask.

"They were by this morning."

"Did anything happen, Auntie?"

She laughs. "Not much. They were hungry, that's all."

I want to ask the meaning of her statement, but I already know. All my life, every time I show up, Auntie has had something on the table as if she was expecting me. She sets a freshly-baked blueberry scone next to the iced tea.

It's buttery and flaky and melts in my mouth.

While I enjoy the taste, I look at my couple. "How are you two holding up?"

The woman perks up. "Yesterday was calmer, but your Auntie has been taking good care of us."

I take another bite. "You're about as safe as you can be here with her."

Both of them smile and BillyBob says, "At least we're being well fed."

The woman speaks. "Auntie seems to know when something's going to happen."

"Yes, I know. She's our secret weapon. That's why you're here."

"Sheriff, I really don't like being referred to as a weapon."

"Yes ma'am."

I do appreciate that she refrains from calling me by my childhood name in front of my charges.

She looks at me. "I'm too old now, but you know where

the cave under the oak tree is?"

"Yes."

"It's best that you escort this nice couple there. My visitors from this morning will be returning soon and we need to get all three of you out of the way."

She picks the big red statue I've seen on her counter since I was a kid. "I'll put the Quan-Yin in the windowsill of the back bedroom when the coast is clear."

As the Harding's and I stand, the woman asks, "Will it be a difficult climb?"

Auntie waves her hand. "It's behind the oak tree where you were this morning. It's easy."

"That's what you say."

Auntie takes her hand. "You'll have plenty of time."

We file out the back door and around the garden fence. I've forgotten the first part of the climb is so hard. The steepness of the cliff leaves me a little shaky.

As a kid, we used to race across this ledge without even thinking about danger or the sixty-foot drop. Now, with everything seen from a different perspective, sixty feet is a substantial distance.

Once past the sheer drop-off, things get a little easier, but not much. No one slips, but I cut my hand slightly on a sharp piece of shale.

When we reach the tree, the woman sits. "How much farther, Sheriff?"

"Under this tree."

"Can we rest here a moment?"

"I don't hear the helicopter, so we have time."

Mr. Harding leans against the tree. "Sorry we put you through so much trouble."

I sit facing out at the amazing view of the desert terrain and that ever-choppy lake. "Our entire county has been waiting for a couple like you."

"What do you mean?"

I tell them the story of Harium and Fatima and how we planned to get him back, leaving out the promise to trade him for the Harding's. No point in giving these folks an unneeded scare.

Mr. Harding asks, "how can these people get away with it?"

I pull a stalk of dried grass, strip it and put it in my mouth. "After the jets hit the World Trade center on nine-eleven, a bunch of new rules came into play."

"But, due process is in the Constitution. How can that be overridden?"

"Actually the Bill of Rights. I don't know how it got done, but it did and now we live under the tyranny of the current administration."

The woman says, "I don't like that I knew nothing about it."

"None of us did, but it's what our government has come to."

Mr. Harding says, "a bunch of frightened lemmings or a pack of wolves."

I pick my teeth with the stalk. "Either one doesn't work for our safety and well being. It only works for those fat cats who run the government. There is a whole contingent of people who think nine-eleven was staged to get the American people to fall into line with fear as an incentive."

I stand and point at the lake. "Looks like Auntie was right again." Although we can't see it yet, the sound of helicopter blades chopping the air echoes up the canyon.

"We'd better get into the cave. She seems to think they're going to be much more thorough this time."

The woman asks as she gets up. "They won't find the cave?"

I smile. I don't know how Auntie does it. She's got some

kind of gift, but you already probably figured that out."

Mr. Harding says, "either that or her timing is uncanny."

I lead them behind the trunk and down to a rocky ledge below the tree. We face the solid rock.

I point. "See the entrance?"

He reaches out and fingers a minute crack that wanders vertically in the rock for eight or ten feet to the bottom of the exposed tree roots. "It's solid."

I give him a nervous laugh. "Until she's ready for us to go in, it is solid."

I look back at the house and Auntie stands in the window looking at us. She raises her hand, as she has done so many times.

I grasp both Mr. Harding and his wife by the wrist and back walk through to the living rock.

I push my head in, then step through like it's one of those hippie bead curtains from the sixties. In a second we're in the dark coolness of the cave.

I walk them back ten yards to a huge stone table that sits in the middle of the large room. I motion them to sit on the benches, then, still standing I look out the entrance at the approaching helicopter.

Behind me, Mr. Harding asks, "how did she do that?"

I don't turn to look at him. "I have no idea. I have tried to ask many times, but she always gives me some coy answer."

The woman says, "it seems magical."

With my back still to them, I'm watching the thumping helicopter chop its way up the canyon. "More like sleight of hand, I think, but the real magic is about to come."

"Really?"

I turn to them. "Unless you want to stay in this cave the rest of your time here, I believe you need a new safe place."

Mr. Harding slaps the table. "It's nice and cool in here."

"In the summer when it gets unbearably hot, we used to come here as kids and explore the depths of the cave."

Mr. Harding asks, "there's more to it?"

"It goes deep into the earth. We never could find the bottom, but I have fond memories of trying."

Mr. Harding glances around. "It looks like one single room. Is it the slight of hand thing?"

"She is special."

The helicopter thunders overhead and I step out of the cave for a moment to watch it land dead center in Auntie's garden. Damn those military guys.

Since there's nothing I can do, I can only hope they don't hurt her. I walk back into the cave. Mr. Harding is feeling his way around the circular walls of the single room.

"You're not going to find them."

"Them?"

"There are several tunnels, but we're not meant to explore them now. Probably Auntie has her hands full and can't focus her attention on us."

"Your aunt has some interesting capabilities."

I sit across from the woman. "She's not my aunt. She's simply Auntie. She's been around here as long as I can remember and she's always been as old as the hills. I don't think she's changed much since I was born, but I can't really tell."

"How old is she?"

"She's been saying ninety-four since I was a kid."

In a nervous anticipation of trouble, I step back to the entrance and poke my head out. A dozen military types are fanning out from the resting helicopter. Three come directly toward us.

I slip my head back in and look at the Harding's. "The military guys are working their way over here."

Chapter 11

D.C.

The Lear lands at Dulles Airport and a limo is waiting to take us into town. I like the way Druckmyer travels. I'm a long way off from bumping up the ladder to her position, but fancy vehicles is incentive to grab for that next rung.

"Eddie, where are we going?"

I turn to Sara. "I have to meet with a few mucky-mucks right away, but for now we'll get you settled."

"I've never been to D.C."

"Yeah, well, it ain't what you think."

She looks out the dark tinted glass window. "It really is a disappointment. For some reason I thought the nation's capitol would be sparkly and fresh."

"Vegas is sparkly. The only fresh thing in this town is the tourists. Everything out here is old and filled with historic tradition."

She turns to me. "Don't get me wrong, it's still amazing to see all of these old icons in real life. They're just so dusty looking."

"Smog's eating away at the marble."

We cruise along the mall, then turn left and drive for a mile to an ancient hotel. Before we get out of the car, I say, "it's not the Ritz, but my government rating doesn't give me those kind of privileges."

She looks at me with her big eyes. "Eddie, I don't care. Remember, I'm about ready to be evicted from my crappy apartment. From my perspective, this is living high."

We get out and the driver carries our bags to the check-in desk. He sets them on the carpet.

The clerk sits in the middle of his long desk with a smirk.

It's not directed at me. They all have smirks in these old hotels, not expensive enough to rate hiding their disdain for the people who stay with them.

I lean on the counter. "I'm Mr. Severs."

"I gathered that."

He has a bit of an attitude to go along with that pencil-thin mustache as he stands there with his worn hotel jacket.

After a longer moment than is reasonable, I ask, "you have a room for us?"

He gives me an all-knowing smile. "You and Mrs. Severs?"

Instead of jumping down this guy's throat in front of Sara, like I normally would, I put one hand over the counter. I could easily grab him and shake the pass card out of him, but I simply snap my fingers three times, then hold out my palm.

The little twerp had the whole thing set up before we walked up, he was simply holding out. He strikes a single key of the keyboard and a receipt and pass card magically appear from under the counter.

I sign the paper, take the card and pick up our bags.

"Five-thirteen," he says as I walk away toward the elevator.

We're alone in awkward silence on the ride up. When the door opens we're met with a group of noisy Asian tourists.

"We aren't sleeping together," she says with an air of

finality as we walk along the hall.

"I wouldn't assume that."

"That's good, because though the other night was wonderful, I wouldn't want you to think. . ." She drops the last part of the sentence.

I slip the pass card through the slot and the door beeps. "We have separate queens, if that's okay?"

We walk in and she takes a breath. "It's beautiful." She rushes to the window and looks out toward the capitol building high on the hill. She points, "look, Eddie, we can see the seat of our government."

I walk up behind her and want to wrap my arms around her cute little waist, but I hold myself back and stand next to her. One can never tell what a woman is thinking and I'd hate to get my face slapped because of an insensitive move.

She points at a skyline I've seen too many times, but through her eyes it looks fresh and exciting. She leans against me and hums.

I'm not sure, but I cautiously wrap my arms around her waist and we stand for a moment until she turns with girlish excitement. "You must take me outside."

"I've got to go to work for a few hours first, but I'll be back."

"I'll wait here in the room."

"No, you don't have to. Go out and walk around. Although it's old and dusty, there still are some amazing things."

I look at my watch. "I'll meet you back here in two hours."

She gives me one of those smiles that melts my heart. "See you here."

I dig in my wallet and produce a hundred. "You'll need some walk around money."

I see caution in her eyes and I say, "no strings."

She smiles and takes the money.

I ride the elevator back to the lobby and walk over to

Frank. "Let's get back to the office."

"Have you there in twenty."

I ride in traffic thinking about Sara and how Las Vegas is so far away. I think about her kids and her mom. Do they all live together? I don't know about having a mom around, but I'll cross that bridge when I come to it.

I walk into the Homeland office as a light shower moistens the sidewalks. An hour later, after talking to three higher ups, I start the process of transporting Harium Hissiam from the Egyptian prison to our Bakersfield field station.

The second I enter the document into the files, the computer locks me out. Three guards show up at my station and escort me to the front door. They are friendly but persistent as I try to tell them who I got the okay from and show them my written orders from Jake. It's a little unnerving, but I also know that when Homeland office is threatened, all unnecessary personnel are shown the door. It's happened before.

I get in the limo and we drive over the state line as the sun comes out, leaving the sidewalks and streets glistening. It's a perfect time to take Sara for a walk because the mall is beautiful just after a rain.

The driver follows me into the hotel and Sara is waiting in a chair reading a newspaper.

She stands and smiles as we approach.

The driver turns to me. "Will there be anything else, Agent Severs?"

"You'll be back at eight?"

"Eight sharp, sir."

"Thanks Frank. I'll take it from here."

He nods, turns and walks out of the building.

Sara elbows me lightly and whispers, "you going to tip him?"

"He's a government employee. He couldn't take a tip even if I offered. He'd get fired if anyone found out."

She slips a windbreaker on and points at the front doors. "Let's walk to the mall."

I'm thinking it's a bit crowded this time of day with all the Sunday tourists crowding the streets and sidewalks, but what the hell. She wants to walk, we walk.

She takes my hand and we stroll toward the front door. She turns to me with glassy eyes. "Since I was a little girl I've always wanted to walk the mall."

"It's not that big of a deal."

"I don't want to tell her how dangerous it is, but I'm a cop with a big gun under my jacket. No one will bother us.

As we step through the front doors a half dozen teenage girls rush around us as they run down the steps, all the time talking non-stop, most of which I don't understand. It's not that I don't get the words, I can't figure out how they communicate using incomplete sentences. Everything is in some kind of female code. I've run into this before. Kathy used to do the same thing. Everything was half-baked and a series of choppy run-on sentences with no end or subject on which to hang the statement. I don't get women.

We walk down the steps as the jabbering races away from us. It's too much fun being around that much excitement if only for a few seconds.

I spend much of my time with Jake and he's no picnic. The only time I've ever seen him even halfway excited was when those two escapees from Quentin turned on us and unloaded a fifteen-shot automatic from twenty yards. Bullets were zinging past our heads like a spray from a waterfall and all Jake could say when it was all over was they were bad shots. Of course they were bad, but hell, I'd peed my pants and I couldn't stop shaking for an hour.

Once we took them, Jack walked into a McDonalds and ordered a burger and fries like nothing happened.

Sara's picked up the excitement as she dances around me like some poodle who needed to relieve itself.

We stroll along the sidewalk at the base of all of these old, stodgy buildings, her pointing out things I've never seen, like a view of the river from one angle. She points at an old car driving by.

We finally come to the corner overlooking the mall and she goes nuts. She can barely contain herself. Her teenager turns into an eight-year-old.

If I can spend the rest of my life with this woman, I'll be a lucky man. I'll need to take her to an ever-growing set of wondrous places to get her excited like this, but it'll be worth it.

We cross the street and stroll along the sidewalk, her looking at the Lincoln Memorial for the first time and me seeing it through fresh eyes, though I've taken relatives and low-level dignitaries on the same walk a hundred times.

As we approach the monument, she takes my arm and squeezes herself close, then kisses my cheek. "This is nice, Eddie."

I want to tell her how much fun she is, but I don't have the words, so I just squeeze her back and look into her amazing hazel eyes. "You having fun?"

"Yes, yes!"

We start up the steps of the monument and the white marble Lincoln stares out at us in his thirty-foot-tall chair. No matter how many times I visit this place, I always get a little choked up, but I manage to hide it with all of the people around.

I turn to Sara and she's bawling. God, this woman. She doesn't care that there are people, tears are rolling down her face. Although it's noisy inside of the monument, Sara's sobs are loud enough to be heard echoing off the stone walls.

I'm not sure what to do. Her crying is infectious. I'm torn between trying to care for her and wiping my glassy eyes when she throws her arms around me and pulls me tight, then really lets loose. It's the moment I'm ready to ask her to marry me. I want this unabashed expression in my life. If I can't do it myself, at least I want to be next to someone who can.

It's embarrassing and exhilarating all at the same time and it goes on. As she eventually calms, we turn to one of the inscriptions chiseled into the wall and she begins again.

A half-hour later, I coax her out of the building and we walk around the backside where the view of the river and Arlington cemetery calms her.

I sit on the edge of the concrete walk with my feet dangling over the ten-foot ledge. She sits next to me holding me tight. "Kinda made a fool of myself in there."

I turn to her. "No, no you didn't."

"It was so much more emotional than I expected."

"Yes, I know. It always surprises me."

"You weren't the one blubbering all over the place."

"I'm jealous of you for it."

She gives me glistening cow eyes. "Really?"

"You were impressive in there. I really don't know how to let go like that. I wish some of that would rub off."

"Come on, Eddie, you're giving me a hard time."

"No, I'm serious. I have all of the same feelings, I just can't seem to let them out. I'll choke them down until I gag."

She gives me a long direct stare deep into my eyes. I'm sure she's looking for a hint of sarcasm, then she says. "I can't help myself. It just comes out."

She stands. "Let's see something else."

We walk around to the front of the building and enter the throngs of people going in and out. We descend the stairs and start back toward the east end of the mall. I purposely walk to the far south of the strip hoping she won't notice the Vietnam Veterans Memorial, but she does and she wants to drop into its darkness. I stop, knowing a deer-in-the-headlights stare is plastered all over my face. "I can't."

In her jubilant nature, she says, "it's important."

"Yes, I know, but I can't. If you want to go, I'll wait here on this bench. I just can't."

She gives me a curious look. "Someday you'll tell me?"

The word someday means she's planning on seeing more of me. It means that I'm not a total loser after all like I thought when Christine left. That's it. Being with Sara, I no longer feel completely lost. A little lost still, but much less.

"Yes, I'll tell you sometime soon."

"Okay then. You wait here and I'll be back in a while." She walks away fast like the ice cream man just showed up.

I step over to the newspaper rack, deposit my fifty cents and pull a paper. When I sit, I skip the headlines about the senate doing something and find an article on page two that I can dive into.

By the time I'm reading the comics, Sara sits next to me.

She looks wrung out. "I didn't know how many died in that stupid war."

I fold the paper. "I was too young, but my brother's name is on that wall somewhere. I went down there once and that was enough."

I stand and we walk east along the lawns looking at the phallic Washington Monument. It's a perfect day and I'm with a great woman. I'm thinking, how could life get any better, when my phone rings. Damn that phone.

I pull it from my coat and it's Ballard. "Jake?"

"Eddie, how's it going with finding Hissiam?"

"Since it's Sunday and I'm off at least one day a week, I'd planned on finalizing it tomorrow."

Jake snigger's. "Hey, Eddie, you don't have to get testy with me."

"I just need some time off, Jake. Homeland isn't my whole life."

"You got that woman with you?"

I pause. "Yeah."

"That's good, Eddie. You need a woman, but I need Hissiam and I need him right now. The shit is about to hit the fan here and I want to have something to calm things down."

I turn to Sara and motion for her to wait, then I walk onto the lawn a dozen yards away. "I got the paperwork done, but the computer locked me out. I'm not sure if the requisition got posted or not."

"Locked you out?"

"Some kind of security breach, because they escorted me out a few minutes later."

"I haven't heard anything."

"Me either, Jake, but it happened and it's got me worried."

"Druckmyer's back on the war path and she's looking for blood. She's got the entire fifth division saddled up and waiting for a signal."

"Holy shit."

"You got it, buddy. That's why I need a bead on Hissiam."

I look back at Sara and wave. "I'll go to the downtown office. I'm sure I haven't been locked out there."

"You wish."

I say, "get back to you in a few hours."

I close the phone and walk back to Sara. "I've got to go back to work for another hour or two."

She looks disappointed. "That's okay. I want to visit a few of the Smithsonian's. They're somewhere at the end of this walkway, right?"

"Yes, but let me put you in a cab."

She gives me a self-assured look. "I want to walk."

I look around. "Normally, I'd say okay, but though this place looks friendly, it's not, especially after dark and the sun is almost down."

"Oh, come on, Eddie, how much different could it be than the Vegas strip?"

"It's different, Sara, just trust me on this. I'll get you a cab and I need to be assured you'll take a cab back to the hotel. Walking around here alone is not safe, especially for a woman."

"We strolled up this walkway and nothing happened."

I pull my jacket back and show my three-fifty-seven tucked in its shoulder holster. I wouldn't come here without this."

She gets a shocked look. "Jesus, Eddie, you carry a gun on your day off?"

I don't answer, but take her hand. "I really have to go put out some fires." I walk her to the edge of the sidewalk and raise my hand to hail a cab. In thirty seconds one stops and I give her a kiss on the cheek. I hand her another hundred. "Please get another cab when you're done and I'll meet you back at the hotel in a few hours."

"Okay, Eddie." She grabs my lapel and pulls me close, then gives me a juicy lip lock.

It lasts so long the cabbie honks his horn. "You two goin' somewhere or what?"

I want to snap back at him, but I'm in the throes of a romantic moment.

She pulls back and looks at me with glassy eyes. "Something to look forward to when you get back."

She gets into the cab and closes the door.

Once the cab is gone, a black Suburban pulls up. The doors open and two big guys get out. I don't recognize them.

I give them a grin splay my arms in a peaceful gesture and start to say something. The bigger one grabs my arm, twists it

D.C.

around to my back and shoves me into the suburban.

~

My ear seems to be attached to my cell phone as Druckmyer give me a constant barrage of orders. She's got the entire fifth division bivouacked outside the county line. As much as I try, I can't seem to slow her down. As fucked up as she is, it's not an understatement to say the woman is a force.

It's been days since I talked to Eddie last and I haven't heard a thing. What's happened to him?

I'm sitting on a cast-iron bench under an old tree in the middle of the little park in the center of town. I'm trying to get a handle on the sequence of events. The sheriff and his charges have disappeared leaving his dipshit deputy to mind the store. As soon as Druckmyer gets out of the hospital, which should be any hour now, all hell's going to break loose on this little town. I know her. She wants to be here in person to take command. When she does, she'll tear this town a new asshole out of spite, enjoy doing it, then walk away like nothing ever happened. She doesn't care if she gets the Harding's anymore, she's out for revenge. God, the woman is a horror.

My phone rings again. I take it from my pocket and don't recognize the caller. I open the door. "Yes?"

"How's it coming with Hissiam?"

"Sheriff, where the hell are you?"

"I'm sure you'd like to know so I can get spirited off to Guantanamo."

"I'm really not the one—"

He yells, "just listen!"

I go silent.

"I don't care who is pulling the strings on this one. If you take this any further we have a surprise for you that will forever

189

haunt you for years to come."

"It's not me, Perkins."

"I'm glad it's not you, Ballard, because I like you, but give this message to your boss. I'm not acting alone here and we've been preparing for years."

"She doesn't take to threats."

"It's not a threat. What I'm saying is fact. I am willing to negotiate with her tomorrow, face-to-face in the park under the old tree."

I look up at the tree and take a deep breath. "You really don't know what you're up against."

"I think I do, Ballard. If she wants to test me, we're more than ready."

"Look, Perkins, the only thing that is keeping the entire United States Marine Corps from being dropped right on your head is my boss is still in the hospital. She's just twisted enough to want to be here to watch your town shrivel up and blow away. She gets pleasure doing things like that."

"Just give her the message." His phone clicks off.

I look across the street at the Wonder Bread truck. A face pokes out the small side window and he shakes his head.

Damn, another few seconds and we could have had a bead on him.

My phone rings again and shit, it's Druckmyer. "That pissant going to give in?"

Perkins' whole message will force her into action, so I candy-coat it. "He wants to negotiate."

I visualize spit flying across the room as she screams into the phone. "No negotiating with fucking terrorists."

Damn, she's turned the sheriff into a terrorist too.

"What do you want to do?"

"They say I'll be out in the morning. I'll deal with that bastard tomorrow. Tell him he has eighteen hours or all fucking hell is going to break loose."

"You'll meet him in the park?"

"In the park at noon."

The line goes dead and I hope somehow she is forced to stay in the hospital a day or two longer. Dead wouldn't be a bad alternative.

This park is so pleasant. A mockingbird sits in the tree across the street and sings an array of songs. A dog saunters up and noses my knee for attention. Absently, I pet him, still trying to think a way out of this mess. Hissium is on his way, but where is Eddie?

I look at my watch and a full half-hour has gone by, me in deep thought and not coming up with a thing. Druckmyer hasn't called.

One of the guys gets out of the Wonder Bread truck, walks over, sits across from me and pets the dog that seems to have adopted me. "What do you want to do, sir?"

"I don't know, Waverly. You and the guys come up with anything?"

"No sir, but we wonder why she's doing this."

"You haven't been around long, have you?"

"No sir, only a few weeks on this detail."

"Druckmyer is in it for the power. She doesn't give a rat's ass about the law or anyone's rights. She has to be top dog and I've never seen her fail."

"Sounds like this Sheriff Perkins has something nasty up his sleeve."

"Yeah, I know and it has me worried."

"Worried?"

"The sheriff's determined. It's going to be the clash of the titans and I'm not sure I want to be around for the fallout."

The next day around noon, I'm back on the park bench.

An ancient woman dressed in thick layered clothing with two or three dresses, a number of blouses, a few sweaters and a lavish lavender shawl over her head. She moves like a snail across the lawn. It must take her five minutes to reach the park picnic bench, then another two or three to find her seat facing out toward what I'm afraid is a mess about to unfold.

Druckmyer calls and I'm forced to answer, but I continue to watch the old woman settle herself on the bench close to me.

"Ballard here."

"Get your fucking ass in gear Ballard and get over to this hospital to pick me up."

"They're letting you out?"

"Ten minutes ago and I'm fucking brewing for a fight. Is that chicken shit sheriff of yours around?"

I want to tell her the sheriff isn't mine, but what is the use. "He's in his office."

"Tell him to fucking prepare himself to be buried."

I just got two orders at the same moment which gives me options. I choose the first. "We'll be right there, ma'am."

I click my radio and one of the guys in the van opens the back door and runs over. "Sir?"

"One of you guys have a car?"

"Yes, Sir. David has one."

The old woman is finally settled. She pulls out two big knitting needles and her arthritic hands are like blurs of light making stitch after stitch. She smiles at me.

While being mesmerized by her knitting, I say, "get David to go to the hospital and pick up Druckmyer."

"Holy shit, she's out?"

"She's out all right and this town is toast."

"Do we need to move the truck?"

"Yeah, maybe around the corner might be safer. For now,

David needs to get in his car and bring her back."

The kid walks toward the van, but I can't seem to take my eyes off of the speed of the old woman's knitting.

I stand and walk over to her bench in the shade. I bow slightly. "Ma'am."

"Auntie to you, Jakey."

No one's called me Jakey in years. "How'd you know—"

"I don't know how I know, I just do. Won't you sit?" She slides over and pats the bench seat next to her.

"I'm sorry, you'd better—"

"I'd better go somewhere where an old woman's safe, is that what you're about say?"

I nod.

"I'm fine here. Sit down, son, we have some talking to do."

Without thinking, I sit next to her looking out on the small park and across the street at the Sheriff's office.

She points up with her needles. "Whenever you look, you need to notice the sky too."

I'm compelled to look up. "It's blue."

She giggles. "Yes, it's blue."

The whole time her hands have not stopped. The stitches are flying across the intricately-patterned knitting.

She says, "I knit to calm myself."

I really don't know what to say. It's the very question I was about to ask.

"I'm here to help. You have a volatile situation and I came off of the hill as your negotiator."

I'm confused, because she answers my every question before I ask it.

"Druckmyer is on her way, right?"

I nod, unable to speak.

"Druckmyer and the Sheriff are going to clash, right?"

"Yes, ma'am."

193

"Okay then, I'm here to defuse the situation."

I'm about to tell her about Druckmyer's unbending intent.

"Tell you what, son, you take care of your people and make sure none of them fly off the handle and muck up the works and I'll handle Druckmyer."

I snigger. I'm about to say that Druckmyer does not get handled, but again she beats me.

"Druckmyer can be handled like any other human. It just takes the right finesse."

The Sheriff steps out of the office and walks to our park bench. "Auntie, you ready?"

She gives him a big smile.

I chime in. "Druckmyer's on her way."

The Sheriff smiles. "I know. You guys aren't the only ones with listening equipment. I came out to see if you got anything on Hissiam."

"I sent one of my guys back to Washington to research him, but he dropped off the radar four days ago. It's not like him, so I'm a bit worried. What's about to happen has me much more anxious."

The old woman pats the back of my hand. "You needn't worry Jakey. You're man was abducted and questioned by your own people. He escaped and is on his way here now."

"How do you know?"

The Sheriff sits across from us. "She just knows, Ballard."

The old woman grins. "I've learned a trick or two in my day."

"Trick or two?"

"The plants tell me."

"What plants?"

She points up. "This old maple for one. She tells me your hamburger is about to arrive."

My car slips around the corner and slides into one of many parking places in front of the park. The kid gets out with two big bags and rushes over. "Sorry it took so long, sir. The burger joint was halfway around the lake and the line went around the block."

He sets the white bags down and fishes into one of them. "Burger, no onions, right?"

"Cheese.? I say.

"Sorry sir, I forgot."

I reach out and he plops the soaked sandwich in my hand.

"Got you some fries too, sir." He hands the soggy fries over and I set them next to the burger. "Where'd our truck go?"

"Around the corner. I suggest you get in that truck and don't move."

The old woman, still knitting like a demon, sniggers. "Son, I told you, Druckmyer is mine."

The kid looks at her, then at me.

I shake my head. "Don't ask. Just get back in the truck."

"Yes, sir."

He walks away and I open the paper wrapper. "Sorry, when we ordered, neither of you were around."

The old woman shakes her head. "Those gut bombs are the last thing I'd eat."

The sheriff smiles. "Even I shy away from that burger joint and I really have no discernible taste."

"I don't care, I'm hungry."

I take my first bite as the old woman speaks. "Eat fast, Jakey because you're not going to be able to finish this."

I crunch down into the burger, then speak while eating. "What do you mean?"

She looks at the empty street and nods. It isn't five seconds later when David rounds the corner and haphazardly pulls into a parking place behind my car. I didn't realize he had one of those jacked-up versions of a truck. I'm sure Druckmyer is irate and I'll get some shit for that oversight. Behind him is an endless line of government military trucks that park, unload fifty fully-armed soldiers, then drive out of town. The soldiers form a line at parade rest in the middle of the street.

By the time I'm halfway through my burger, Druckmyer is squeezing herself out of the Chevy truck onto a ladder.

I force as much of the second half of the sandwich in my mouth as possible, but don't finish the last bite when it happens. I couldn't finish the last bite if I wanted.

~

That shithead of a doctor finally releases me. I would have left last night, but if anything went wrong, I'd be on my own insurance-wise. Government insurance doesn't allow for patients to take matters into their own hands. Hey, fuck those insurance pencil-pushing dickheads. Ballard's on his way.

I can't believe this hospital doesn't have an extra-wide wheelchair for full-figured women like myself. When I get back to Washington, I'll be giving them a shitload of trouble for their oversight. It's me, Director of Homeland and they're wheeling me out on a gurney because they didn't allow for slightly overweight people. Maybe I'll just sue. On second thought, suing them will only cost the hospital's insurance company. I want to get them where it hurts, so fuck the suit, I'm going to have them shut down. How dare they treat me like this? It's embarrassing.

They push me outside and the nurse lets me get off of the gurney. This bitch has a special place in my thoughts of revenge. She'll fry in the fucking electric chair and I'll make sure of it.

Ballard pulls up and I walk over to the car almost without help. I'm slightly dizzy, but it's probably from the drugs the bitch gave me to keep me quiet.

Nurse Ratchet grabs my elbow. I pull my arm away. "Leave me the fuck alone."

A kid gets out of the car. It's not that sleazy bastard Ballard, and immediately he's third on my list, that's for this morning.

I bark at the kid. "Who the fuck are you?"

"David, ma'am."

Well, David, if you don't want everyone of your pubic hairs pulled out one at a time, I'd suggest you open the door of this ridiculous truck and get me a fucking ladder."

He races around the front of the truck and grabs the door handle at eye level. "I've got a ladder in the back for my girlfriend."

He pulls out an aluminum ladder with a label that clearly states a maximum capacity of 250 pounds and sets it in front of me. I give the first step a test and hear it creak under my weight. When I step on the first rung, the ladder collapses and I almost ruin my right knee from the drop to the concrete. "What the fuck, you trying to kill me?"

By the time I've extricated myself from the aluminum scrap of metal, the nurse races down the entry with a reasonable hospital stepladder. It has rails to hold on to.

The climb into the truck is much easier and I tell the kid to put the hospital ladder in the back. I look at the nurse for any back-talk. "Charge it to my tab."

The kid closes the door and races around to his side.

Once the truck is started and pulls away from the curb, I get why overly-testosteroned men buy these things. I feel like queen of the highway, impervious to everyday traffic. I hide my grin as the kid merges onto the highway.

I open my phone and hit speed dial. A three-star General answers with his gruff voice. "Potraious here."

"General, you got your men ready?"

"Waiting your command, sir."

'Sir' is his only way to show respect. The dickhead probably doesn't even have a feminine equivalent in his vocabulary.

"Okay then, get 'em rolling. I want that town surrounded by the time I get there."

"We already have the town surrounded. I'm pushing my men closer to squeeze everyone into the park."

"Like we talked about, General. I like your style. I'll be arriving in a jacked-up black Chevy truck with big wheels."

His phone goes dead and I slide mine into its pouch on my hip as we come to a red light. A half dozen cars wait for the light to change.

I wave the kid on. "Run that fucking light. I don't have time for lights."

The kid wheels his truck into oncoming traffic, lays on his horn and bolts through the light without a hitch.

When we roll into town, the military follows us. Guns are up and pointing at the citizenry. Good, I want to scare the fuck out of them. I want that dipshit sheriff to know his town is lost and it's all his fault. I want whoever is left to get a town hall meeting together in the ruins of this fucked up little village and point their finger at him. He'll suffer. You're fucking well right he'll suffer.

The kid parks behind the Sheriff's cruiser, but I yell over the loud mufflers. "Drive fast upon the lawn and park directly in front of that piece of shit park bench."

He climbs the curb, rolls across the lawn and pulls in sideways right up to the bench. When he shuts his engine off, he looks at me and grins. "Don't just sit there, you twerp, get that fucking ladder so I can get out of this piece-of-shit truck."

He leaps out and fishes the ladder from the back of the truck, then sets it up in front of my door.

It takes an awkward moment for me to climb to the earth, but once I do I turn to the bench and Ballard.

The kid gets back in his truck and drives away.

"What the fuck are you doing here, Ballard?"

In an apologetic voice, he says, "this isn't right, Ma'am."

"I decide what is right, Ballard." I slur his name with disdain and turn to the Sheriff.

I swear when we drove up, I saw Ballard, that little-dick Sheriff and some old woman in ragged clothes, but now a little girl sits next to the Sheriff in a summer dress with long blonde hair and a red ribbon to hold it in a ponytail. She might be seven. I want to focus on the sheriff, but the girl distracts me.

Something is terribly wrong. "What the fuck is going on?"

The girl's voice is sweet and innocent. "My name is Annie, what's yours?"

I recognize her tone. My words catch in my throat. I glare at her, then at one of my subordinates. "Get that girl the fuck out of here."

He jumps like I was a snake and rushes around the bench to grab the girl, but stops and falls to his knees bawling. "I didn't mean to."

"My name is Annie," she says again. "What's yours."

There's something I recognize in her voice. Even her ribbon is familiar. What is it?

I really don't need to get engaged in a conversation with some dopey little kid, so I turn toward that dickhead Sheriff. "Do you really want this entire town destroyed?"

His answer surprises me. "Her name is Annie. What do you have to say to that?"

I turn to the little girl. She smiles. I drop both hands on

199

the table and lean in close to face off with the Sheriff. I yell, "you really want a piece of me, Perkins?"

When I refocus, and I have no idea how they did it, I'm six inches from that button-nose little girl. The dickhead Sheriff is sitting on the opposite side.

The girl smiles bigger. "I'm Annie, what's your name?"

I turn to the old woman who seems to be the only constant in this macabre scene. "Who is Chatty Kathy?"

The girl says, "Annie. My name is Annie, not Kathy."

I turn to the Sheriff and the two have shifted positions once again. I look back at the Sheriff and they switch again. "I'm Annie."

"Stop!" I scream.

I glare at the old woman. "What the fuck do you think you're doing?"

Her almost toothless mouth breaks into a full grin. "Helping you to remember, my dear."

I pull one hand off of the table and swing my arm to backhand her hard across the face. I misjudge the swing and miss. I've swung so hard I'm off balance and I topple on top of the table. A few boards crack, but they hold.

I look up as the little girl comes into view. "Hi, I'm Annie. Who are you?"

Something in my resolve breaks. I choke out the words, "Annie. My name is Annie, too."

Then it all floods in. All of the memories of abuse. All of the beatings from Dad. Mom's insistence that nothing was wrong. The emotional beating from my classmates because I was heavy. I've always been heavy. The ridiculing remarks. My first husband who refused to have sex with me. My last husband who wouldn't leave me alone. It all floods in at once. I'm sprawled on the park table crying. It's the first fucking time I've cried in twenty years."

The floodgates open and tears roll down my face. My nose drips. I can't catch my breath. I gasp for air between open sobs. I feel seven again. Maybe it's the last time I sobbed this way. I feel like that little girl. Then something so strange happens that I stop breathing. One second, I see out of my eyes looking up at the little girl. The next second, I'm seeing from a completely different perspective. I'm looking out of the little girl's eyes at myself. I'm frightened and intrigued at the same time.

The old woman takes my hand. I want to pull away. I want to slap her. I'm ready to tell her to leave me the fuck alone. All I can do is break into another bout of bawling.

Her hands are gentle, something I've never felt. She kisses the backs of both of my hands and looks at me with her old, blue eyes. She has so much compassion in her eyes, I break down and cry harder. God, will I ever stop?

Then, as if things aren't weird enough, another face comes into my vision. It's the Sheriff and he's like an angel. He smiles, but doesn't speak.

"I'm sorry," I say. "I didn't know."

He mouths words, but no sound emerges. I know what he's saying.

"I've been so angry and I didn't even know it."

He nods and his smile gets bigger.

Chapter 12

The Park

I'm sitting with the old woman and Ballard as Druckmyer squeezes herself out of that ridiculous truck and rushes over with some military guy in tow. She pushes through the spring air like it's molasses. With that much weight it must be hard to move at all.

She reaches the table and slams both hands hard on its wooden surface. I almost flinch, but I'm not going to give her even this small satisfaction.

She's loud. "What the fuck are you doing here, Ballard?"

In an apologetic voice, he says, "This isn't right, ma'am."

"I decide what is right and what isn't right, Ballard."

She turns to me. "You really want this town destroyed?"

I don't know what to say.

She turns to Ballard like he gave her some kind of smart-ass remark, then turns back to me. "Who, is Chatty Kathy?"

I have no idea what she's talking about. There's only five of us here; the General, Druckmyer, Ballard, Auntie and myself.

My answer surprises even me. "Her name is Annie."

Why did I say that? I don't have time to think of an answer when Druckmyer does the oddest thing. She lifts her right hand off of the table in a lightening fast move and backhands Auntie. I'm used to odd things happening with Auntie around, but Druckmyer's hand, instead of breaking the old woman's jaw and with the power and directed intensity it's sure to happen, her hand goes right through Auntie's face like she's a ghost.

The swing is so hard it throws Druckmyer off balance. She flops on the table then bawls for almost five minutes.

As she comes back to the world of the park bench and old shade tree, Auntie reaches over and takes her hand. It brings on a whole other bout of tears and unintelligible blubbering's. It's downright embarrassing.

～

There were many tall tales back on base about Druckmyer. General Burkheart gained a lofty reputation for slugging her, but he also got demoted.

I talked to him yesterday and he said, "it was worth it. She's hell on wheels. I wanted to punch her the second I met her."

I'm not going down the same road as Burkheart, so I'm ready for anything she has to throw at me. I promised myself this morning while shaving that this woman would not get to me.

When I get out of the Humvee to meet her for the first time, I'm prepared for her short temper and I've been well schooled on her attitude and how much power she actually wields, which is substantial, but, I'm not ready for her obesity.

Once she's extricates herself from the truck, she summons me and I rush to meet her. "Got your men ready?"

"General Williams. . . Sir." I'm not sure if the "Sir" is appropriate.

"Move on my command."

I salute, because I know she likes this sort of groveling bullshit from a man. It's not her command, it's mine, but I let her live out her personal little fantasy and I don't say a word. Already, I'm figuring out a way to chop her off at the knees, I don't know how yet.

I follow as she waddles up to the park bench with the Sheriff, that spook Ballard and some old woman dressed like a street urchin.

Druckmyer's a ball cutter. She chops at Ballard and the Sheriff, but then something happens and I think it's with the old woman. Druckmyer has a heated conversation with some invisible person, then backhands the old woman. I'm positive she's crushed that old woman's skull, but she misses and falls sprawled on the picnic table. As if things aren't odd enough, Druckmyer starts to bawl like a baby. I've served four tours, faced three enemies, shot my share of men and been shot twice, but I don't know how to handle this.

She keeps blubbering about some child named Annie. Damn, it's downright embarrassing. I actually back up a few paces.

Then, if things aren't strange enough, Druckmyer lifts onto one elbow, looks the old woman in the eyes, then apologizes in every way she can. She gets so overly apologetic, I'd say she's groveling. Jesus, fucking H. Christ, do I really need to witness this bull, especially from some government pencil pusher.

I'm ready to turn and walk away, but the warning voice of my commanding officer rings in my head. I stand at attention waiting for her to get down to what we came to this fucked up little town to do, turn it into a battle zone.

Chapter 13

The Past

Once I stop my bout of crying, the old woman takes my hands and in a split second I am whisked away from the picnic bench, away from under the tree and the entire town out into a darkness I've never experience. I stiffen from some kind of old, familiar fright.

"It's okay Annie," she says, "we're going on a small journey."

"Where are we going?" the little girls voice asks. I look about to see the girl and she is no where in sight. I realize the voice came from me and the next logical step is I am the little girl, or at least I was the girl and somehow through this old woman's magic, I'm revisiting her/me.

"Where are we going?" my woman voice demands. I'm frightened. I can't see. All I can feel is the old woman's hands.

"Not to worry, Annie, we're almost there. Once we're done, I promise to return you to the park bench."

Her words are settling. My fear dissipates and once again I relax into a cradle of safety I have not felt since I was a kid.

Far off in the darkness I notice a pinprick of a light. It

gets larger, like going through a long, straight train tunnel. The end is minuscule, but bright. As the light gets bigger, the old woman comes into view. The light envelopes us and we're ejected into a warm, cloudy day on a train trestle overlooking a small creek. I remember this creek.

I look at the old woman. "Where are we?"

She gives me her toothless grin. "In your past, my dear."

I realize I feel light, like gravity has lessened or I've gone on some crash diet and it actually worked for the first time in my life. I look at myself and I'm thinner like I always wanted to be. Not as thin as those magazine models I always despise, but thin nonetheless.

I feel so free and light, I put my hands in the air like a ballet dancer and make a pirouette on a single board of the bridge. Two train rails are on either side of me. "What happened, I'm so thin."

The old woman leans on the rough-hewn rail. "You're in your past, Annie."

I look at my hands, normally rough and blistered from the eczema I've struggled with for years. My fingertips are smooth and unblemished. My arms are well-proportioned again instead of the sausages I normally live with.

"Is there a mirror? I need a mirror."

The old woman motions and a full-length mirror appears leaning on the handrail. I dance in front of it and there I am, myself forty years ago, a girl of twelve. I'm so happy to be alive. I'm free again of the darkness that overshadowed my entire life. What was that shadow? How did I not notice it? Where did it come from?

I turn and look at myself from the back and I actually have a cute little butt, not those boxcar buns I've lived with since I was in my twenties. Where did all that weight come from?

I turn to the old woman who has an angelic grin. "How

did you do this? What's your name, anyhow?"

"I'm Auntie."

I can't believe it, for the first time in years I actually care enough to ask someone's name and I really want to know.

I try out the word. "Auntie. . . How did you do this?"

She shrugs. "I don't know how. All I know is I can do it. Isn't it time for you to get out of that downward spiral you've set into motion and touch your roots again?"

I look again in the mirror and there is my pretty little face, not that horror of a pockmarked scared mess I've been trying to hide from all these years. I touch my cheek and start to cry. Between sobs, I ask, "What happened to me?"

The woman puts her arthritic hand on my forearm. "What happened to you is about to happen. Do you remember?"

"Remember what?"

She points down the rails back toward a distant town.

Three men walk along the rail toward me and a piece of some long, lost memory floods in. These men are not friendly.

I freeze and turn to Auntie. "These men don't belong here."

She gives me a pained grimace. "No, Annie, they don't but they're here."

The three men step onto the bridge and I hear their shoes clunk along the wooden slats. I look at them and see the malice in their eyes. They spread out, blocking off any way of getting around them and back to the safety of town. I already know retreating to the far side of the bridge is no alternative because there are only dense woods for miles.

I turn for help from Auntie, but she's gone.

≈

Four men pile out of the black Suburban and surround me. The biggest one has short-cropped blond hair and a thick, well-developed neck. "We can do this the hard way, Eddie, or you can come peacefully."

I put my hands up slightly with palms open as an offering of peace. "I'm always up for easy."

The blond guy points. "Get in the car."

I climb in and sit sandwiched between two line-backers. As we pull away, one digs for my service gun, while the other cuffs my hands behind my back. "I thought we were doing this the easy way?"

The driver looks back and grins. "It's all a matter of our perspective, now isn't it."

Once I'm trussed and a smelly black bag is pulled over my head, I ask, "Where are we going?"

No one answers.

We drive for an hour and stop. I hear a big steel door open. We drive in and the door closes behind us.

The engine is off and one of the bruisers drags me out of the car and forces me into a small padded area. When he pulls the hood off, I'm in some kind of eight by eight concrete cell with a steel door and a single light bulb over my head.

He removes my cuffs and I sit on the single cot with no mattress. "What am I doing here?"

He says nothing.

"You guys know I'm Homeland Security, right?"

I reach for my badge, but of course, they took it with my gun. "I'm on your side."

He snorts and leaves the room. When the steel lock snaps into place, for the first time in my life I feel scared.

It might be an hour later when the door lock snaps again and Bruiser opens it. He motions for me to come with him and we walk down a makeshift hall made of raw plywood. The rafters and sodium lights of a huge warehouse are high overhead.

We wander through the maze of plywood walls until we

finally are dumped into a gigantic waiting area with three chairs in the center. This could be an airport hanger except I hear no airplanes.

Bruiser sits me in the middle chair. "You wait here."

It's the first words I've heard from him and it's shocking how high his voice is compared to his size.

I look around and other than the arched beam ceiling, all I can see is sheet after sheet of plywood surrounding me. There is something about the plywood that is disconcerting.

My internal diatribe goes on until a small man opens one of the twenty-two doors, I sat there long enough to count each one a few times. He motions for me to come in.

I stand and walk across the polished concrete floor and enter the cheaply carpeted room with a single desk and Bruiser standing in the corner. The little guy closes the door and motions for me to sit in the steel folding chair.

He sits on his side of the desk and studies a folder. Five minutes goes by before he looks at me and asks, "Do you know a hooker names Sara Summers?"

"Yes, but she's no hooker. She was—"

He interrupts, "How long have you known her?"

"Five days."

He looks at me. "Five days Agent Severs?"

"Maybe six, I can't count clearly right now, but look, if you already know I work for Homeland what the fuck am I doing here?"

I guess my voice rose a little to high in volume, because Bruiser steps forward in a threatening way. I lean back in my chair and take a breath. Quietly I ask, "What am I doing here?"

"You never met Sara Severs before six days ago?"

In a quiet voice I answer. "No, never."

He drops a photo on the desk in front of me and turns it

around so I can see it. He points at me. "Is that you, Agent Severs?"

"Yes, of course it is."

"That photo was taken last year in Saint Louis. Who is that standing next to you?"

I look more carefully and though she has long black hair and her makeup is thicker, there is no doubt it's Sara.

"Holy shit, I was in Saint Louis last December." I look at him. "I swear, I never met her before six days ago."

He drops another photo and turns it toward me. "And this one?"

It's Sara all right, this time a redhead. She's walking past me. The photo is slightly blurred, but it's her.

"I never met her before."

He drops another photo on the desk of her and I naked, entwined in one another arms at her apartment in Vegas.

I point, "That one I know. That was four days ago at her place."

"Yes, Agent Severs, we know. What we don't know is if you never met her before the blackjack table in the Flamingo, how is it that we have these other photos?"

"Jesus, how long have you guys been following me?

He digs back in the file and looks at the top of the paper. "Two years."

"Two years?" I yell. Bruiser steps forward.

"Two years?" I ask more quietly. "What the hell for?"

"Sara Summers, also known as Nadia Kraskoff, currently works for the Turkish government and we have believed for a long time that you have been passing secrets to her."

"Secrets? I'm an agent for Homeland. I have no secrets."

He gives me an all knowing smile. "Druckmyer seems to think different."

"Holy shit," I say almost to myself.

I look at him. "Druckmyer is a twisted bitch who would torture her own mother if she thought it would better her career."

"Yes, we know."

"You'll take her word anyhow?"

The little guy digs in the file and pulls a half-dozen photos, then drops them on the desk in front of me. "It's not like we don't have corroborating evidence, Agent Severs."

"So, you think I'm a spy?"

"No sir. The word spy doesn't carry much weight these days, because it is so hard to prove, but terrorist is a much better term and it gives us so much more leeway."

I slump in my chair. "I'm a terrorist?"

He taps his finger on the photos. "We can certainly build a case for it, don't you think?"

I look at him direct. "You and I both know that all you have to do is tag the word terrorist onto someone and you don't need to build a case."

"Precisely the point, Agent Severs. Looks to me that we've pretty much got you by the short hairs. I don't have to remind you that under the new laws, we can pretty much do with you as we like."

"Yes, I know. So, what do you have in mind?"

He leans back in his comfortable looking office chair and puts his hands behind his head. "Tell us about Sara Summers, or should we say Nadia Kraskoff."

"Kraskoff sounds more Russian than Turkish."

"Born and raised in northern Ukraine. Once the Russian government folded, she started working for the Turks."

I look at him. "Truly, I never knew she existed until six days ago."

"Oh, I'm sorry to hear you say that Agent Severs."

"Not as sorry as I am, because I know where this is leading."

"You're very right, sir. It doesn't look good."

Well, shit, the first time in a long time I find a woman I like and I think she likes me and I pick a spy. It's just the way my luck is running these days.

I turn to Bruiser. "Got a cigarette?"

He pulls a pack of Camels from his shirt pocket, taps one out and puts it in my mouth. The little guy strikes a match. "Thought you quit?"

"Almost a year now, but if your shipping me off to Egypt, what the hell, it may be my only pleasure for a long, long time."

He leans forward and lights the smoke then sits back in his chair. He nods to Bruiser who touches my arm. I turn to the little guy. "You're not going to ask me any more questions?"

He gives me a sardonic smile. "No need. You'll give us all the answers we'll need tomorrow morning in Egypt."

"That quick?"

He stands and waves Bruiser on. "No point in wasting time."

Bruiser tugs at my shirt and I stand. We walk out of the little office and back into the huge warehouse. After walking the maze of plywood walls, we step out of the hanger and onto the tarmac with the Lear waiting with its engines running.

I'm thinking fast of a way out of this mess, but nothing comes to mind. My hands are cuffed and the big guy has a firm grip. Plus, where would I run that airport police wouldn't have me in ten minutes. There isn't even a single tree that I could hide behind.

I get to the steps of the Lear and halt for a moment. Bruiser pushes me. "Give me a second to have a last look at my home."

He stops and lets me look around. I wish I was standing next to a brook, or on the coast having a last look at the

Atlantic, but I guess the paved and concrete slabs of an airport I don't even know the name of is going to have to do. I take a deep breath and step into the plane.

Sara sits in the third seat facing forward. One side of her face is bruised. When she sees me, she gives me a frightened look.

Her handler, a huge woman I would never want to tangle with, holds up one hand as if to backhand Sara, glares at her and says, "not a word."

Sara's eyes are not those of a cold war refugee or a spy. They're the eyes of a frightened woman not used to being handled like this.

I'm seated in the front facing the cockpit with my back to Sara. Bruiser buckles me in. He grins then walks to the back as the plane taxi's away from the terminal. I have one chance left albeit a slim one. I know I'm as good as dead if I leave American soil.

Without wiggling too much I slide my hand up to the back belt loop of my Levis and feel the seam. Hidden in a minuscule pocket I'd had stitched in all of my work pants, just inside of the waist I feel the lump and work it to the surface.

Jake laughed and called me paranoid when I told him about the pocket, but I had that dream two years ago when I first started this detail and other than the woman being a brunette, and me meeting her in Vegas rather than D.C., this is the exact scenario. I dreamed I was cuffed sitting inside of Druckmyer's Lear and I reached for the key stitched inside of my waist seam.

It comes out painlessly and I unlock myself keeping my hands behind me. God, I can't believe my dream is coming true.

I look outside the window and the plane taxis onto the active runway. The engines, always so friendly, now hopelessly threatening, roar to life. The plane rolls along the runway gaining speed as the momentum pushes me back. I reach forward and unclip my seatbelt. Not in a million years would I attempt such a stupid maneuver, but either I die now or in some Egyptian prison having my fingernails pulled off by some twisted guard trying to extract information I don't have. Plus, the dream was so clear and I do survive.

The plane is gaining speed. I lean forward without looking back. I jump. I propel myself forward. I crash into the flimsy closed cockpit door. I slam the two pilots forward. Their chests push the controls. I grab one control and turn the wheel sharply. The plane veers to the left skidding into the grass. The front wheel digs into the soft earth. I hear it snap. The nose drops to the ground. Were spinning. I feel the horrible sound of metal against pavement. Sara screams somewhere behind me. The back wheels fold or break off. We're spinning faster now. I see the marsh as in my dream.

The pilot is frantically trying to regain control. The plane scrapes across another stretch of asphalt. It breaks through the fence still going a hundred and plunges into the marsh. It digs up plumes of water and cattails then flips. I'm on the roof of the cabin. I take a deep breath like in my dream. The front windows shatter. Water floods in. It's a horrible sound of metal ripping away from the body. I'm in a cushion of water waiting to stop. The plane never seems to stop. I'm almost out of air.

~

Auntie is gone and I stand alone. The men are coming at me. I remember what happened. They took me below the bridge. Forty years my hate for the world has been directed at these three men and I didn't know it.

"It's okay, Girlie, we aren't here to hurt you," says the one with a graying goatee.

The big one giggles high-pitched like a girl. "We'z here to set you'z free, Missy."

They spread out and block my way as they move closer.

I back up to the rail and look down at the shallow creek. No jumping here.

The third one with an overly baritone voice speaks. "We have something to show you."

I back up along the bridge but the big guy blocks my retreat. It's going to happen again. They'll take me down to the rocks and force me to my knees then split me open, ruining any future chance of a pleasurable sex life. They'll ruin my ability to have a baby. They'll have their way with me one at a time and I can't do anything about it but whimper.

The big guy leaps forward and grabs my arm. Holy shit, it's the same arm, at the exact same place that has ached all of my life. Could it be some kind of memory of this moment?

"Got you, Missy."

The other two leap forward and grab me. I can't scream. I can't speak. Is this going to happen again?

They drag me along the bridge. I'm so frozen with fear, I can't resist. The little girl part of me has no idea how much pain these three are going to inflict. The fully grown adult part of me knows and braces herself for the violation.

But wait. . . I have the adult side of me. I know what I know. Although I'm in a small body, I know what to do.

We're at the end of the bridge. I pull my restrained hand up to my mouth and give the back of the big guy's hand a viscous bite. It draws blood. He screams and lets go. I swing my free hand around. I slam the balls of the small guy who holds my other hand. He doubles. I knee him in the nose.

I spin in a perfect Kung Fu pirouette I learned in my

twenties. I slam my heal into the third guy's stomach. I turn back to the big guy and judo chop him hard in the neck. He grabs his throat. I spin once more and catch him across the nose with my left foot. He goes down and slams his head on the track.

Mr. Middle-size rushes me. I step aside. He slides past and falls to his knees on the wooden slats. I rush him before he can right himself. I slam my fist under his ribcage. He drops to his knees gasping. I kick with the tip of my cute little Sunday school patten-leather shoes. I hit him under his chin. I hear a satisfying snap of his jaw. Before he falls, I give one last spin and clip him at the bridge of his nose.

The one I first dropped is running at me. He swings his fist. I take that hand and help him over the rail of the bridge. He drops ten feet into the brambles and rocks. I lean over the rail as he lands flat on his back. I'm sure some bones are broken.

The adult part of me is satisfied with my work. I hardly raised my level of breath. The child side of me is crying for the pain I caused these three men.

I look in horror at the damaged and moaning men, then speak in a deeper voice than I am used to. "Fuck off, Assholes."

The whistle of a train comes from far off. It's the same train of my youth that roared over the bridge while these three raped my little eight-year-old.

I walk over to the guy on his knees gasping. The one who I ruined his voice for probably the rest of his life. I give him one last satisfying slam with my knee into his face. He sees it coming but can't move fast enough to get out of the way. He slumps across the tracks.

I scream, "fuck off Asshole."

I turn to the one with the broken jaw. "Fuck off, Asshole."

I wipe my hands and walk along the track toward town.

My knee hurts from hitting that guy, but other than that I don't have a hair out of place.

Auntie appears next to me. "You'll make church today after all."

I smile. "Yes, I never made it to church that day did I?"

We walk together along the track as the whistle gets closer. I feel light and happy for the first time since that day. It's like nothing ever happened.

I turn to Auntie. "This is what's been under my craw all this time?"

She smiles. "Yes."

"How did you know?"

"I didn't, you did. I simply got you back here to the root of your rage."

"I don't understand?"

"You're anger brought you back to this moment so you could work through what you've been carrying around all these years."

"I've been furious at the whole world because of those men, haven't I?"

She smiles as we step off the bridge and walk between the shiny rails.

The white steeple of the church peeks above the thick forest. I haven't seen that steeple since I was a kid.

I look down at my slender hands, my Sunday dress, black patent leather pumps with white bobbie socks and I'm still the child I was on the bridge.

I turn to Auntie and take her hand. "I'm going to get to go to church?"

"Yes you are, child."

Tears well up in my eyes. "I can't remember why, but that days was a special day and I'd never made it."

She smiles as we round a bend in the track. The train

passes with it's noisy clickey-clack of wheels on rail. Once it passes, I see Dickerman's grocery, then Red's barber shop and the little thirty seat movie theater. On the cheap Marquee above the entrance it reads, "South Pacific."

I turn to Auntie once again. "We really are back on that Sunday?"

"You need to go into the church to complete a missing part of your life, then you'll be able to find your humanity again."

We reach the tree-lined Main Street and the short string of stores, Peterson's drug, the hair salon, Bill's auto parts, Sanderson's ice cream parlor where I stopped with my quarter after church every Sunday. On the opposite side was Henderson's hardware, Bristol's small engine repair, the bakery where mom bought donuts on special occasions, Jimmy's dad's Appliance repair shop and at the end of the street, the church. I really liked Jimmy and later he would be my first boy friend.

Doc Flanders sat back on his property in the oldest building in town, a Victorian with a full porch and huge shade trees. I tear up again when I see it.

A crowd of Sunday dressed people are filing into church.

"I'll wait here," Auntie says as she sits on a bench under one of Doc's trees.

I step forward with excited anticipation and find myself skipping the hundred yards toward church. The day is crystal clear as I pass Mr. and Mrs. Jamison with their new baby.

"Hi Annie," she says as I skip by.

I slow to a walk and turn to her. "No one's called me Annie in years."

She gives me an odd look and I remember I'm eight again. It's hard to keep both of these experiences straight.

I turn and skip up the ten steps of the church. I know ten because I can't believe how many times I counted them. One, two, three, as I climb. "Hi pastor Bloom," I say as I pass him.

"Hi Annie, how's your mom doing?"

I stop and turn to him. "My mom?"

"She's been a little under the weather, hasn't she?"

She found out that Friday she had advanced throat cancer. I was coming to church to pray for her and I never made it. She died two weeks later and I blamed myself for her death. God, the whole thing went down hill from that day, or this day, it's so confusing.

"She's fine, Pastor Bloom."

I step into the big room with its single stained glass window and its rows of pews and the smell of something I grew to hate. I never went back to church after that day. I got raped, mom died and dad fell apart with his drinking. I was left to care for him for the next ten years until I ran away to D.C. and my new life.

I sit at the back pew where I always sat and start praying.

Chapter 14

Escape

Driving forward the plane finds dry land —just like in the dream— and finally stops upside down. The water drains from the cabin. I take a breath. Both pilots are coughing, but alive. I push through the broken door and scream. "Sara."

Other than the sound of dripping water and the high pitched whine of a distant engine, everything is quiet.

"Sara," I scream again before I realize that the entire back side of the plane is missing. I run along the roof for ten yards and look out the gaping hole. To my left a hundred yards away the body of the plane lies on its side, wings missing, one engine still wildly spinning. The other engine is almost buried in water and mud.

Far off, the sound of a siren brings me back to the problem at hand. I just survived —like in my dream— but I'm now a fugitive.

I turn and run north away from the airport. Did I do the right thing?

The underbrush is thick, but passable as I zig-zag around

big clumps of blackberry and deer brush.

The siren's are much louder by the time I run to the edge of dry land and leap into three feet of mucky marsh water.

I wade thirty yards to the next spit of land and sprint away from the burning mass behind me.

The whining engine finally runs out of fuel and sputters into silence.

I'm a half-mile away when a helicopter comes thumping from far behind me. I continue to run on dry land, leap into the smelly water, climb back onto land and run again. The chopper is close enough that I find an animal burrow under the brush. I climb as far as I can into its safety. The chopper roars overhead and turns back toward the crash.

Ten seconds later I'm out of the tunnel. I leap to my feet and continue my run for freedom.

I'm forced to repeat this duck and cover maneuver three times before I reach a grove of cottonwood trees that allows me enough cover to take a break and watch the scene a mile behind me. A car rushes by on a road above me.

News helicopters, rescue trucks and police vehicles are all parked at the edge of the runway above the wreckage. Hundreds of people swarm the three separate pieces, probably all looking for me.

I'm sitting in the shade of the cottonwoods, drenched to the bone and mud splattered over my entire body. I laugh when I realize that no one is looking for me except the Agency. It'll take another five hours to realize I'm missing then to mobilize the troops to find me. I've got time, but I need to get out of here.

I climb into the mucky water, remove my shirt and wash the excess mud, then hang it on a tree branch. I scrub my face and arms and try to comb my hair with my fingers.

I remove my shoes and levies and rinse the mud from

them, then carefully climb out of the water and redress. I don't look normal by any means, but I'm passable.

I climb the embankment and stand on pavement as three cars rush by.

I walk west on the side of the road and put out my thumb every time a car goes by. Twenty long minutes later an old station wagon pulls to the side of the highway fifty yards in front of me. I run to the passenger door. When I open it, an old guy greets me with a stub of a cigar in his mouth and his little dog yapping. Once I'm in, the dog sniffs my wet clothes. The old guy pulls onto the highway. "Where you goin'?"

"About ten miles, if you're going that far."

"Oh yeah, I'll get you there."

We ride in silence for a minute, until he asks, "How come you're so wet."

I look at him. "It's a long story."

"Look son, part of the deal when your hitchhiking is you got to entertain the driver, otherwise what's the point. I've been driving five hundred miles. A long story, though you may not be able to finish it, is just what I need.

"I was fishing and my boat capsized in the marsh."

"Come on, you were fishing in a sports jacket?"

If I tell him the real story, this guy is going to turn me in, so I try a different tack. "We were walking along the banks of the marsh and my girlfriend got mad at me and shoved me in then got in her car and drove away."

He looks at me and shakes his head. "Entertaining, yes, but not the truth is it?" He points out the window. "That marsh is not only the dumping ground for the airport, but there are billions of mosquitoes floating around on its waters. Look at em. No one in their right mind would take a stroll in that mess."

I look and there are clouds of mosquitoes hovering. "I

thought you didn't live around here?"

"I said I drove five hundred miles. I live ten miles from here. When I was a kid, before the airport fucked up the marsh, we used to come down here in the middle of the day when the mosquitoes weren't as bad and fish bluegill. It was good fishing back then."

"I can't really tell you what happened."

"It's okay, son, I'm an old man. You can spill the beans and it will get no further than this car. I'd like to think it has something to do with that plane wreck all over the news. It's certainly close enough and the police were crawling all of that area just before I saw you."

"Police?"

"I fucking hate police, so whatever happened, you're safe with me."

So, I tell the story in reverse order, starting with hiding from the helicopter and going back all the way to meeting Sara in Vegas and the couple in the ultra-light.

He listens to me without interrupting until he pulls off the highway. "I turn here, but it sounds like you don't have a place to go. My house is at the end of this road. You could rest there for the moment and get your thoughts together."

"Thank you, sir, I'd like that."

"Name's Pete."

"Pete."

He smiles and drives two miles deeper into the underbrush then turns into a dirt driveway and pulls up to a run down shack with two small out buildings. "It ain't much, but it's got a shower and a pretty comfortable couch."

"Thanks, Pete."

He smiles and gets out. The little dog runs to the front door and barks incessantly until Pete finally hobbles to the door and opens it. The dog bolts in.

The interior is dingy, but neat with a little thirteen inch TV on the kitchen counter and a portable radio on a fifties red Formica table with rusting chrome legs.

He immediately flips the radio on with the volume low and Charlie Parker softly plays background music.

With his back to me, he says, "You probably want to get some of that mucky marsh water off of you."

"Yes, if you don't mind."

He points at the back of the little house. "Showers out that door 'round back. I'll get you some sweats to change into."

"Thanks Pete, you're very kind."

He turns to me and smiles. "Towels are in the cabinet just before you go out the door."

I walk down a short hall and out back onto a concrete pad that might have at one time been a half basketball court, though all that is left is a rotting pole five feet tall and the remnants of yellow paint on the crumbling concrete. At the far end of the court, a camp type outdoor shower stands against a building with three wooden walls big enough to cover a persons torso, but that's all.

The water is hot and refreshing and the shampoo feels good, though there's something about the marsh water that is hard to get out of my hair.

Half way through my shower, he hobbles out and hangs blue sweats on a nail next to the shower. "It ain't all that much fun in the dead of winter, but most of the time it's not bad watching the birds and squirrels."

I rinse soap off of my face. "It feels great."

He goes back in the house and in a minute I follow wearing the sweats and drying my hair.

He tosses me a comb and points to the right of the back door. "Mirror's in the bathroom."

When I'm finished I come out. He has a sandwich and

some chips sitting on the table. "Figured you'd want to eat."

I sit and take a bite of the ham and some kind of sharp cheese. "I am hungry."

The radio softly plays a Miles Davis tune from the Kind of Blue album. It's my favorite.

The atmosphere is calm for the first time since those goons pushed me into the Suburban.

Pete asks, "You can stay the night, but what's your plan?"

"I really don't know, Pete. I can't go back to where I live or any of my old haunts. Either I turn myself in or I go build myself another life somewhere."

"Sounded like that little town in California has a Sheriff who'd protect someone like you."

"You might be right. Whiskey Flat could be the only town in America."

"Canada's an option."

"I can hardly handle Baltimore in the winter as it is. I wouldn't want to live ten months out of the year in cold."

In the morning he drives me to a truck stop on the highway and buys me breakfast in the diner. When we're done, he slips me a hundred dollars.

"I can't take this, Pete."

He waves me on. "Left over from my disability check last month. I ain't got no use for it. You already know you can't tap your bank account, right?"

I nod.

"Well, what're you going to get to California with, certainly not your good looks or them fancy clothes you're wearing."

I look at the sweats and at the grocery bag of dirty clothes. I take the money. "Thanks Pete, you've been more than kind."

"Anything to spit in the eye of my fucked up government."

He gets up. "You ask around for a ride from inside this

restaurant. There's a lot of long distance driver's come through here, so wait for one going all the way to California. You don't want to get stuck out there in Kansas or Colorado." He pronounces it, coal-o-raid-o.

I shake his hand. "Thanks again, Pete."

He smiles. "Don't mention it. You pass it on someday."

"I certainly will."

He hobbles out of the restaurant as the portly waitress pours me another cup of coffee. "You look like you're going somewhere."

"California."

"Pete told me to get you a ride."

"You know Pete?"

"He comes in here every morning. You just sit tight, Honey, and I'll get you that ride."

∼

I've never been outside of Nevada and California, much less lived in Russia or Turkey like they say.

When they snatch me at the stoplight less than thirty seconds after Eddie puts me in the cab, I think I'm in some James Bond movie. Harry, the bastard who abandoned me, loved James Bond.

No one asks any questions. No one tells me where they're taking me, they simply put a smelly black bag over my head and give me some kind of shot in the arm. The next thing I know, I'm strapped to a folding chair staring at a bright light.

When they accuse me of being a terrorist, I freak.

The big guy backhands me and I shut up. They ask one question after another and I answer as best I can considering my jaw is swollen. An hour later, I'm on the same Lear jet as Eddie and I flew in just a few hours ago. I remember the small chip hidden in a back corner of the cocktail table. They have me handcuffed, so I can't run my fingers over the imperfection like I did on our way to D.C., but I recognize it.

I turn to a gruff looking woman in a military suit. "Where are you taking me?"

The woman backhands me. "No words from you!" Her accent is Russian.

When the door opens and Eddie is escorted up the steps, I begin a yell for help, not realizing he too is shackled.

Half way into my attempt to yell Eddie's name, the big Russian woman draws her hand back readying it to break my jaw this time. "Not a word," she growls.

I look at her and cringe.

Eddie is led to the front of the plane. When he sits, he looks back only once. His tormentors says something unintelligible and Eddie turns to face the cockpit door.

The plane races along the runway.

At the last second before we are in the air, Eddie leaps to his feet. He tosses his handcuffs to one side and shoulders the cockpit door. I watch in horror as both the pilot and co-pilot are slammed into their instrument panel. The next second the nose of the plane dives the few feet to the pavement. I can see right out the front window as the plane hits the marsh. The front window shatters. Water pours in.

The plane shutters like we're in an earthquake. The seats rip from the floor. The table with its minuscule chip in the Formica, flies over my head.

The second my seat dislodges, the plane opens and breaks in half. I'm catapulted high into the air. I'm spinning. I know the ground is coming. The jet explodes behind me. I feel the heat. I close my eyes knowing I'm going to hit the ground. I'm as good as dead. What about my kids?

The General steps back a fast five paces. "What did you do to her, Sheriff?"

I respond with a shoulder shrug. "Nothing."

The General raises one hand and two underlings run across the grass, leap to attention and give him a snap of a salute. In unison, they both say aloud, "Sir!"

"I want a medic, get me a mask and a gas specialist."

They both salute again and yell, "Yes, sir!"

He turns to me. "What did you do?"

I stay seated. "Look General, you were here, I didn't do a thing. Both of them passed out. Since no one else is affected, I'm guessing Auntie did something. This isn't her first time."

"Auntie?"

I point at her laying with one hand gripping Druckmyer's left wrist. "The old woman."

A smallish soldier rushes up with a gas mask on and one in his right hand. He hands it to the General. A pack is strapped to his back and a wand connected to it in his left hand. His right hand salutes. "Sir, you wanted me?"

"Check this area for gas."

He flips a red switch and takes a minute passing the wand over the two reclined women, over me, the table, and the lawn around us. "Nothing, sir."

The General hands him the mask. "You're relieved, Sergeant."

The young man salutes and rushes off. A middle-aged man in white runs over. He salutes. "Sir, you called."

I interrupt quickly before he can give orders. "General, I've seen this kind of thing before with Auntie. If we disturb them, it may not turn out well."

He turns to the medic. "How do they look, Captain?"

He comes in close. "Color's good. Both of them are breathing normally. Looks like they're asleep."

"Thanks Captain. You're relieved."

The medic walks away.

The General turns back to me and walks closer. "You say the old woman did this?"

"She's done stuff like this before."

"When will they wake up?"

"Hell, General, I can't tell you. I'm just the Sheriff. I don't know things about old women or agents from Homeland security for that matter."

Auntie opens her eyes and lifts her head off the table. She looks at the General as if she'd been present the whole time. "Druckmyer is resting for the moment, General. She should be back with us in ten minutes. If you care to have a seat and wait."

Auntie looks at me, "Jackie, would you mind getting me three lemonades from Sally's? I need to have some private time with Melvin."

The General gets a worried grimace and looks around. He leans forward. "No one knows that name."

I smile as I unravel myself from the picnic bench and stand. "I'll be back in a jiffy, Auntie."

"Thank you, Jackie."

I walk toward Sally's restaurant. About half way across the lawn, I look back and the General is sitting on the bench. Auntie takes his hand and his head slumps toward the tabletop like he's nodding.

I cross the side street and walk into the restaurant.

Sally, in her plump smock with a fresh apron pulls a lock of blonde hair out of her face. She gives me her sexiest smile. "What's going on out there, Jack-o."

"Auntie's at it again."

She sighs. "That's good, because I hear the military boys are here to rip our little town to shreds."

"She's got the General and that ain't nothing."

"She want a lemonade?"

"Three. Can you believe it, Auntie took the Homeland agent like she was a little child."

She pulls out three paper cups and the pitcher. "I hope The agent sees the light when she comes back, cause we could use a little help around here."

She pours the cups full and hands them to me. "You want tops?"

I shake my head and reach for money.

"Jack-o, you know your money's no good around here. You could take me to a movie or something."

Sally's a good woman, just not my type. She is a good friend too, so I throw her a bone. "Not ready yet."

She smiles.

I walk across the creaky wooden floor and out the front door. As I'm crossing the street, the General lifts his head off of the table and I swear I see him smile.

By the time I've walked across the lawn, he's taken her hand and is kissing it. "Thank you, Auntie. Thank you."

I don't dare ask what happened, because I already know.

I set the cups in front of Auntie and she slides one to the General. "Drink this, it'll take the queasy feeling away."

He picks the cup up and takes a sip.

Druckmyer awakes, lifts her head and looks about until she sees the General sitting next to her. "General, you didn't go through with our plan, did you?"

"No ma'am."

"Good. Wrap up your troops and go home, that's an order."

Auntie hands Druckmyer the lemonade and says, "drink this, it'll help your queasy stomach."

Druckmyer turns to Auntie and breaks down crying. "How did you know that happened to me?"

Auntie hands her the drink and pats the back of her hand. "You knew, child. I simply reminded you."

The tears roll down Druckmyer's cheek. "I'm happy. . . for the first time I'm really happy."

"Yes, I know, child. Drink your lemonade, it'll help."

Without even looking at what it is, Druckmyer lifts the paper cup to her lips and takes a long drink of the icy liquid. When she puts the cup on the table, half of it is gone. "I'd forgotten how it feels to be happy." She cries again, then breaks into a tearful grin. "I'm so happy."

Auntie speaks in a soft voice. "There is much work to be done, Annie. You must begin this work as soon as you get home."

"Work?"

"Now that you know the core of your pain, work with that pain until you come to terms with it."

"I have come to terms, Auntie. As of now, everything is different."

"You're in an elated place. You have not come to terms with it yet. This feeling will fade."

"How could it fade? I'm free for the first time since the bridge incident. I want to scream out my relief from the top of the capitol building."

Auntie smiles and turns to the General. "Mel, though you feel the same, you must keep yourself under control for a few days. Don't do anything out of the ordinary until your feet are back on the ground."

"I'm done with being a General. I want to go to Central America and help save the rain forest."

"Sir, give yourself a few days before you do anything rash. This is a life changing experience, but you don't want to throw away everything you've worked for."

"What's the point of staying now that I know why."

234

"Take another drink of your lemonade, General."

He takes another sip.

Auntie takes his rough left hand. "Like Annie here, you're in a very unique position to make some major changes in the way things are run. With the stroke of your pen, you have the ability to change many peoples lives right here in our country. There is plenty of time to help Central America. Right now, North America needs your help."

His road map of a wrinkled face softens. "Yes, I see what you mean, but how can I be a General any longer?"

"You can be a General for love."

His grin widens. "I never thought I would ever say this, but I want to be a soldier for love."

He raises one hand and his aid runs across the lawn, gives him a snappy salute and yells, "Sir?"

"Round up our forces, we're moving out."

The young man turns and rushes off.

The General looks at me and points at Auntie. "Sheriff, you have a gift here in your community. Take good care of her."

"Yes Sir, we do." I say as I snap a respectful salute.

He looks at Druckmyer, then at Auntie, gives her a serious salute, smiles and marches away.

Druckmyer turns to Auntie. "How did you know?"

"Remember, Child, all of that knowledge is inside of you. All you have to do is tap back into it whenever you want. Us humans get so distracted with our 'doing' that we forget how to just 'be.'"

Druckmyer points to her heart. "I'm afraid I'll forget and this feeling is going to disappear."

"Some of it will in time, but the more you keep checking in with who you really are, the more you can create the who you really want to be. For most of your life the who you wanted to be was the angry person we knew a few hours ago. If you

235

wish to be this new you, keep your mind focused on who you are now. It won't be easy, there are so many distractions, but the rest will follow."

Druckmyer grabs a layer of fat hanging from under her arm. "First I get rid of some of this body armor. I can't believe I did it to protect myself from further attacks."

"It worked, didn't it?"

"Yes."

"It no longer serves you."

"Right, it no longer serves me. I guess I'm going to be asking that question a bunch in the next months."

Auntie smiles and pats the back of Druckmyer's hand. "Drink some more lemonade, it'll settle your stomach."

Druckmyer finishes the cup.

Ballard, who's been silent, finds his voice. He looks at Auntie. "Can you take me to the same place you took Druckmyer?"

She turns to him. "It's not a carnival ride, Son."

"I know, but she seems so happy. I've never seen her like this and my life could use a little happiness."

"Annie's journey isn't for everyone. A journey like hers would tear your life apart."

"But, she looks so happy."

Druckmyer grins. "I am, Ballard. I certainly am."

Auntie takes his hand. "You could use a good woman in your life. When you get back to D.C. go to the steps of the capitol and wait. When a single Canadian goose lands on the steps next to you, your future bride will be close."

"What does she look like, so I don't miss her?"

Auntie smiles. "You won't miss her."

"How long do I wait?"

She gives him a sly look. "How long do you have?"

He frowns and drops his head. "Forever."

She raises one thick eyebrow. "How long do you wait?"

"As long as it takes."

Druckmyer takes in a sharp breath of air. "Holy shit, I had Eddie Severs arrested. He's on his way to Egypt. I've got to stop that."

Ballard looks at her. "Egypt?"

She clicks her radio and speaks into it, "Get me the status on Eddie Severs."

The radio squawks, then a voice says, "Yes ma'am."

This is the perfect moment so I speak. "What about our local citizen, Harium Hissiam. He's been in Egypt for two years. We'd like to have him back."

Druckmyer click the radio. "Check on Harium Hissiam too."

"Yes, Ma'am."

"We'll get your Hissiam back, Sheriff."

"Thank you. Our whole community misses him."

The radio clicks and a voice says, "Some problems, Ma'am."

"Problems?"

"Seems your plane crashed four days ago while you were in the hospital and Severs went missing. No one is sure if he escaped or is stuck below the marsh. They've been dredging the mud for two days."

Auntie laughs. "He's close."

Druckmyer turns to her. "Close?"

"I can't tell you where he is, but he's been hitchhiking across the country."

Chapter 15

Hitchhike

Eighteen hours of breathing this guys cigar and he won't let me open a window. Except for how dangerous it is for me to be hitching in Kansas, I'm ready to get out and find another ride

He pulls off the interstate and takes another drag from his rank cigar. "Let's get some breakfast, I'm starved."

Thank God, I'll get a little breathing room.

The truck stop is like every truck stop in America. It's a big open parking lot, lots of trucks, restaurant, even cute waitresses to draw the men in for meals.

When we sit, a young woman with blonde hair bounces up and with a friendly grin puts waters on the table. In doing so, she leans forward with her low cut blouse. Her ample bosoms heave forward. My truck driver, Hank, almost jumps her right there.

"You boys need some time?" she asks in a squeak of a voice that only adds to her appeal.

Hank looks at me and winks. "I'm ready."

She pulls out her pad. "Okay, what'll you have, handsome?"

She speaks to Hank and he's about as ugly as a hog, though he's soaks it up like a spaniel.

"Coupla' egg's over medium, extra bacon, English muffin."

She gives him a grin. "Coffee?"

"Lots of it."

"And, how about you soldier?"

I pause. "Do I look like a soldier?"

"You look like you been through a tour in Iraq, or your wife just left you. Either one, you've been through a war."

I point at the stained menu. "A coupla eggs scrambled with toast. Big coffee."

"What kind of toast?"

"Dry rye."

I can't believe it, she gives me a wink, turns and walks away.

Hank grins. "I skip meals to stop here. The chicks are too much."

I raise my eyebrows like I'm agreeing with him, but I'm only pitying him.

The meal is adequate, considering the cigar smoke and each time the waitress walks by Hank ogles her and whispers snide comments to me about what he'd do if. . .

I look around the restaurant and every poor sap sitting at a table is doing the same thing. Maybe it's the fate of truckers?

We split the bill and he stands. I remain seated. "I'll stay here a while."

He smiles. "I saw you checking out my blonde. Give her one for me, would ya."

I smile and wave him on as he walks out of the restaurant. God, the guy is a lost cause. The last thing I'm here for is to pick up some blonde in a restaurant in the middle of Kansas.

She comes by after ten minutes to pick up the check and

give me a smile. "You staying with us a while?"

I look up from reading a scrap of newspaper left on the next table. "Looking for a ride out west without the cigar. You know of anyone?"

"This isn't exactly a good place to get a ride."

"I couldn't stand that cigar one more minute."

She giggles. "It did seem permanently attached to his face."

"You don't know the half of it."

She puts her hand on my shoulder. "See what I can do."

She walks away and I delve deeper into the business section of the paper.

A minute later she comes back to my booth, drops a New York times on my table and refills my coffee. "You seem like a Times sort of guy."

"Thanks, Ma'am, I really appreciate—"

"Samantha, but my friends call me Sammy."

"Thanks, Sammy?"

She gives me an overly friendly grin and walks away.

I've gone through every article in the Times and four cups of coffee as the lunch crowd slowly fill up the restaurant. Samantha has come by a dozen times for a momentary chat, keeping me updated on possible rides west, but nothing pans out.

She stops again with a worried look. "Carson, my boss, says you have to give us the table back through lunch. I get off at three. I could give you a ride to the state line. It's not too far. It's easier to get a ride in Colorado. Some archaic law prohibiting hitching in Kansas."

"I wouldn't want to put you out."

"It's only thirty miles to the border. I live that way anyhow."

I refold the paper. "Any good places to go?"

She points south over the overpass. "Town's that way about two miles. It's not too interesting, but they have a nice park in the center. I could meet you at the park at three fifteen."

I automatically look at my watch, then realize it's gone along with everything else I own, including the life I once knew.

"Thanks, Samantha, I really appreciate this."

"Sammy. My friends call me Sammy."

Once I reach the top of the overpass, I see corn and soy fields for fifty miles. The single story structures of the town poke above the corn stalks on a painfully straight road that leads off into a distant haze with no end in sight.

She was right, nothing in this town is interesting, but it's a working town in the middle of nowhere. I'm probably the only visitor since the interstate bypassed the town years ago. Hardware, small market, drug store, sheriff's office of which I steer clear of and the park with hundred year old Elm trees, a bandstand in the center and an acre of well-tended lawn.

I buy a Washington Post and a day old deli sandwich in the market. I sit on a park bench in the shade to read and there on the front page is Druckmyer's crashed Lear and the story. Sara and the three agents are in the hospital. The two pilots were released a few hours after the crash. There's no mention of me.

I smile to know that Sara made it, but the rest of the article sheds no new light on the crash.

By three, I've read the newspaper, talked to an old man feeding the birds and took a nap next to the trunk of one of those massive trees.

In my dream, I'm back in Whiskey Flat single-handedly fighting off the troops and Druckmyer when something attacks my foot. The second attack awakes me and Samantha stands there kicking at my feet. "Having a bad dream?"

I smile, but don't answer. I get up and brush the lawn clippings off of my sweats with both hands.

She takes my hand and leads me along the path toward the edge of the park. "My car's in front of the drug store."

There's something possessive about her taking my hand, but I can't put my finger on it.

Her car is a dark, pumpkin orange, completely restored, mid sixties Volkswagen Beetle. I get in the passenger side. She starts the engine and it purrs to life.

"Where did you come up with this beauty?"

"My ex builds 'em. He finished this one for me six months before he beat me for the last time and I left."

I look around. "He doesn't live here, does he?"

She laughs as she backs out of the parking place. "He lives in upstate New York. I had to move this far to get shut of him for good."

"If you're from New York, why live out in the middle of no where?"

She turns right at the first corner. "I've ask myself that same question for the last year, but the place has grown on me. It's quiet and calm. I guess after Al, I needed a big dose of calmness."

She drives out of town in an easterly direction. I point out the window. "Thought you were taking me to the Colorado border."

"I am. I just need to stop at my house a moment and get out of these greasy clothes. That's okay, isn't it?"

I shrug. Under my breath I recite, "says the spider to the fly."

Four blocks of pot-holed back streets and she pulls into the driveway of a run down Victorian.

She looks at me with the innocence of a nun. "Come on up while I change. I think I have a beer in the fridge."

Spider or no spider, a beer sounds good right now, so I open the door and follow her up the ten rickety wooden steps, through the oval beveled glass front door and into the middle of the eighteen nineties. "Wow, this place is beautiful.

Where did you get all of this furniture?"

She tosses her jacket over a high back couch and I follow her to the kitchen. "Most everything came with the house. I bought it completely furnished for twenty five thousand. It's one of the advantages of living out in Nowheresville, Kansas."

"What's that?"

"Houses are cheap."

She points at the original nineteen twenties refrigerator, the kind with the big coil exposed on top. "There some Coronas in there. Get me one too, would you."

She steps into the next room and half way closes the door. "Rather than go through a drawn out divorce process and messy division of property, I cleaned out the bank account for thirty grand and left Al with the house and his shop. He got the better end of the deal by far."

She half steps around the door with only a black bra and lacy panties. "You got that beer?"

"I can't find an opener."

"Top drawer on the right."

I turn away from the female spectacle and awkwardly search the drawer, but the opener isn't there. I turn back and shrug.

She fully opens the door and traipses across the kitchen like it's no big deal. She reaches in the drawer and hands me an odd looking Donald Duck opener.

I uncap her bottle and hand it to her.

She clicks her bottle to mine and takes a long drink, then walks back to her bedroom.

I turn and with my eyes follow her rotating hips and her shapely butt in those thong panties hardly large enough to cover anything.

When she gets to the door, she turns quickly and catches me ogling her backside. She smiles. "You like?"

I stumble my words. "Very much."

"Want some?"

What red-blooded guy is going to pass up this kind of offer? I push away from the counter as she drops her bra on the floor.

She disappears around the door and in a flash I'm chasing her to the bed. She screams a yelp and fights me with all of her strength, ending up on top. She pulls at my sweatshirt, but I stop her. "I need a shower."

"Fuck a shower," she says, "You take me if you can now or you don't get me."

I laugh and press on pulling my sweat bottoms down, tearing at her thong underwear, all the time fighting off her ability to slip out of any position I try to get her in.

For twenty minutes she wrestles me across the bed, onto the floor, across the room and up against the far wall. The whole time I'm trying to mount her and she slips out of one hold after another, laughing, moaning, egging me on, twisting her body so I can see her wetness, but not letting me get close.

When she lets me, and she certainly has control of situation, she leaps on me like a cat on a mouse. She pushes me deep into her. When I earnestly meet her, she leaps to her feet.

She jumps across the room and lays face down on the edge of the bed. "Take me from the back."

I get to my feet. I rush to the focus of my attention. My maleness is pointed like an arrow.

I find the bulls eye of her target. When I shove myself hard into heaven, she pushes hard against me and moans loud, then slips away and I find myself rubbing the coarse bed sheets.

When it is over and we both find our moment, we lay exhausted in a tangle of blankets and sheets on the floor wrapped in each other's arms.

I wake in the middle of the night and search for a pillow,

then again in the morning when she stirs, gets up and goes into the bathroom. I get a glimpse of her sexy backside, then doze as she takes a shower.

She wakes me a few minutes later. "I've got to get to work in a few hours. If you want that ride to the border, I'd say it's time to get in the shower."

I get up and shower while she puts herself together in the bathroom mirror.

When I get out, she's in the kitchen and yells, "try the clothes on the bed."

The pants are a little loose, but serviceable and the shirt, a red Hawaiian flower arrangement feels comfortable.

I step into the kitchen with the smell of eggs and toast. Before I can say a word, she turns her back and hustles to spatula eggs from the frying pan. "We got to eat quick if I'm going to get you to the border and back to work in time."

I slurp down the eggs and rush the toast, then we're out the door without as much as a dozen words between us.

A half-hour later, we cross the Colorado border and she pulls into a rest stop. "You'll have some good luck here. Lot of truckers come through."

Since things have gotten very business like, I put out my hand. "Thanks for the ride."

She doesn't take my hand, but gives me a half grin. "I gotta go. Good luck."

I get out and the little Volkswagen rushes off leaving me wondering what happened and if last night was a dream.

A minute later, her horn blares from the opposite side of the freeway as she roars back toward Kansas and her life.

My new life has yet to be revealed. All I know is I might find some kind of help in Kern County, so Whiskey Flat here we come.

I walk to the on-ramp and stand in the shade all day with

my thumb out trying for a ride.

That night, I sleep on the backside of the rest stop in the grass with my dirty sweats as a pillow, a marked contrast to the night before. Lucky it's not too cold.

Sometime before dawn, someone kicks my foot and shines a light in my face.

~

"BillyBob?" I ask quietly in the darkness of the cave. The helicopter has left. The soldiers crawled every inch of the rock formation without finding us and why I don't know.

The Sheriff, who snores softly in the back of the cave, stops. Did I awake him?

BillyBob reaches over and touches my fingers. "Yes, Myrt?"

"Do you think it's time to find out what happened?"

"What happened to what?"

The Sheriff speaks from the darkness. "To Auntie and to us?" He shuffles and walks to the front of the cave. "It's dark out, so we're not going to see much. The climb back to the house can be a bit dangerous."

BillyBob stands, pulls me to my feet and leads me forward. We carefully feel our way through the ever-narrowing tunnel to the entrance.

The Sheriff is outside.

We step through the entrance onto the rocky ledge and climb to the base of the huge oak tree. The moon shines on the ground showing us the way back.

Sheriff Perkins points toward the house and a small porch light. "Think Auntie is still there?"

The climb back is difficult. We move slowly and methodically along the ledges. I take a breath of relief when we step onto Auntie's ruined vegetable garden.

BillyBob knocks and gets no answer. He looks at the Sheriff, then me in the ghostly moonlight. "Think she meant for us to go inside?"

I say, "Try the door."

BillyBob twists the handle and the door opens. I follow him in and for the first time in twelve hours BillyBob turns on a switch and we're bathed in light.

The Sheriff picks up the phone. "I've got to call in."

A note and a set of keys sits on the kitchen table. The note tells us to make ourselves at home and just before dark at seven o'clock to take the car and find our way to the park across from the police station.

I show the note to the Sheriff as he hangs up the phone. "I've got to get back. Meet you at the park later tonight."

He rushes out of the house and pulls the little motorcycle from the shed.

BillyBob and I make a sandwich from left over chicken, drink a few gallons of water and listen to the radio as we eat.

Later, when we get to the car, BillyBob points. "Look at this car, will you Myrtle."

"It's a car, BillyBob. So what?

We get in and he starts the engine. "It's a seventy-two dodge dart and it's in perfect condition."

I shrug. "Seventy-two, ninety-two, who cares?"

He huffs. "It's a classic all Detroit car, maybe the last of its kind."

"All Detroit?"

"Every part made in America. Not one piece made in Japan or China or Mexico. Listen to that engine."

I shake my head. Men get excited about the oddest things.

Chapter 16

Rectify

I come back from another in a long series of journeys into my past to rectify the horrible wrongs done to my little girl.

The sun has gone down and a yellow streetlight bathes the park with a strange glow. Have I been gone all day?

The old woman sits across from me. I break down and cry again. In the middle of my sobs, she reaches out and takes my hand. "It's okay, child, crying is good."

When I calm, I look at her. "There is so much pain in the world."

She smiles, still holding my hand. "Yes there is and what are you going to do about it?"

"First thing is I'm quitting this horrible job."

"You can quit now if that's what you really want, but think about how much suffering you could alleviate before you leave."

"Suffering?"

"You could bring Harium back to his wife. You could find a way to help Sheriff Perkins keep the system from gobbling up the Harding's. You could help Eddie Severs. You could bring back the hundreds of innocent people in overseas prisons being tortured and maimed."

"I couldn't do any of that. All of those decisions are out of my hands."

She squeezes my hand lovingly. "It is true that you're one person, but are you willing to stand idle while the rest of the world suffers, especially the ones you're directly responsible for their suffering?"

I break down into sobbing again. "I am responsible aren't I?"

She rubs the back of my hand with her twisted arthritic fingers and I'm soothed. "You know again what suffering feels like and you no longer can ignore this feeling. Go to the world and help the ones you can from your position."

I look at her. "I can't go into the office Monday morning and declare that I'm going to start being compassionate. They'll lock me up."

"As a terrorist, I suppose."

"Exactly, as a terrorist."

"Then don't declare your change of heart. Just go into the office Monday morning and do your job like you always do, except with a secret compassion. There are many borderline cases that can be set aside, like the Harding's. Start working on getting those resolved from your new frame of mind."

"Yes, you're right, the Harding's are a good example. I could interview them and find that, though they have some charges to face, they are innocent of terrorism. It really is in my hands. I can do that."

"Would you like to interview the Harding's?"

I nod.

From behind me an older couple walk to the park bench and sit next to Auntie. "I'm BillyBob Harding."

I look at Auntie. "How. . . how did you do that?"

She smiles. "Here's your interview, just in time."

I look at the couple for the first time as more than a file name. The Harding's are right out of the hippie sixties. He with his white ponytail and her still with no bra though her tits have been pulled by gravity for way too long.

I put out my hand to shake. "I'm Druck... Ann Druckmyer."

He cautiously looks at Auntie, then back at me. "The same Druckmyer who's been after us?"

Auntie says, "Maybe she's not chasing anymore."

He puts out his hand and shakes. I shake the woman's hand too and I pull an inch-thick file from my briefcase magically sitting next to me. I open the file. "I have some questions if that's okay?"

I look at Auntie and she smiles. "You're doing fine so far, Child."

I give her a short, tentative smile and open the file. "You are BillyBob and Myrtle Harding, is that right?"

He looks at Auntie with a fearful grimace. She encourages him with a nod.

"Yes."

"You live at 32321 Cyrcuse Way in Boseman, Montana?"

"Not any longer. We sold that house and we live in our RV full time."

"You lived there for thirty-three years though, right?"

The woman speaks for the first time. "We raised three kids in that house."

I point at the file. "Yes, I can see. All of your kids are active member of their community."

BillyBob tries to look at the file, but in automatic reaction learned from years of secret service work, I tilt the file so he can't see.

After twenty minutes of questions I already know the answers, including Frank Deluchi, I ask the one question I don't know. "Why did you do it?"

Both of them look at me with blank stares.

"Why did you take the chance of bringing down the wrath of the government on your heads pulling such a stunt?"

Mr. Harding answers first. "It sounded like a good idea at the time, plus I like flying. Seemed like a perfect match."

The woman gets an embarrassed look and fiddles with her hair. "It was sexy."

"Sexy?"

"Something about being bad sparked up my libido for the first time in ten years. When that kind of thing happens I don't want to waist it."

Jesus, these two did it on a whim. How is that possible? I turn to the husband. "How can anyone toss away their freedom on a whim?"

He grins. "As I said, it sounded like a good idea at the time. If I'd known how much trouble I was getting into I probably would have given it a second thought, but then again, maybe not?"

These two are about as much a terrorists as Walt Disney. I put a few scribbles in the first page of the file, close the folder and look at them. "In this political climate, your act of resistance, for whatever reasons, was seen as harmful to our government."

Mr. Harding puts one finger up. "Can I ask a question?"

I nod.

"If what the news has such a spin on things that in some circles it could be considered a lie, then isn't what we're doing in some ways patriotic?"

"Some could say that, but if you look closely most patriots spent much of their lives in prison."

"Don't we want the truth?"

"It depends on who you think 'we' are?"

He grimaces. "Who we are?"

"If you're the mass of humanity out there living your lives, working every day, raising a family, you really don't want to know that the government is barley holding it together. It's too unsettling to realize how fragile our system really is."

The woman says, "I'd want to know so I could make plans for my future."

I ignore her statement. "If you're part of the government, you want to stay part of the government, and you will do anything to maintain your position, including spin the truth to fit your needs. That's really how government works. Someone like you comes along and all we want to do is get rid of you."

Mr. Harding speaks. "I thought we all were in this together."

I give him a sardonic smile. "We are in this together and you're in this together. The we's control the world and the you's are here to serve the we's."

"How could that be?"

"I don't know how, but it's been this way for millenniums and I don't see much changing anytime in the future."

~

I'm dead.

Lashed to this seat, flying too high in the air, spinning dizzily toward either the swamp which is sure to drown me or the hard brush that will decapitate me. Either way, I'm dead.

The earth is coming. I see it from one angle of my spin. Each time, I'm closer, too close. I close my eyes.

I can't believe I came all this way only to die at the end of some runway. What's going to happen to my kids? Why did those people abduct me?

A thousand thoughts go through my head as I spin in an arc toward my impending doom.

When it happens, it's with the suddenness of the plane diving into the swamp. I hit so hard I'm sure my entire body is dislocated, every bone shattered. I pass out.

It must not be much later, because when I awake, I'm looking at the sky with a soot colored cloud. A seagull flies past my line of vision. I'm still alive? I wiggle my arm and it's still in one piece. I move my head and my neck isn't broken. I look forward at my feet and wiggle each shoe. My legs are fine.

Beyond my feet is the swamp, then a set of trees and the shattered plane with the plumes of smoke billowing. The clouds of mosquitoes are horrific.

I reach to unbuckle my belt and feel the handcuffs once again. Everything is like a dream. I look at the side of the seat as a trail of swamp goo slowly oozes over the edge and fills the crack behind where I'm sitting.

Just before everything goes black once again, in the distance I hear sirens.

When I awake, a neck brace is being attached and someone is unbuckling me from my seat.

"I'm not Nadia." I say with a weaker voice than I expect.

A guy in a blue jumpsuit pats my shoulder. "It's okay, ma'am, we're taking you to the hospital. You'll be fine."

"I'm not Nadia, I'm Sara."

Everything goes black once again. When I awake, I'm tucked in a warm bed surrounded by light green walls.

"Where am I?" I think I said this aloud, but the nurse tucking in my bed doesn't hear me.

I try again, but no sound comes out of my mouth.

The nurse turns without looking at my face and begins to walk away. With as much effort as I can muster, I lift my right arm and find it handcuffed to the rail. I swing my left arm and hit her on the elbow with my wrist.

She turns and looks at me. "You're awake."

I nod.

She winks. "I'll be back in a second."

She returns five minutes later with a short, emaciated looking doctor. He checks my eyes with a flashlight, then gives me a big smile. "You're a very lucky woman."

"Where are my children?" I try to say, but no sound comes.

He looks close at my moving lips. "You're voice is gone?"

I nod.

He opens the drawer beside my bed, pulls out a pad of paper and pen, then hands them to me.

I ask the question again.

He reads as I'm writing, then looks at me. "We didn't know you had children, Ms. Kraskoff."

I grimace, shake my head and write that I'm not Nadia Kraskoff. I am Sara Summers from Las Vegas. I have two children and a mother. I scribble Mom's phone number, rip the page out and hand it to him.

"I'll check into this, ma'am."

A light shines in my eyes. "What are you doing here?"

Still half-asleep I shield the flashlight from my eyes. "Got stuck hitching and was forced to spend the night on the grass."

"Can I see some identification?"

I'd been considering this eventuality since the plane wreck and I have a plan solidly in place. "Got robbed two nights ago. They took everything and my car. That's why I'm hitching."

I already know what the next question is and I jump to the moment. "I've got my number though."

I've been saving this particular identity for two years just for this kind of situation. My neighbor Jan Flanders, a drug dealer, disappeared without a trace one day for no apparent reason. He left me a note to take care of his cat, but nothing else. After a month, I quietly shut down his phone, his gas and electricity and stopped postal deliveries, then told our landlord he'd moved.

I look like him and it was easy from there to get his drivers license and social security number through Homeland data banks. Once a month, I'd check on him and enter a fake location for him to keep the records current.

"What's your name?" the cop asks.

"Jan Flanders." I give him my social and driver's license from memory and one of the cops goes back to his cruiser.

"Where do you live, Mr. Flanders?"

I give him the Virginia address and fake phone number.

"Why are you in Colorado?"

"My sister's in California and she's sick. I was going to see her."

"Where did your car get stolen?"

The questions continue as his partner runs my information. Dawn breaks over the flatness of Eastern Colorado. The partner comes back in a hurry. "He's clean Jimmy and we just got a call from H.Q. about a wreck west of here."

The cop who was grilling me says, "You can't sleep here."

"Yes, sir. I'll start hitching again."

They get in their car, put their siren on as they race past me and onto the freeway.

An hour later, I get a ride from a convention salesman going to Reno. He feeds me and put me up that night, then drops me in Reno and hands me a twenty and three quarters. "Before you go south, step into one of the casinos and drop these three quarters in one machine."

I want to just keep moving, but I'm compelled to follow his slot machine instructions.

It's mid day, so the casino is slow. I find the first machine, insert the three quarters and pull the handle. I win six quarters. Before I play out those six, I win another six and the barmaid brings me a free drink. Life seems pretty good for a half-hour as I win and play lose and play, but eventually, the quarters are gone and the second drink is gone.

I feel a little dazed as I walk out and put my thumb out going South along Virginia Street.

Three short rides later, I get to an on-ramp and stand there for an hour before a guy in a pickup pulls over.

I open the door and look in. He sits with a cigarette hanging out of his mouth and a beer between his legs. "How far you going?"

"Bakersfield."

"I'll get you to Bishop, about half way."

I climb in and close the door. It's the last second I feel safe until he drops me in Bishop three hours later. There are many times I'm sure he's going to flip his truck he drives so fast. He tailgates slow moving cars enraged that he's forced to go slow, then honks and flips them off as he passes in an outside turn on a mountain road. He's destine to remove himself from the gene pool long before he has procreated. When I get out of the truck, I swear I'll never get into one of those huge macho trucks again.

Three hours later, after walking to the south end of town and standing on the side of the road with my thumb hanging out, another macho truck pulls to a stop. I take a breath and climb in.

The kid, a pimply-faced teenager, gives me a friendly grin. "Where are you going this fine day?"

"Whiskey Flat by Lake Isabella."

"Sure, I know it. I'll get you to the South side of the lake. I'm going down the hill to Bakersfield."

I smile. "That's great."

He puts his foot on the gas and pulls onto the roadway with those ridiculous tires whining so loud we can't talk. I don't feel like talking anyhow and within a half-hour, I fall asleep.

I awake when the truck pulls to a stop. "Where are we?"

The kid looks at me. "Just turned toward Isabella. We've got another thirty miles to the lake."

The big tires howl again as he comes up to speed and we have to yell.

When I get out of the truck, he points north. "Up that road ten miles is Whiskey Flat."

"Thanks for the ride." I close the door and the truck pulls away. I walk along the road and realize it'll be dark soon.

Three full Marine troop carriers drive past going the same way as my pimply-faced ride. A moment later another half dozen military vehicles pass, turn right and roll down the hill.

Did Druckmyer finally overpower the Sheriff and take the Harding's? Did Perkins give in?

Whatever happened, the siege is over.

I put out my thumb and an older red sports car pulls over and stops. I run to the car and open the door and a pleasant looking young blonde gives me a grin. "Where you going?"

"Whiskey Flat."

"Me too."

I smile and get in.

She pulls onto the highway. "Ever been to Whiskey Flat?"

"A week ago. It's a nice town."

She looks at me as the car shifts into high gear. "You must have been apart of the whole scene there."

I'm so close to what I hope to be safety that I can tell her. "I was one of the agents."

"Really?"

"Until they turned me into a terrorist."

She gives me a wary look. "Terrorist?"

While I was in D.C. trying to get Mr. Hissium released, Homeland all of a sudden saw me as a security risk. I barley escaped. I'm here because this may be the only place in America a person like me can find safety."

"That's my dad."

"Sheriff Perkins?"

She nods. "I'm going to see him now."

"Me too."

"Well then, I'm your perfect ride, aren't I?"

"The only perfect one in a list of many crappy rides getting across the country."

We climb a small bluff overlooking the lake, then drive into a suburban environment with gas stations, real estate offices, burger joints and hardware stores along the two-lane highway. I know we're still in the desert, but this side of the lake is indistinguishable from any town with lawns, one story houses and kids playing in front yards as the street lights come to life for another American summer night.

"You know my dad?"

"Met him once."

"He's one of the original good guys."

"Anyone who pits themselves against Homeland Security has to be a bit of a lunatic."

"I tried to talk him out of it."

"We did too."

She looks at me as we're slowing for a red light. "Looks like we were both wrong."

"How's that?"

"I think David just chopped Goliath off at the knees."

I snap my head and look at her face, pink from the reflection of the car red dash lights. "How's that?"

"I think Homeland's backed off and let the old hippy couple stay in Whiskey Flat."

"No kidding."

"That's what I'm going to find out. I think my dad's pulled it off."

"Wow."

The light changes and she drives slow as we come into the twenty-five mile speed zone. A sign welcomes us to Whiskey Flat: elevation nine hundred twenty-three feet, population twelve hundred sixty-two.

She pulls to a stop in front of the police station and points across the street at the park. "Would you look at that, Auntie's come to town. I don't think she's come off of her hill since I was a kid."

I'm thinking it couldn't be too many years ago since she was running around in diapers, but I say nothing."

"Who's Auntie?"

The young woman opens her door and gets out ignoring my question. I follow suit and look across the street once more. "Holy shit, it's Druckmyer."

"Druckmyer?" the young woman asks.

"Homeland security."

~

I'm trying to explain to Auntie how everything changes from this day forward and how I am in a position to make that kind of difference, when my first test walks up from behind.

The Sheriff looks up and smiles.

I turn and there is that little sleaze-ball Severs walking up the lawn just like he owns the place with some little twit in hot pants and a slinky blouse. God, do I hate those sluts who can flaunt their femaleness like it's cheap perfume.

The Sheriff smiles. "Hi honey."

I look at her again. She better be his daughter and not his

latest girlfriend. I fucking despise it when older men hook up with some twit with tits just to prove that they still can.

"Hi, Daddy."

I give an internal sigh of relief. I was beginning to respect this Sheriff, as much as a pain in the ass as he's been.

Eddie is a whole other ball of wax. My first response is to pounce on that bastard and beat the hell out of him, then throw him on my fucking ruined plane and light the spilled fuel.

The old woman puts her hand atop mine and I look from Eddie to her hand and I'm calm again. I look into her old cataract eyes. "Here is your first test, Child."

"He wrecked—"

"First test. Take a breath and let yourself relax."

I follow her suggestion and relax my midsection, the place where I always hold tension.

"Remember, Child, if your tensing from that old place in your stomach, it relates to what happened on the bridge.

I look at Eddie again, this time from my new place. "Eddie."

"Ms. Druckmyer."

"Call me Anne."

He's shocked into silence and stands shifting from one foot to another.

"Eddie?"

"Yes ma'am?"

"Did you get any information on Hassiam?"

"Yes, Ma'am, but maybe we should speak in private."

I wave him away with the back of my hand. "Speak here."

He takes a breath. "He's in Zaperadth prison in northern Egypt."

I take out my cell and speed dial. When I get an answer, I speak with my old gruff voice. "Jason?"

"Yes ma'am?"

"Send a plane to Zaperadth and have Harium Hassiam delivered to Whiskey Flat, California."

"He's not in too good a shape, ma'am. Maybe we should fatten him up a bit and let some of the bruises heal."

I wink at Auntie and bark. "Look mister, you're not paid to think. We're in the middle of negotiations here. Whiskey Flat as soon as humanly possible, you got that."

"Yes ma'am. By morning."

I close the phone and put it back in my pocket. "We should have Hassiam tomorrow."

Eddie speaks, "What about me? Do I turn myself into this Sheriff so he can protect me too?"

I wave at him with the back of my hand, pick up my phone and speed dial Jason. "Yes Ma'am?"

"Eddie Severs."

"Ma'am?"

"Take him off the wanted list."

"What about your plane?"

"He's a Homeland agent, for God sakes, and a good one at that. Get him and his girlfriend off that list."

I look up at Severs. "Will that do?"

He smiles. "Yes ma'am. Thank you."

I've been in this bed, chained to the rail, for five days. I got my voice back yesterday. From the guard standing at my door, I know I'm in some kind of big trouble, I just don't know what. No one has told me a word. At least they know my real name.

The guard steps into my room for the first time since I've been here and digs in his pocket as he approaches. He gives me a dopey grin. "Guess they want you free."

He unlocks my cuffs as the doctor walks in. He looks at the officer. "Is she ready?"

"She's free if that's what you mean."

He gives me a grin. "Ready to be released?"

"Released?"

The nurse steps in with my clothes freshly laundered and hands them to me. "There's a shower in the bathroom. Maybe you want to freshen up before we take you to the front door."

"I would like that."

I swing my legs out from under the cover and put my feet on the cold floor. When I stand, I'm a bit woozy, but the nurse escorts me to the bathroom and helps me get in the shower.

The hot water feels good, but I'm so excited about getting out that I soap down and rinse in a few minutes. Once I'm dressed, with wet hair, I step out of the bathroom.

The nurse has a wheelchair. "We have to wheel you out the front door of the hospital."

I sit and she pushes me to the elevator, down to the first floor and through the busy lobby. When I get to the door, a limo is waiting. My two children pile out and run to see me.

Eddie gets out behind them and as we're hugging and I'm crying, Eddie stands waiting at the car.

I wave him over. "What happened?"

He rolls his eyes. "You really don't want to know, but if you insist, I'll tell you on the way back to Vegas."

～

I look at the Sheriff. "I'm bringing Hissiam back in rough condition. We could have him wait for a few weeks, which is standard so he's more presentable, but I'm counting on you to soften the repercussions. I bring him back now and no law suits, okay?"

"I don't have that kind of power."

I grimace. "Do what you can, because I'm breaking all the rules. It'll cost my job if there are a lot of waves."

Auntie looks at the Sheriff. "You can do it, Jackie. I can help with Fatima if needed."

He looks at me, then back at Auntie. "From what I know of Fatima, I'm sure it'll be needed."

Auntie says, "we want Anne to stay in her position as long as possible, because this is where she can do the most good."

Mr. Harding speaks. "Does this mean we're free to go."

The Sheriff shakes his head. "There is still a matter of the F.C.C. and probably some huge fine. I've still got you in custody and unless you can come up with the twenty thousand dollar bail, we will need to extradite you to Las Vegas in a few days."

"How about I pay their bail?" A tall man steps out of the shadows and walks fifty feet across the lawn. "I'm the attorney for Frank Deluchi.

He gives me a slight bow and looks at the Sheriff. "How about it Sheriff. I'll put up the bond and make sure these two are back in Vegas for their day in court."

Sheriff Perkins speaks with a flummoxed voice. "Yeah. . . I guess. . . . sure." He unfolds himself from the park bench. "Come to think of it, my butt is getting a little raw from this bench. He stands. "Maybe we'd better step into my office to take care of the paperwork for the bail."

The attorney waves one hand as if to let him lead the way. "I'm at your service, Sheriff Perkins."

The two men walk across the lawn and cross the street, then go inside the Sheriff's office.

I turn to Mrs. Harding. "All of this goes away if you can tell me where Frank Deluchi is."

"Frank is maybe the ultimate patriot. Singlehandedly he

has awoken—"

I glare at her. "You're in enough trouble, ma'am. I'd keep those thoughts to myself if I were you."

She shrinks and Harding takes her hand. It's the simple act of him slipping his hand into hers to support her —something I've never experienced— that gets me. I try to concentrate on the second page, but tears well up in my eyes and blur the text. When I feel a hand on mine, I pull away like it is a snake, then realize it's Auntie. "It's okay, Child."

I burst into tears right in front of the Harding and everyone.

Auntie takes my hand once again and I let her, feeling her support and her caring. "It's going to be all right, Anne. Life just dealt you a raw deal, but you can change that."

"I can?"

She takes me in her arms and my few tears turn into a full blown, snot-dripping wail. I can't stop. Five minutes goes by, but it feels like an hour as Auntie holds me and pats my back. When I finally calm and she lets me go, I wipe my eyes and nose on a paper napkin Harding gives me. I look at everyone and feel embarrassed. "I can't seem to help myself."

Mrs. Harding gives me a shy smile. "Crying is good."

"Not if I want to keep my job."

I look at Auntie. "How long am I going to be this way?"

She gives me a big, crooked toothed smile like she sports a mouth of fresh dental caps. "For the rest of your life, we hope, but first you need to make up for all of those years."

"Years?"

"It might be good to take a month off and go somewhere you always dreamed of so you can cry this out."

"A month?"

"Not the whole month. Go some place nice where you can relax."

~

Everyone has left the park. Auntie and I sit on the bench under the oak tree. The sound of Hank Williams filters out from the bar across the street. The evening color is disappearing. A single streetlight buzzes then flashes on and three or four bats swoop in to scoop up the spring moths. I'm sipping on a lemonade from the restaurant.

"Once again Auntie, you saved our butts."

She gives me her old woman grin, a smile I've never seen change since I was a kid. When she speaks it's with her crackly voice. "Twarnt nothin', Sheriff."

A lone coyote makes his familiar yowl on the side of the hill behind us. Another answers from down by the lake.

It's been a hectic few days and I'm relieved that peace has returned to our little town.

I turn to Auntie. "We're even getting Hissiam back."

"Your world of sheriffing is back in order?"

I smile.

The End

Discussion Guide on back page

Other Books in Print by Nik C. Colyer

"This compelling adventure series teaches solid ways men and women can be together and enrich their lives."

Bill Kauth Author and co-founder of New Warrior Training

Channeling Biker Bob 4 part series
Nik C. Colyer

Avaliable through

Singing Reed Press

www.NikColyer.com

Nik's Favorite Story

"... a very interesting metaphysical science fiction novel structured around the soft science of psychology, sociology and futurism. The plot is fast paced and shoots off in unexpected directions." Bob Spears Grit Lit

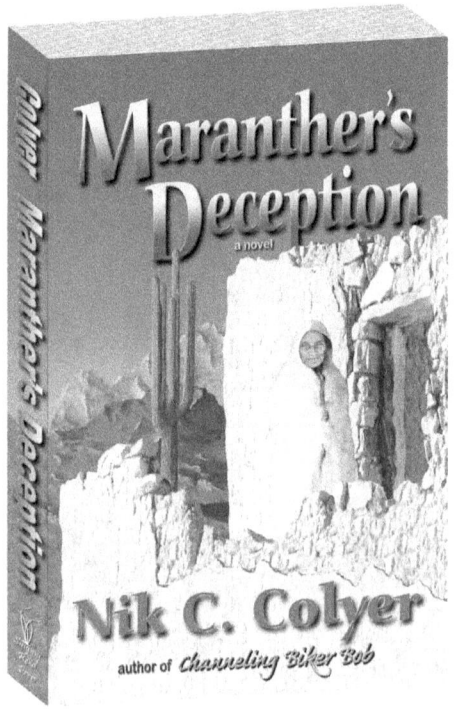

"Nik Colyer's poetry is so emotionally honest it shoots directly into one's own heart. His raw, naked truths touch that hidden place we all share. Never a dull moment, his poems are evidence of a life fully lived."

Will Staple - Author of I *Hate The Men You Sleep With*

Trillian Rising

Jason Oakley's Jungle vacation turns to a nightmare when his
buddy smuggles a gold medallion out of the Amazon.
The cursed medallion is both the cause of a world pandemic
and the only hope for life saving vaccine.
Time is of the essence, and for Jason time is running out.

Available through
Singing Reed Press
www.NikColyer.com

Flamenco Flood

This screwball comedy floats through the little town of Marysville like the ever-threatening floodwaters of the mighty Yuba river.

Avaliable through Singing Reed Press

www.NikColyer.com

Books to come from Nik C. Colyer

Guerilla TV Discusion Guide

1. Why is Frank Deluchi doing what he does?
2. How does BillyBob talk Myrtle into broadcasting?
3. Why is the broadcast so controversial?
4. Why does Homeland see the Hardings as terrorists?
5. What happened to Eddie and the hooker?
6. When they met, why so secretive?
7. Does the fight in the bar remind you of anything?
8. Why is the doctor so helpful with their escape?
9. Why Whisky Flat?
10. Is a county sheriff sworn to serve and protect?
11. Why was Druckmyer so bent on getting the Hardings?
12. How did the sheriff protect the Hardings?
13. What brought the military into Whisky Flat?
14. Why did the General break Druckmyer's jaw?
15. What magic did Auntie posess?
16. What was the reasoning in taking Druckmyer back?
17. Why was the sheriff not interested in the local women?
18. Eddie had a dream that helped him how?
19. What was Eddie's surprise in Kansas?
20. When Eddie returned, why wasn't he areested?
21. What caused the military to finly pack up and leave?
22. Why was Druckmyre so set on quitting her job?
23. Where did Auntie take the General?
24. Whisky Flat does exist?
25. How does this story apply to your life?